WINDSWORN
GRYPHON RIDERS BOOK ONE

Windsworn:
Gryphon Riders Trilogy Book One

Copyright © 2017

♠ Derek Alan Siddoway ♠

First Edition

Published July 2017 by Derek Alan Siddoway
Editor: Jason Whited
Formatting: James Downe

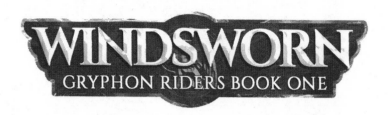

DEREK ALAN SIDDOWAY

Chapter 1

Soot heard the thrum of gryphon's wings and the scrape of talons on cobblestone long before the knock ever reached the door. Even so, he hesitated to rise from his chair by the fire, heaving a sigh as he did so.

The smith's singed and callused hand paused when he reached for the door latch. He'd half made up his mind to pretend like he hadn't heard anything when another knock came.

"Wayland! I know you're in there."

"Who's there?" Soot asked in a gruff voice — even though he knew exactly who it was.

"It's Andor."

The smith sighed again and lifted the latch. Pulling the door open, Soot could see by the small fire crackling in the hearth a tall man standing on the threshold, dressed in leathers and royal blue. Shoulder-length blond hair framed a weatherbeaten and worried face, aged beyond its twenty-something years. When he saw Soot, the visitor's piercing eyes softened, and his stern expression broke into a grin.

"By the Tempest, it's good to see you again, old friend!" the man said, gripping the smith's shoulder. He looked past Soot, taking in the small room and its meager contents.

"So, this is where you ran off to," Andor said in a low voice, half talking to himself. He glanced back at Soot, answering his friend's unspoken question. "It wasn't hard to find you, Wayland. What other forge in the city has a golem working in it?"

Soot grunted and shrugged his burly shoulders. "It's the middle of the stormin' night, Andor. What're you doing here?"

"You didn't have to leave," Andor said, ignoring his friend's question.

Before either man could speak again, a baby's cry filled the darkness in the street. In the flickering torchlight, Soot made out a pale gray gryphon, standing stock-still in the middle of the yard.

While Andor walked around the gryphon's side toward the sound of crying, Soot approached the creature's head.

"Hello, Stormwind," he said, running a hand down the gryphon's beak. The gryphon gave a small scree in recognition and leaned into the smith's touch.

A few moments later, Andor appeared holding the wailing bundle. Soot looked down at the child, a frown creasing his brow, and jerked his head toward the cottage. Inside, Andor sat down in one of the chairs by the hearth, rocking the infant until it fell silent once more.

"Thank the winds," he said. "I'm not cut out for this parenting business — I guess I should count myself lucky she slept that long."

Soot sat down across from the pair, never taking his eyes off the swaddled baby.

"Is that?"

Andor nodded.

The smith's throat bunched into a knot. "Marien?"

"Didn't make it," Andor said, voice breaking. Tears welled in his eyes.

Soot ran his good hand over his bald head and covered his face. After a moment, he cleared his throat and looked up at his old friend again with tears of his own.

"Adelar won't speak with anyone," Andor continued. "He shut himself in his room and ordered her out of the citadel as soon as he found out Marien died."

Soot rose for the door, hand tightened into a fist. "Enough is enough! I'll pound some sense into him if it's —"

Andor raised a hand to quiet his friend. "Soot, please. You'll wake her. He's beyond reason. I…I'm not leaving her with some strangers. He'll change his mind someday, realize what a thunderstruck fool he's been. But for now, she can't stay."

Soot's face changed from outrage to horror as it dawned on him what his friend was asking. "Oh no! I can't, Andor, I don't know the first thing about babies. You take care of her!"

"The Gyr is no place for an infant," Andor said. "Please, Soot, just for a little while. I'm certain —"

"If anyone, her father should be the one to raise her!"

Andor shook his head. "That's impossible."

Soot raised the capped stump where his right hand should have been. "You know how hard it is to be a one-handed smith? Even with Seppo, it's all I can do to keep up, let alone try and raise a child. I've given enough to your stormin' family and the crown."

Without realizing it, Soot towered over Andor, chest heaving. His friend looked up from his chair, still holding the baby. When he spoke, it wasn't in the barking tone he used to command his riders; it came out so soft Soot almost didn't hear it.

"I wouldn't ask you to do this for Adelar. This is for Marien."

Only the snap of coals in the fire broke the stillness. Soot's shoulders drooped, and he nodded. Before the smith could change his mind, Andor placed the bundled child in his friend's thick arms. Soot stared at the sleeping baby, captivated as Andor reached into the pocket of his royal-blue uniform. The gryphon rider pulled out a white stone set in silver on a matching chain.

"Marien wanted her to have it," Andor said. "She gave it to me almost a week ago — almost…like she knew."

Soot stared at the white stone as it spun on the chain twinkling lights of sky blue, blue and gold. He nodded to Andor to lay it on the table, still holding the swaddled infant in awkward arms.

"I'll see to it you're sent whatever you need," Andor said, stopping at the door. "But Soot — she can't know. Not anything. Understood?"

The smith replied with a grunt, still trying to figure out how the night had ended with him holding a newborn. Andor reached for the door latch.

"And Soot...thank you. You don't know what this means."

"Wait," Soot said as Andor stepped into the street where his gryphon waited, clawing at the cobblestones. "What's her name?"

Andor paused and stared up at the night sky. "Evelyn. Marien named her Evelyn."

Chapter

2

E va."
    "*Eva.*"
"Evelyn!"

The girl started at Soot's shout, almost knocking her bowl of porridge off the table. Shaking his head, the smith tried again

"You paying attention now?"

Eva nodded, her long blonde hair sliding across her face with the motion. "Yes. Yes — sorry! Just…thinking."

"How about you think about what you need to pick up at the market?" Soot asked. "And no dallying, girl! Now that summer's on, we've got plenty of work to do — there's that big order of horseshoes from Hawk's Ridge due by the end of the week."

Eva ran over the list of items again in her head, mouthing each one to help her remember better. "Can I take Seppo to help carry things?"

Soot scratched his three-day growth of beard and frowned. "I suppose…but I'll need him back soon to work the smelter, so be quick about it."

Excited at the prospect of a morning at the market, Eva scooped up the last of her breakfast and shot out the door. "Don't worry, I've got it!"

As the door continued to swing on well-oiled hinges, Soot shook his head.

Outside, the morning sunlight flashed bright on the white stone buildings of Gryfonesse, promising an early arrival of summer. Eva paused to stretch and smile in the yard situated between the small cottage and the smithy. The sky above shone blue, empty of clouds and gryphons alike. Below, the city stirred with the sounds of people and songbirds calling out their good mornings, along with the apprentices and journeymen beginning their day's work in the Craftsman District.

Eva paused to scatter some corn to the chickens squawking and scurrying after her then ducked into the forge, already hot from the never-ending fires she helped feed.

"Seppo! Where are you? We're going to the market this morning and —"

She stopped short as a giant suit of armor clanked toward her from the back of the smithy. Seppo's rounded iron head skimmed the ceiling of the forge as he crossed the shop to deposit a stack of firewood that Eva couldn't have carried in five trips. Clapping his iron hands together to free a piece of bark wedged in a joint, the golem turned to Eva.

"Good morning, Mistress Evelyn," Seppo said in a tinny, proper voice. "I hope you are well. While you and Master Wayland slept, I took the liberty to chop more wood and fire the smelter."

Eva shook her head in awe of the golem's prowess. Although even Soot wasn't sure what powered him, Seppo didn't need to eat or sleep, so he often got bored in the middle of the night and began work on the next day's projects. Soot and Eva didn't mind most of the time, but every once in a while the golem made such a clatter with hammer and anvil that he woke everyone on the street. Eva supposed if all she needed to sustain her was a little oil now and then, she'd probably go out of her mind sitting still all night, too.

Although Soot was known through the capital — and all of Rhylance — for his skill as a smith, they would never have been able to handle to volume of work they did without Seppo. No matter how much Soot grumbled and cursed the golem, he worked harder, faster, and more efficient than a whole group of apprentices and journeymen could.

Even so, Soot kept Eva plenty busy. Skinny girl of seventeen years that she was, Eva could pump the bellows, shovel slag, and swing a hammer for just as long and with as much skill as any boy.

"Thanks, Seppo," Eva said. "Ready to go?"

"I would be delighted to accompany you, Mistress Evelyn."

They returned to the well in the yard just as Soot came stomping out of the cottage. He took one look at Eva and then up at Seppo and shook his head. "You do her chores for her again?"

"I am here to serve, Master Wayland." Seppo answered in the same level tone he always had. "I became restless during the night and —"

Soot cut him off with a wave of his stump like he did every time the golem started, as the smith put it "rambling on like a rock in a tin cup."

"How many times I have to tell you to stop spoiling that girl?" Soot grumbled, walking off toward the forge.

Eva looked up at Seppo and grinned. Soot talked like he was all slag and sharp edges, but on the inside she knew the smith was soft as a bar of iron right out of the fire. He worked Eva to exhaustion many a night but still made time to bring her a new book or one of Gryfonesse's famous yellow roses every now and then from the market.

Together, Eva and Seppo made their way down the lane to the marketplace a short walk away. On their way, they passed several craftsmen who greeted them as they passed by on business of their own. Eva shook her head as Seppo stopped in the middle of the street to raise a hand at a passing butterfly. It alighted on the back of his iron hand for a moment, and Eva swore she heard a small giggle escape the big suit of armor before the butterfly fluttered away. Behind them, a barrel maker pulled up his pony and cart and cleared his throat, eager to continue on his way. "Come on, Seppo," Eva said, wrapping her hand around one of the golem's giant fingers to give it a gentle tug.

As they drew nearer to the market, the streets grew more crowded as they spread into wide boulevards. Eva led the way with Seppo clanking behind her. Although most of the citizens had seen or at least heard of Soot's golem and knew Seppo was harmless, they still cleared the way when the giant suit of armor came into sight. Eva was grateful she didn't have to push and squeeze her way through the morning traffic, but it always felt a bit disconcerting when the crowd parted and stared as they walked past. Embarrassed, she solved the awkward exchanges by focusing on the ground just in front of her feet. She only looked up when the street opened up into the market circle, a giant ring of shops, stalls, and wagons that formed the heart of Gryfonesse.

Here, a person could find almost anything from all across western Altaris — salted and smoked fish from Pandion's coast, melons and pottery out of the summerlands of Maizoro to the north, furs and hides from the south and much, much more. At one time or another during the year, trade of every sort passed through Gryfonesse, Rhylance's capital and the largest city in western Altaris. Soot had his own stall spot for the big fall and spring festivals, but a long list of needs from dozens of patrons made it unnecessary to set up their excess wares in the weekly market. Although Eva enjoyed their short trips, the thought of spending all day in the crowds and noise made her head spin and stomach churn.

A quick trip to their regular stops yielded fresh bread, milk and cheese, and some early season squash and corn from Maizoro. With Seppo carrying the morning's haul, Eva worked up the nerve to fight through the crowds to one last stop. When she neared their final destination for the morning, a gray-haired woman looked up and smiled at the girl and golem.

"Good morning, Eva," the woman said. She sat on the steps of a fountain, the centerpiece of which was a large, rearing gryphon, wings spread and front talons stretched wide. A small basket with a scattering of coins was in her lap, and her right arm and hand were wrapped in dirty rags. "I was wondering if I'd see you around today."

"Good morning, Rose," Eva said, just loud enough to be heard over the bustling patrons and shouting merchants hawking their wares. She reached up into one of the baskets Seppo carried and handed the woman a loaf of bread. "Got a story for me today?"

The woman shifted her ragged, stained shawl up over her shoulders and smiled, revealing a scattering of missing teeth in her wide grin. "Got something better than a story today," she said. "Did you hear —"

A series of shouts made Eva spin around. From her vantage point atop the fountain, she saw several guards pushing their way through the market, pausing now and then to question random citizens before moving on. Looking around, Eva saw several more groups of soldiers and realized by their gold-trimmed cloaks and winged helmets they were from the palace.

"What's going on?" Eva asked.

"You ain't heard?" Rose said. She let out a dry cackle and shook her matted head. "Some thief stole a gryphon egg from the Gyr last night!"

It took a long moment for Rose's words to sink in as Eva's head rose to look at the giant, barren mountain towering over the city to the east. As she looked, Eva noticed several groups of what looked to be birds way off in the distance, flying away from the mountain. Although they seemed no larger than eagles at the distance, Eva knew they were gryphons, likely carrying riders on a search for the missing egg — if what Rose said was true.

"Who would steal a gryphon egg?" Eva asked. Out of all the people to cross, Eva put the gryphon riders at the very bottom of the list

"Someone real brave or real stupid," Rose said. "Rumor has it a group of Scrawls was meeting with the king about a border negotiation. One of 'em went missing this morning."

Eva looked out over the crowd and saw the royal-blue uniforms of several gryphon riders working their way through the crowd as well. By now, everyone in the market seemed aware of the armed soldiers threading through their midst, searching stalls and questioning bystanders. She didn't know why, but the sight of the famous warriors in armor and mail sent her stomach fluttering, and she turned back to Rose, eager to get the rest of the story and return to the forge.

"Why would the Scrawls steal a gryphon egg?" Eva asked. "We've been at peace with them for almost a hundred years!"

Rose tapped a gnarled finger against the side of her head. "Don't know, but it don't bode well for the negotiations — the king's got 'em all locked up while the city's being searched. "

"I...I better get back to the forge," Eva said, as a sudden burst of anxiety clutched her. "Come on, Seppo."

Eva turned as someone shouted and saw a pair of palace guards pushing their way through the crowd at the foot of the fountain steps.

"You there!" the front guard, a man with a shaved head and round face said, pointing to Eva. "Hold up, girl."

Eva felt her stomach twist as the two guards, the man who'd yelled and a dour-faced woman, approached. She looked behind her, but Rose was nowhere to be seen, no doubt eager to stay out of mind of the guard.

"What's that thing with you?" the man asked, pointing to Seppo.

"Looks like some kind of Scrawl contraption," the female guard said, gesturing to Seppo's breastplate. "Thing's covered in runes."

"I beg your pardon," Seppo said in an irate voice. "I am not a *thing*. My name is Seppo."

The pair started and reached for the swords. "By thunder," the woman swore. "It spoke!"

Eva's stomach coiled tighter, caught between the spooked guards and Seppo. She opened her mouth to tell them Seppo didn't mean any harm, but the words wouldn't come out.

"Hey, what you got in those baskets there?" the male guard said, gesturing toward the items in Seppo's hands. "Something's been stolen from the palace. Show us what you got."

"I most certainly will not," Seppo said, twisting so the baskets were farther out of reach.

Eva's heart leapt into her throat, but she finally managed to speak. "Seppo, just let them see —"

14

"Move aside, girl," the female guard said, pushing Eva. She tried to back out of the way and tripped on the fountain step, falling on her rear.

"You will not lay a hand on Mistress Evelyn," Seppo said. Dropping the groceries, the golem stepped between Eva and the guards, fists bunched. The guards fell back, drawing their swords. Eva tried to tell Seppo to stand down, but all that came out was a squeak. At the same time, a woman screamed and the crowd pushed out of the way, leaving the four of them in an open circle.

"Hey!"

A young man around Eva's age fought through the onlookers, furthering her embarrassment and fright. He wore the silver wings and royal blue of a Windsworn — a full-fledged gryphon rider. He shot Eva a reassuring look that sent her heart pounding even faster before turning to the guard.

"Get out of the way, kid," the male guard grunted. "Palace business."

"I didn't know the palace made a habit of picking on girls shopping at the market," the young man said. He looped his thumbs through his sword belt, feet spread wide in an easy, confident manner.

"You're not on your mountain now," the female guard said. "So, quit strutting around like a rooster putting on a show."

"Is there going to be a fight?" Seppo asked with genuine curiosity.

The young man jerked his head toward the guards. "I don't think these two really want to tangle with us, my giant iron friend."

"Why you little —"

Eva's breath caught as the male guard stepped forward, swinging his sword overhead. With speed belying his size, Seppo caught the blow across his arm, knocking the blade aside. Before the man could react, the golem grabbed him by his mail shirt, hefting him into the air. Eva stared aghast as the man kicked and squirmed, but Seppo held firm and turned to present the guard to his mistress.

"What shall I do with this offender, Mistress Eva?"

Everyone — especially the young gryphon rider — turned to

Eva, whose face burned. "Just put...put him down," she muttered, dropping her eyes to the golem's feet.

The guard collapsed in a pile, struggling to his feet as the onlookers continued to stare. When Eva looked up, the gryphon rider stood over her, hand extended, a crooked smile on his face. "May I?"

Speechless and wishing she could melt into the fountain, Eva held up her hand and allowed the young man to pull her to her feet.

"May I have your name, fair maiden?" he said in such a way that Eva wasn't sure if he was making fun of her or not.

"It's uh...Ev-Eva."

The young rider smiled again, dark brown eyes shining. A whirl of butterflies flitted through Eva's stomach as he spoke, still holding her hand. "A pleasure to —"

"What's going on here?"

Almost as Eva didn't exist, the rider dropped her hand and turned around as a golden-haired man stepped through the crowd. A small frown sat on his face as his piercing blue eyes surveyed the scene.

"Lord Commander Andor," the female guard stuttered. "We were just performing a search of this young woman when your rider —"

"They seemed to believe we were harboring something sinister in the squash," Seppo chimed in. "Greetings, Andor. It has been far too long."

The golden-haired man nodded to Seppo, his cold gaze falling on Eva. For a brief moment, Eva thought she saw his eyes widen in recognition, but the look disappeared as soon as it came.

"What's your name, girl?" the lord commander asked.

"E-Evelyn, sir," Eva managed to spit out a second time. Her legs felt like a pair of green willows, apt to fold beneath her at any second.

The lord commander nodded and turned back to the guards. "I can assure you, Seppo and...Evelyn here had nothing to do with the stolen egg. I think it best we let them go on their way after this debacle."

Lord Commander Andor looked at the young rider as he finished, and the easy smile dropped from the boy's face faster than a hawk making a stoop. With one last dirty look at Seppo and the young man, the guards left, shouting for the onlookers to disperse.

"You should try and stay home the next few days," the lord commander told Eva. Once again, he stared at her for a long moment before shaking his head and slapping Seppo on his breastplate. "Tell Soot hello for me."

With a final nod, the golden-haired man turned with a swish of his cloak, beckoning the young rider to follow.

"It was good to meet you, Eva," the confident Windsworn said with a wink. "Stay out of trouble."

Chapter
3

I'm sorry to have upset you, Mistress Evelyn," Seppo said for the dozenth time.

"It's fine," Eva mumbled. She felt a wave of relief as Soot's forge appeared. The exchange in the market had left her as drained as a morning working the forge, and she looked forward to the somewhat solitary work ahead of her. Unbidden, the thought of the cocky young gryphon rider rose to her mind again, and another flutter of butterflies rose inside her. She hadn't even been able to untie her tongue long enough to get his name.

After storing their morning's groceries away in the cottage, Eva joined Soot and Seppo in the forge. The wave of thick, hot air smelling of hot metal and the clangor of Soot's hammer welcomed her back, pushing all thought of the market and the gryphon riders from her mind.

Eva buried herself in her work throughout the rest of the day. Although she could help out with the hard labor when necessary, most of her time was spent doing finish work — grinding, polishing, and any other final touches required. By the time they finished for the day, the strands of golden hair fallen from her ponytail hung lank with sweat, and ash and smoke marks streaked her face.

The evening sun painted amber streaks across the white stone of

Gryfonesse's Craftsman District. A cool spring breeze washed over Eva as she stepped out into the yard, and she shivered a little washing away the forge grime at the water pump. Before going into the cottage, she paused and let out a long breath. A good day to be over.

"Seppo said you had a run-in with the guard at the market," Soot said while Eva cleaned up after dinner.

Eva's chest tightened at the mention of the ordeal, but she told him about her conversation with Rose on the fountain steps and the ensuing conflict.

"Bah," Soot said, waving his good hand, dismissing Rose's news. "That beggar woman loves to tell a good story."

"But they *were* searching the marketplace," Eva insisted. "And the guards stopped us because they thought Seppo had something to do with the Scrawls."

"Well, whatever it is, the lord commander was right to tell you to stay at home the next few days," Soot said. "You don't want to get mixed up in any business with the Gyr."

"How do you know him?" Eva asked. "Isn't he the king's brother?"

Soot fell silent for a long moment and cleared his throat. Eva already knew what was coming — her foster father did the same thing whenever Eva asked about Soot's past, her parents, or any other subjects he didn't like to discuss.

"We've met once or twice," Soot said. "When I was an apprentice and journeyman, my master was a smith at the Gyr."

Eva's head jerked up as she put their last bowl away in the shelf. "You've been in the Gyr? You never told me that!"

Soot mumbled something under his breath and rubbed his bald head. "For a short time."

"What's it like?" Eva asked, rushing to his side. Hardly anyone other than the gryphon riders ever set foot in the mysterious mountain fortress. As a child, Eva often imagined what the halls of the Gyr must look like — according to the stories it was a stronghold of the Ancients, abandoned for hundreds of years until the Sorondarans and

19

their gryphons settled the valley of Rhylance.

The smith shrugged. "I didn't see much other than the forge. It was a fine workshop but nothing out of the ordinary to speak of."

Eva's hopes fell, and she gritted her teeth in frustration. Getting anything out of Soot was like trying to wring water from a stone: in the end, your well of information was as dry as when you started.

"But the lord commander knew you *and* Seppo," Eva said. "And I know you didn't have Seppo around while you were a journeyman."

"Right," Soot said. "Well, how many other golems have you heard of in the capital?"

"But —"

"Gryphon riders aren't folk you want to get mixed up with," the smith said in a tone conveying the conversation was over. "They're… trouble — whether they mean it or not."

Eva's mind flashed back to the dashing young rider who'd come to her rescue that morning. "They can't be that bad," she said. "If they get into trouble, I'm sure it's just because they're protecting Rhylance."

"You'd be surprised," Soot muttered.

"What?"

"Nothing!" Flustered, her foster father rose from his chair. "We've got a full day ahead; you won't get the morning off to get into trouble at the market tomorrow. Time for bed!"

Agitated but knowing she wouldn't get any more out of Soot, Eva retired to her small room and flopped down on her straw mattress. No sooner had she closed her eyes than she opened them again, restless and tired but unable to sleep. She listened to Seppo's heavy footfalls outside as he wandered around the yard, no doubt tempted to pick up work in the forge again, in spite of Soot's nightly reminders. They'd tried locking him in the cottage before, but the golem's size meant he could hardly move with knocking over chairs or breaking something.

Eva replayed her run-in with the gryphon riders and Soot's begrudging conversation over and over. Frustrated, she rolled on her side and slid a hand beneath her mattress. When she pulled it free, a soft white light glowed through the cracks in her fist.

As Eva opened her fingers, the opaque stone's glow lit up her room like a full moon. Twisting the stone's silver chain around her fingers, Eva held it above her face, watching the lights fade and change from white to gold, pink, and sky blue. Eva felt a familiar calm settle over her, just like every time she held the necklace.

Soot called it a Wonder, an artifact from the days of the Ancients. They came in all shapes and sizes and did all sorts of things — crystal lanterns with endless light, weapons and tools that never lost their edges, and more. Although some were rarer than others (Eva once heard a customer at the forge talking about a cauldron that boiled water without a fire), few even among the nobility could claim to own such a treasure. As such, Soot had kept a close eye on Eva whenever she played with the Wonder as a child. He'd also made her promise not to tell her friends or anyone else about the stone.

To Eva, it was more than just a peculiar shining stone and pretty necklace. It was the only thing she owned that had belonged to her parents and almost the only thing Soot had ever told Eva about them. Her father had given it to her mother before he died in battle. Not long after, Eva's mother had died, too, giving birth to her.

"They were good friends," Soot would say whenever Eva persuaded him to share what little he would about her parents. "And they loved each other like you wouldn't believe."

Eva stared at the stone for a few more minutes, thinking of the gryphon rider once again. For all the stress and embarrassment she'd been through, he'd almost made it worth it. Once more, she berated herself for being so shy and awkward. Chances were they'd never meet again.

Trying not to think about it, Eva curled her hand around the Wonder stone and rolled onto her side. She pulled her blanket up and soon drifted to sleep.

It felt like only moments later when a ruckus from the chickens pulled Eva from her slumber. Silently cursing the dumb birds, Eva readjusted herself on the mattress and started to doze again.

The chickens squawked and fussed again. This time, Eva sat up in bed. As she did, her blanket slid down, and the light from her mother's stone spilled across the room once more. Eva grabbed the Wonder, stuffing it under her mattress, and peeked out the window.

Outside, the yard was empty and silent. Eva held her breath, listening for the sound of Seppo going to investigate. He often whiled away the night on the lookout for foxes or raccoons brazen enough to steal one of the chickens or raid the nests. It couldn't be him upsetting the birds — they'd grown so accustomed to the big golem that Eva had to constantly shoo them off his shoulders or spend the next few hours scrubbing their white droppings from his iron plates.

The chickens set up a third distress call, and Eva rose out of her bed, wide awake. Where was Seppo? She'd just thrown a cloak over her nightgown when the golem's clanking footsteps and shadowed figure passed her window, heading for the coop. Eva relaxed as he passed out of sight then listened for the sound of Seppo chasing off whatever kept harassing the chickens.

Her senses spiked again when the golem spoke. "Who are you?"

A flash of light illuminated Eva's window, followed by the crash of iron plates.

"Seppo?" she whispered out the window. Although the chickens remained silent, the golem didn't answer.

Heart pounding in her chest, Eva crossed her room and made to wake Soot, still snoring in the room next to hers. She paused, hand poised over his door, and for reasons she couldn't explain, slid out the cottage toward the chicken coop.

In her bare feet, Eva crossed the yard in silence, footsteps muffled by the short grass. Something squished under her foot, and Eva bit back a hiss when she lifted it up and found chicken dropping smeared across her heel.

Eva paused at the corner of the forge. Over the nervous clucks of the chickens a voice whispered something in a strange language. She risked a peek around the side of the building and stifled a gasp of surprise.

Seppo lay stock still on his back, arms and legs clasped to his sides. A small, hooded figure bent over him, one hand hovering a few inches from his chest plate, still muttering in an indiscernible tongue.

At first, Eva thought the golem was dead — until she saw the glow of his sapphire-colored orbs.

Eva froze as the person paused, pressing herself against the wall, hoping they hadn't seen her. She held back a sigh of relief as the mumbling continued. Looking down, she spotted a rock the size of a crab apple at her feet and squatted to pick it up with a shaking hand.

Eva peered around the corner, saw the figure still crouched over Seppo, and let the rock fly.

The stone hit the person in the hood, and they toppled over sideways with a grunt before struggling to rise. At the same time, Seppo's limbs came back to life, and the golem rolled over with surprising speed, grabbing the mysterious assailant around the ankle.

With a firm grip on his attacker, Seppo rose, the hooded person dangling upside down from the golem's outstretched hand. As they kicked and squirmed, the hood fell away, revealing a boy no more than a dozen years old. Eva knew at once he was a Scrawl from the dark blue rune tattoos covering his shaved head and exposed arms.

"Lemme go!" he hissed before dropping back into the same strange tongue he'd been speaking before. Eva jumped back. The boy's rune markings started to glow.

Surprised, Seppo dropped the boy on his head, and the intruder crashed to the ground. The Scrawl moaned and sat up, shaking his head. As soon as his chanting stopped, the glowing script on his body faded and a satchel at his side fell open. Eva gasped as a large, rounded object rolled out of it, stopping at her feet.

It was a gryphon egg.

A blood-red egg the size of Eva's head.

Chapter 4

The Scrawl boy scrambled forward, but before he could snatch up the egg Seppo clamped a hand around his neck and lifted him off the ground again.

"Let me go, I said!" He kicked and squirmed but this time didn't utter any incantations. "I've done nothing wrong!"

Eva stared at the egg. Almost as if compelled by another force, she sank to her knees and reached out for it. In her mind, she became aware of a steady thumping, a heartbeat not her own. When her fingertips brushed the egg, she was surprised to find it warm to the touch. She picked it up in both hands, and the heartbeat increased until it pounded in her ears. She couldn't be sure, but she thought it quivered in her palms.

"What shall we do with this intruder, Mistress Evelyn?" Seppo asked. The boy hung from the golem's grip like a kitten in its mother's mouth, surly and pouting. Seppo gave him a slight shake and watched to see if anything else fell out of his cloak. "I think we should break his legs."

Eva broke her gaze away from the egg. "What? No! We're not going to hurt him!"

Seppo sighed, from wounded pride, Eva guessed, when the boy had rendered him immobile on the ground. "Very well. Shall I take him to Master Wayland?"

Without waiting for an answer, he began to stomp toward the cottage, both Eva and the boy hissing in quiet protest.

"Wait!" Eva said, jumping in front of him and holding up a hand. "Just wait!"

She wrapped the egg in her cloak and nestled it close to her, feeling an odd urge to protect it, similar to the feeling that compelled her not to wake Soot. "How did you come by this egg, thief?"

The boy frowned at her, still fidgeting in Seppo's grip. "I'm not going to say anything until this thing puts me down!"

Eva nodded at Seppo, who responded by raising the Scrawl higher in the air before letting go to let him fall in a heap on the ground.

"I am not a thing," the golem said for the second time that day. "I am Seppo."

"Don't try to run," Eva warned the boy, attempting to sound braver than she felt. "He's almost as fast as a horse, and he could snap your legs like twigs. Now, where did you get this egg?"

"I saved it!" Scrawl said. "The egg was in danger — someone wanted to destroy it!"

"I think he stole it," Seppo said in a matter-of-fact tone.

"No! Please, you have to believe me," The Scrawl paused and took a deep breath. "I...I had a vision. If I hadn't stolen the egg, it would have been destroyed, and...it was meant for you. It's no coincidence that I'm here. I saw this place — and you. That's how I knew where to come."

Eva stared. "What?"

The boy nodded his tattooed head toward the egg nestled in the crook of Eva's arm. "It feels right, doesn't it? The egg? It was meant for *you*."

The egg pulsed again, and she felt its warmth through her clothes, making her skin tingle. A second thought struck her and replaced the tingling with a weight in the pit of her stomach: she was holding the stolen gryphon egg — the egg the entire palace guard and Windsworn were looking for. Even so, for reasons she couldn't explain, it felt like the boy told the truth.

"Here," Eva said, unwrapping the egg and pushing it into the boy's hands. "It's not meant for me. You've made a mistake. I'm...no."

"May I make an observation, Mistress Evelyn?" Seppo cut in. "It seems a very poor idea to give the egg to the person who stole it in the first place."

Eva held a finger to her lips, afraid the golem would wake up Soot if he carried on much longer. She looked down at the boy, a head shorter than her. For some reason, she felt he was telling at least part of the truth. Of course, the egg couldn't be for her, but she couldn't help but believe he really was looking after it.

"Look, I don't know why you think I'm the one you needed to bring the egg to, but you got it wrong." She paused. "You can sleep in our woodshed overnight, and I'll bring you something to eat in the morning. But then you have to leave."

The Scrawl wrapped the egg up and placed in back in his satchel. "I appreciate your...hospitality...and I'm sure after a night's sleep you'll come around."

"No," Eva began. "I think you misunder —"

"Eva, what in the Tempest is going on out there?"

Eva froze at the sound of Soot's voice, but Seppo filled the ensuing silence.

"We have apprehended the thief, Master Wayland!"

The boy's eyes went wide, and he stared at Eva.

"Quick!" she hissed, spinning him around and shoving him toward the shed. "Get inside!"

Without further encouragement, the boy ran for the woodshed and ducked inside, closing the door behind him. Eva turned around just as Soot rounded the corner, rubbing his eyes.

"You two are raising enough racket to wake the dead," the smith said. He looked at Eva. "Why aren't you in bed?"

Eva jumped in before Seppo could reveal anything else, the lie spilling out easier than she expected. "Something was in with the chickens. I ran out to scare it off. Sorry for the noise."

Soot studied her, and Eva wasn't sure if he believed her or not.

"And you?" he said, looking at Seppo. "Where were you, you big pile of slag?"

"I was here!" Seppo protested. "It was I who caught the thief and —"

"Yes!" Eva said in a loud voice. "It was a raccoon, trying to get inside the coop to steal the eggs. I chased it out, but Seppo caught it. Don't think we'll have to worry about that one again."

She finished with a weak laugh, stomach rolling, and hoped her foster father bought the story. Sure as sky, Soot wouldn't believe the boy's story — even if he gave the Scrawl half a chance to explain himself in the first place. Eva did her best not to glance toward the woodshed as Soot looked around the yard.

After what felt like forever, the smith yawned and headed back to the cottage. "All right, back to bed," he told Eva. "You'll be dragging your feet as it is tomorrow." Soot paused to point a gnarled finger at Seppo. "And you. Keep it down!"

As Soot turned away, Seppo looked at Eva, and she knew the golem was dying to say something. She held a finger to her lips and gritted her teeth, shaking her head. Exasperated, Seppo shook his head and stomped away, muttering.

When morning arrived, Eva woke early enough to sneak out a heel of bread and bucket of water to the woodshed. Crossing the yard, she found herself hoping the boy was gone — or better yet that the whole thing had been a wild dream. When she opened the door, however, Eva found the Scrawl sitting cross-legged on the ground, the red gryphon egg nestled in his lap.

"Here," she said, handing him the bread and setting the pail down beside him. "You need to leave soon. If Seppo sees you again, I can't promise he won't hand you over to Soot."

The boy shook his head. "You *have* to take the egg. And I'm not leaving until you do."

Exasperated, Eva opened her mouth to argue, but the Scrawl cut her off.

"Who's Soot?" he asked through a gigantic mouthful of bread.

"The blacksmith!" Eva said.

"Your husband?"

"What? No!" Eva wasn't sure to laugh or be appalled. "He's…he raised me."

The boy nodded. Stuffing the rest of the bread into his mouth, he offered up a hand, covered with rune tattoos. "My name's Ivan."

Eva hesitated. Like everyone else, she'd heard the old wives' tale that Scrawls could kill with a touch. Ivan extended it again, however, and she took it feeling the same when their hands fell apart as before. "Good to meet you, Ivan. I'm Eva. But really, you've got to go. I —"

Ivan nodded as she spoke. "I know who you are. I told you, I saw you in my vision. That's why I'm staying. You've got to take the egg."

Once more, he reached into his satchel and held it out for her. On impulse, Eva's hands rose. She wondered if the egg was still warm, if it still pulsed…but no. Eva shook her head, pulling her hands back.

"You should be gone by nightfall," she said. "Soot usually has Seppo or me fetch the wood for the furnace, but I can't promise that Seppo won't reveal you — he's still upset about whatever you did to him last night."

Ivan shook his head after taking a long draught of water. "I'm not going anywhere," he said, folding his arms over his chest and the satchel. "I'm supposed to be here, with you and the egg."

"It won't go well for you if Soot finds you. He'll turn you over to the gryphon riders."

The boy shrugged again, as if Eva were a little girl telling him about her imaginary friends. The gesture infuriated her more each time he did it. But before she could argue with Ivan anymore, Soot's voice rang out over the sound of hammer striking anvil.

"Eva, where's that water? I'm getting parched in here, girl!"

"Don't say I didn't warn you," Eva said as she closed the door. In answer, Ivan smiled and waved.

Throughout the remainder of the day, Eva couldn't stop thinking about Ivan and the egg, especially the way she'd felt when holding it. She wondered how long the boy would wait before he gave up and left. And what was all that nonsense about seeing into the future? Although the Scrawls kept much of their rune lore to themselves,

Eva felt certain none of them could use it to see things that hadn't happened yet. Rune magic, as far as she knew, only worked on real things, like people, animals, objects, and the elements. Fortune-telling and all that sort of mystic mumbo jumbo had nothing to do with real magic. It just didn't work that way.

But that didn't explain how Eva felt while holding the gryphon egg. The thought sent a shiver through her. She'd never felt so... complete. Ever since, there'd been a pressing need to experience that again, like an itch she couldn't quite reach to scratch.

A shower of sparks brought Eva back to the present as Soot pounded away at a cherry-red wagon axle. She smacked the tiny embers stinging her neck and pulled her leather cap down tighter to cover her hair. The forge was no place for daydreaming, and Eva had her fair share of burn marks and scars like any other smith's assistant. Whenever she got careless in her work, Soot told her stories of careless smiths who'd lost limbs, been killed or horribly disfigured. Chastising herself for her carelessness, Eva refocused on the job at hand.

Due to their heavy workload, the day passed by without a chance for Eva to check on Ivan again. Even so, something told her the Scrawl hadn't gone anywhere. For his part, Seppo acted as if the whole thing hadn't happened — at least while the forge preoccupied him. Soot held a deep-rooted love for the forge that Eva shared to a lesser degree, but the golem lived to work with hammer and hot iron.

On rare occasions when work ran slow, Seppo grew restless and they'd wake up one morning to find random pieces of intricate metalwork he'd crafted to pass the time. Once, he'd made a rose so lifelike that, aside from its metal color, looked like it could have just been picked. At the moment, Seppo pounded away with a hammer Soot could barely lift, humming a weird noise akin to a cat's purr mixed with wind chimes.

When they stopped for the night, Eva felt even more tired and dirty than the day before. After picking up their tools, she and Soot and walked over to rinse away the grime. When Soot finished, Eva waited until he'd gone in the house before sprinting over to the woodshed. She opened the door and blew out a long sigh. Ivan was gone.

Chapter 5

Eva prepared dinner for the night and tried not to think about Ivan, or the gryphon egg. Now that he was gone, Eva wondered if she'd done the right thing by letting the Scrawl go, wondered if she should have told Soot. The more she thought about it, the guiltier she felt. What if the Windsworn captured Ivan and the Scrawl confessed she'd helped him? She swallowed hard and tried not to think about it, although the implications weighed on her until it felt like Seppo stood on her chest.

"Why so glum?" Soot asked after he'd finished eating. He wiped his whiskered face with the back of his hand and smacked his lips. "I swear, each stew you make is better than the last!"

Eva managed a weak smile as she cleared the table. Soot continued to watch, face softening. "Eva, maybe we've been working a little hard lately — how about you take the afternoon off tomorrow and visit the library? Seppo and I can take care of things."

"All right," Eva said, trying hard to sound more excited than she was. It didn't work.

"Look here," Soot said and put an arm around her. "I'm sorry about the other day. All that talk of Windsworn caught me off guard. It's... been a long time since I had any reminders of that life. Some things are hard to remember."

Eva nodded, too flustered to even attempt to pry more information from Soot about "that life." After washing their bowls at the water pump, she excused herself to bed. Leaving Soot to his nightly ruminations out on the porch, she opened the door to her bedroom. Ready to collapse on her straw mattress, Eva instead stifled a scream.

Ivan sat cross-legged on the middle of her bed. When their eyes met, he grinned. "I thought you'd *never* go to bed," he whispered. "Didn't bring any food, did you?"

Eva shot a worried glance out her window. "What are you still doing here?" she hissed, afraid even the slightest noise would alert Soot. "I thought you left!"

"I did. Well, the shed anyway. It got too hot and cramped — this is much better!"

Eva stared in disbelief, her throat tight as panic gripped her. Not only was she hiding a thief wanted by the king, but what if he'd found her Wonder?

"You can't stay here!" Eva said, rushing to her mattress and pushing the Scrawl aside. She shoved her hand underneath her bed, her panic doubling when her hand found nothing.

"Are you looking for this?" Ivan said, holding up the twinkling Wonder stone. "I've been studying it. It's really quite the thing — of all the places to find a relic of the Ancients, I never would have guessed a blacksmith's daughter would have one! Where did you get it?"

Eva snatched the necklace out of the Scrawl's grasp and held it close, smothering its light.

"Get out!"

"Fine," Ivan said, voice rising. "I just wanted a little company after a whole day in that woodshed, and this is the thanks I get." Shooting Eva a dirty look, he hitched one leg over the lip of the window.

Eva's heart raced, and she stumbled forward, dragging the Scrawl back down onto her bedding. "Not now!" she hissed, fighting to keep her voice down. "Soot's out on the porch — he'll see you!"

"Well, how was I supposed to know?" Ivan whispered back. "One second you say I have to go; the next you're telling me to stay — you Sorondarans don't make any sense."

"You have to wait. Until. Soot. Comes. In," Eva said, teeth gritted. "Now go over there in the corner, and don't move until I say."

No sooner had Ivan slumped down in the corner than Eva heard the porch creak as Soot rose to retire for bed. She held her breath when his heavy footfalls paused outside her door.

"Eva?" Soot said. "You awake in there?"

As quiet as she could, Eva lowered herself onto the mattress and closed her eyes, her thumping heart pounding in her ears. After a long moment, she heard her foster father sigh and walk away. Eva's eyes shot open, and she help up a hand as Ivan started to cross the room.

"*Not yet*," she mouthed, holding up her hands to show Soot had to fall asleep first. Ivan winked, which irritated her even more, and sat back on the floor. He only sat still for a few moments before reaching into his satchel and pulling out the gryphon egg again.

Eva stared at it, transfixed by the way the faint moonlight shimmered on its blood-red surface. Seeing her looking at it, Ivan held it out to her. Eva hesitated and bit her lip, torn by indecisiveness. Ivan stretched his arms out again, encouraging, and Eva relented.

As soon as her hands wrapped around the egg, a thrill rushed through her. Stifling a gasp, she sat back cross-legged and sat it in her lap. The beating sound filled her mind, matching the rhythm of her own heart. When she stretched out a trembling hand again, the egg quivered at her touch. Eva held it for a long time, lost in the sensation until sleep started to overtake her.

She looked up to see Ivan already asleep and heard Soot snoring in the next room. Fighting to keep her eyes open, Eva lay down and curled around the egg, lulled to sleep by its reassuring heartbeats.

When morning came, Eva bolted upright in bed, the sounds of drums filling her head. She looked around her room, still half-asleep. The sight of Ivan scratching runes into the floor jolted her awake.

"Why are you still here?" she asked in a loud whisper.

Ivan shrugged. "You fell asleep! I didn't think it would hurt anything."

Eva glanced out the window and saw the sun already high in the sky. For some reason, Soot had let her sleep in. Panic overwhelmed her, and the beat of the gryphon egg pounded in her mind like a drum.

"What am I going to do?" Eva asked herself, running her hands over and over through her long, tangled hair. "What am I going to do?"

A shadow crossed her window, followed by the sound of heavy wings beating. Eva's insides froze. Outside in the yard, feathers shook, and a screech sounded, deeper and louder than any eagle's. The gryphon riders were visiting.

Shaking, Eva pulled herself up high enough to peek over the bottom of her window. Three gryphons filled the small yard between the cottage and the forge, riders just sliding off their backs. Eva's breath caught in her throat, terror momentarily forgotten at her first sight of the magnificent creatures up close.

The white, gray, and brown plumage of each gryphon glowed like burnished metal in the sunshine. As each rider stepped aside, they folded their enormous wings and shook their great eagles' heads, causing a shiver to run down Eva's back. The gryphons were shorter than most horses but carried more muscle on their feline frames than even the war-horses Eva saw knights riding in the parades. From the curve of their yellow beaks to their long, wicked front talons and massive back paws, each creature made a fearsome sight on its own as they switched their long, tufted tails.

As Soot and Seppo came out of the forge to meet the riders, Eva noticed for the first time who their visitors were: Lord Commander Andor and his dashing young rider, alongside a surly girl Eva hoped she never had reason to meet. With a mop of spiky dark hair and a sharp nose, she looked every bit as fierce as the giant half-eagle she rode.

"Soot!" the lord commander shouted, slapping Eva's foster father on the shoulder. "By the sky, it's good to see you, old friend. How are you?"

Although Soot looked uneasy, a small smile crossed his face, surprising Eva. "I'm well enough. It's been awhile, Andor."

"Too long," the lord commander said. "I saw Seppo with your… assistant at the market the other day — I hoped you would have been there with them." Stepping back, he gestured to the two riders standing behind him. "These two are wing leaders in training: Tahl, and the young woman is Sigrid."

As the lord commander started telling Soot about the egg theft, Eva stared at the young rider from the market. *Tahl.* His wind-tousled hair only accented his good looks. Eva wasn't sure, but she imagined he looked around the yard while the older men talked, as if searching for her.

"— don't know how this is going to turn out. Devana was one of our greatest," Andor continued. "And we still haven't found her egg or the thief."

"How'd they do it?" Soot asked

"There was a Choosing," Andor said, "But Devana wasn't ready to give up her egg — she was back in the nest. That's how the thief got away: Most of the riders were in the city for the night. Whoever stole the egg killed Devana and somehow escaped the Gyr before anyone knew something was amiss."

Eva felt a sickening burning, like a lump of iron in the bottom of her stomach. She slid down onto her bed and looked at Ivan.

"You…" she said, fighting the urge to throw up. "You killed a gryphon?"

"No!" Ivan hissed. "No, I never! I found the gryphon like that — I told you I stole the egg to protect it."

Eva shook her head. "I-I don't know what to think," she said. A million thoughts raced through her mind, the beating of the egg muffling and mixing them even more. Before she could say anything else, however, the lord commander's voice carried through the window.

"Speaking of which, where is the girl?"

"I let her sleep in a bit this morning," Eva heard Soot say. "She wasn't feeling well last night, but she should be up by now. Eva! Seppo, go see if she's awake."

Fear coursing through her, Eva snatched up the gryphon egg and held it out for Ivan. "Quick! Seppo's coming; you've got to go!"

Ivan took the egg for a moment and then held it out to her again as Seppo's iron-shod footsteps neared Eva's window. "I can't take it — it's hatching!"

Before she knew what was happening, Ivan passed the egg back into her hands. Sure enough, the egg wobbled and jerked. Eva's head spun, and she pushed it back to Ivan.

"Take it! *Take it!*"

The Scrawl folded his arms and shook his head. "Look, you're just not getting it, Eva," he said in a tone far too condescending for his age. "And I'm tired of explaining things."

"What's *he* doing here?"

Eva squeaked in surprise and almost dropped the egg as she spun around to find Seppo's head poking through her open shutters. She glanced at Ivan. Beneath his dark blue rune markings, the Scrawl's face went pale. The gryphon egg continued to shudder in Eva's hands, tiny cracks spreading across its smooth surface like spiderwebs.

"Eva, what's going on?" Soot asked as more footsteps approached. Finally deciding it might be time to leave, Ivan yanked opened the bedroom door.

"Not this time!" Seppo yelled. Eva heard the front door slam open, followed by a brief scuffle. Rooted to the spot, Eva could only stare at the egg as the pounding in her head magnified even more and a little beak poked through the blood-red shell.

"Aha!" Seppo's voice rang out triumphant. At the same time, Soot, the lord commander, and Tahl appeared in the window. When they saw Eva standing inside with a hatching gryphon egg cupped in her hands, their eyes went wide.

No one spoke.

"I...I can explain." Eva began.

Before she could say anything else, an angry peep filled the silence. A curved talon burst out of the egg, followed by another. Eva lowered the half-broken shell to the floor, and in one sudden motion the entire gryphon hatchling burst free of the egg.

A crashing sound rose in the kitchen, and Eva's bedroom door flew open. Seppo held Ivan tucked under one arm and ducked down to fit his head inside. His eyes fell to the gryphon chick on the floor, and he shouted in delight.

"Now that's something you don't see every day!"

Chapter 6

Eva opened her mouth to speak, but the words wouldn't come. No one else said anything either. Shaking the last of the eggshell and ichor free from its rusty fur and rose-colored down, the gryphon chick growled and screeched again. It was about the size of a half-grown cat, tumbling around as it tried to stand on its little paws and talons.

"I see you've had some adventures since we met," Andor said. The tone of his voice matched his piercing, cold eyes.

"How?" Soot began. "Why —"

"I meant to tell you," Eva said. Like a dam overflowing, the words rushed out. "He just showed up two nights ago, and he told me he'd seen this vision and the egg had to stay with me and I didn't know what to do because it felt so strange but Ivan wouldn't go away and —"

Soot held up a hand. "Slow down. Take a deep breath."

"I believe I can be of assistance," Seppo said in a cheerful voice. "We found this Scrawl in the woodshed two nights ago. He had stolen the gryphon egg. I wanted to tell you right away, but Mistress Evelyn said not to."

Eva groaned. "Thanks, Seppo."

The golem missed the sarcasm. "Of course!"

"Do you realize what you've done?" Soot asked. "That stolen egg could start a war, and you were the one hiding the thief from the king and the Gyr!"

Eva looked at the floor, fighting the urge to vomit as she started to quake. The gryphon hatchling let out an angry squawk and turned its bright yellow eyes to her. Kneeling down before she collapsed, Eva stretched out a cautious hand to comfort the chick.

"Ow!"

The gryphon's tiny beak bit down hard, and Eva yanked her hand back, blood welling out of a gash in her finger.

"Careful!" Andor warned. "That's no stray kitten."

While Soot and Tahl left to search for a pair of irons to place on Ivan — the Scrawl had remained tucked under Seppo's arm throughout the whole ordeal — the lord commander and the dark-haired girl, Sigrid, joined Eva in the kitchen, where she'd carefully picked up the nipping gryphon chick and placed it on the table. When she sat it down, it screeched louder, drawing a series of concerned cries from its full-grown relations outside.

"Sigrid, go calm them down, will you?" Andor asked. The girl nodded, a deep scowl on her face as she watched Eva and the hatchling before leaving the room.

"He needs fresh meat," Andor said, watching the chick stumble across the table, pecking and scratching at the wood with its beak. "I'm afraid one of your chickens will have to serve."

"What are you going to do to Ivan?" Eva asked. "Please don't hurt him! I...I think he's telling the truth."

Andor studied her for a long moment. "Don't worry," he said at last, "the Scrawl boy will get a fair trial according to the king's law. Right now, you've got plenty of your own problems, Evelyn."

Eva's fear rushed back tenfold. "Am I...will I be arrested, too?"

The lord commander shook his head. "No, but I hope you know you did a damn foolish thing and got very lucky."

"I'm sorry," Eva said, staring at the floor. "I guess I made a mess of things."

Andor's expression softened. "It could have been worse. But this little terror needs to be fed. Let's get him taken care of, and we'll talk more."

As soon as Soot and Tahl had a compliant Ivan secured and placed under Seppo's watchful eyes once more, the smith stomped off to the chicken coop, returning soon after with a limp Ms. Cluck Cluck swinging from his fist. To stave off the guilt when Soot began to pluck the dead chicken, Eva reminded herself of all the times the hen attacked her when she'd gone to gather eggs.

"Tahl, let the Gyr know the egg's been found," Andor said as soon as the young rider joined them around the table. "Let the Council know everything is fine. I'll give them a full report later this evening."

Shooting her a reassuring smile, Tahl tapped his right fist against his heart in salute to his commander and left. Eva watched him go — until Soot walked in, with the plucked chicken, blocking her view.

The smell of fresh blood drove the chick wild, and Eva stretched across the table to grab him before he fell off, intent on reaching Soot as the smith cut the meat into small chunks.

"Watch your fingers this time," Andor cautioned when Soot handed Eva the first bits.

"Sorry, Ms. Cluck Cluck," Eva said under her breath. She held out the first bit of raw chicken to the gryphon hatchling. The chick's head shot out and snatched the meat from between her fingers faster than Eva expected. With a flick of his tiny head, the baby gryphon swallowed it whole and hissed for another.

By the time it stopped shrieking for more, the chick had eaten almost half of the hen. Hunger sated, the baby gryphon curled up in a fluffy ball on the middle of the table and fell asleep almost at once. Under Andor's guidance, Eva slid her hands under the chick and transferred it into a crude nest made of her blankets, careful not to wake the gryphon.

"Eva, please excuse me to talk with Soot for a moment," Andor said.

Exhausted, Eva nodded and stepped out of the cottage, shutting the door behind her. By now, a small crowd stood on the edge of the street, talking and pointing at Sigrid and the two remaining gryphons still standing in the yard.

"Everyone, stay back!" Sigrid commanded the onlookers. "Windsworn business; be on your way."

Eva ducked around the house out of sight before anyone thought to come question her about what was going on. There she found Seppo standing over Ivan. The Scrawl's wrists and ankles were in irons, and a strip of cloth kept him from uttering any kennings. When he saw Eva, his face brightened, and he raised his manacled hands in greeting as if they'd just run into one another on the street. Eva shook her head, wondering how the Scrawl could be cheerful as she sat bound in chains and about to be arrested. Part of her thought she might trade him places, though, given the chance.

"My, what an exciting day it's been already!" Seppo said as if it all were some treat. "I wonder what's in store for the rest of it?"

Not feeling like talking, Eva slumped down on the ground beneath her window and buried her hands in her face. Instead of relief, however, she heard the lord commander's voice from the kitchen.

"She can't stay here, Soot. The chick bonded with her."

"You know she can't go to the Gyr," Soot replied. "What if —"

"It doesn't matter now. The egg hatched for her, Soot. *The red egg.* The gryphon of a generation."

Eva sucked in a sharp breath, a lump forming in her throat. After a long pause, she heard Soot sigh.

"I'll go speak with her," Andor said.

Eva blinked back her tears and stood, pretending like she hadn't heard anything. When Andor rounded the corner, she met him with a blank expression.

"Come with me," the lord commander said and gestured toward the forge.

The murmur of the crowd faded, and Eva felt like she was walking down a tunnel. Inside the forge, Andor led them out of sight before turning to face her. Her chest tightened. Twice, Andor opened his mouth to speak. Eva couldn't do anything but stare, wide eyed, heart pounding.

"Eva, there's something you should know," he began.

A long paused followed. Eva didn't know if she was supposed to ask what, or if she could talk even if she needed to.

"When the chick hatched, it bonded to you," the lord commander said at last. "Do you know what that means?"

"I…" Eva surprised herself by speaking. "I'm not sure."

"It means you have to return to the Gyr with us," Andor said not in an unkind voice. "You will live with the other new recruits and train to become Windsworn."

Eva felt her world crashing down around her. "No! You don't understand. I…" She trailed off, not sure where to even begin. "I'm not Windsworn material. I belong here, with Soot and Seppo!"

For some odd reason, Andor's lips twitched in a brief smile at that. "I'm afraid you don't have a choice in the matter," he said, serious once more. "Had the egg not hatched, it would be a different story. But the bond between gryphon and human is not something that can be broken. And Devana's egg held a very special gryphon."

If that was intended to make Eva feel better, it didn't. She felt tears welling her eyes again but couldn't stop them a second time. "I didn't mean for it to hatch," she said. Alone with Andor in the forge, she felt small and alone. "I only did what I thought was right."

"I'm sorry, Eva," the lord commander said. It sounded more like a remark on the weather than an apology and left no room for debate. "It's not like you'll never see Soot or Seppo again, however. You'll be allowed to visit them on leave. Right now, I need you to be brave and trust me. Please go pack your things and say goodbye."

And that ended it. Tears rolling down her face, Eva nodded. Body numb, she walked across the yard in a daze, struggling to grasp the morning's events. Lost and confused, she almost ran into the cottage door. Instead, Soot opened it and beckoned Eva inside, out of sight of the growing crowd.

As soon as the door shut, Eva collapsed into her foster father's embrace, sobbing. Soot didn't say anything, just held her tight, which somehow made it all worse. After a few minutes passed, Eva shuddered and pulled herself away, gulping air while she wiped away the tears with the back of her hand.

"I'm sorry," she said in between gasps. "Don't make me leave, p-please. I'm s-s-sorry…"

She looked up and saw tears running down the grooves in Soot's forge-beaten face. "It'll be okay, Eva," he said and forced a rare, awkward smile. "You weren't meant to stay here forever! This is an opportunity hundreds of boys and girls all across Rhylance would die for."

Eva swallowed and nodded, wishing Ivan had hidden in one of the sheds of those hundreds of boys and girls. Soot gave her a gentle squeeze on the shoulder. "Remember what I always say: when you've got a job to do, it's better to face the fire head on."

It didn't take long. Although Soot's business prospered and they never went without, Eva had few personal belongings. Her mother's Wonder stone, a few coarse shirts and leather leggings spattered with tiny burn holes from working in the forge, a dress for festivals and holidays, a carved bone hair comb, and a couple of battered books made up the extent of her belongings.

As she placed each item in the bag, Eva's mind whirled, still trying to grasp everything happening. Two mornings ago, she'd just been a smith's assistant. Now…she didn't know what she was now, but she would have given anything to go back.

In the kitchen, a basket with lid straps sat on the table. Soot stood in the middle of the room, looking lost and unsure, for the first time Eva could remember. Outside, Eva heard the crowd gasp and the calls of at least one more gryphon.

"They're coming to get the Scrawl," Soot said, voice dull and muted compared to its normal booming ring. He gestured to the basket on the table. "Andor put your gryphon inside."

Eva rushed forward and wrapped her arms around her foster father once more. "Oh, Soot!"

The smith wrapped her in his arms, once more patted her on the back. "You go up to that mountain, and show everyone what you're made of, Eva," he said. "You're like good steel; you bend, but you don't break. Just remember that — when things get hard."

Eva pressed her face harder against Soot's rough leather apron, trying to fight back the tears. Soot cleared his throat again.

"Your parents…they'd be proud of you," he said at last. "I know I am."

It was high praise from Soot, who didn't dole out needless compliments. Swallowing hard, Eva nodded and wiped her face. She blew out a long breath then turned for the door.

Outside, two more gryphons stood in the yard, sunlight shining on their bronze-and-tan bodies. Their riders escorted Ivan between them, toward the large creatures. A long line of city and palace guards separated the crowd from the proceedings.

"Where are they taking him?" Eva asked, awful images of Ivan being fed to the gryphons or dropped out of the sky flashing across her mind.

"To the Gyr," Andor said, taking the basket with the gryphon chick from Eva. "He'll be held there until a trial is set. Sigrid will take the chick, and you will ride with me. Ready?"

Eva felt her stomach sink and a dull emptiness fill her. So, this was it.

"Goodbye, Mistress Evelyn," Seppo said. He spread his arms in an awkward invitation for a hug. Eva let out a dry laugh at how funny it looked but wrapped her arms around the golem's waist anyway.

"Goodbye, Seppo," she said after. "Take care of Soot for me, all right?"

"An almost impossible task, but I will do my best," the golem said. Eva laughed and looked at Soot, who scowled at Seppo. When his eyes met Eva's however, he looked away, shifting from one foot to the other.

"Stop by when you can," the smith said, his gruff voice strained. "You hear, Andor? You send her to visit."

Unable to speak, Eva rushed forward and embraced the only father she'd ever known. She felt Soot's thick arms enfold her and sobbed into his coarse shirt.

"None of that now," Soot whispered in her ear. He held Eva at arm's length and wiped away the tears from her aching red eyes. "Show 'em what you're made of, eh?"

Andor walked away toward his gryphon, and Eva hefted her packed bag to follow. She was painfully aware of the dozens of people watching, which only made the moment worse. "Goodbye," she said in a hoarse voice. "I love you, Soot."

"I love you, too, girl," the smith said. The sight of tears running down his face broke Eva's heart even more.

Eva turned away and forced herself not to look back again as each step widened the gap between her and the only family she'd ever known. Andor held up a hand when she was about a half-dozen paces from his gryphon. To their left, Sigrid and the Windsworn who'd come for Ivan mounted and rose into the air. Eva ducked her head as dust scattered from the beating wings of the gryphons until they were gone.

"This is Stormwind," Andor said, gesturing to his gryphon. The creature looked at Eva and cocked its great gray eagle's head to the side, clacking its beak. "Go on, say hello."

Eva swallowed and took a cautious step toward Stormwind and then another. As she neared, she couldn't help but notice the way the sunlight gleamed on the gryphon's vicious beak and curved talons. An arm's length away, their eyes met, and Eva froze.

"It's okay," Andor said behind her. "Go on, say hello. Hold out your hand."

Growing up in a forge with a one-handed smith had taught Eva to be careful where she stuck her appendages but she raised a shaking hand anyway and tried not to shy away as Stormwind nudged her open palm.

"Good, Eva," Andor said. "You can pet him now, if you want."

Stepping closer to pet the gryphon was about the last thing Eva wanted, but on the other hand, disobeying the lord commander first thing didn't seem like a good idea either. Stormwind nudged her hand again, and Eva relented, running her hand down the feathers of his powerful neck. Up close, the gryphon seemed even bigger — Stormwind's back stood as tall as Eva's shoulder, but his muscular frame and wings made the creature seem twice as big as a horse.

Andor's hand fell on her shoulder and guided Eva around to

Stormwind's backside as the gryphon spread his wings for them to mount. Once he'd taken his seat in the saddle, the lord commander jerked his head for Eva to join him. Heart pounding, Eva could hardly think straight as Andor pulled her up behind him.

"I, uh…" Was it too late to tell Andor that heights scared her? Would that disqualify Eva from being Windsworn and put an end to the madness? She glanced at Soot and Seppo, watching from the awning of the forge and wanted to yell at them to save her.

"What's that?" Andor said over his shoulder.

"Never mind," Eva muttered, hoping she could shut her eyes and the lord commander wouldn't notice.

"All right then, hold on!"

Chapter

 7

Andor whistled, and Eva's insides froze as Stormwind gathered his powerful lion's legs beneath them. In the next instant, the gryphon sprang forward, and Eva bit back a scream as the creature's body jerked and lurched beneath her. Concerned more with self-preservation than impressions, Eva clutched Andor so tight she felt his chain mail pressing into her bare arms

Stormwind's beating wings blasted cool morning air into Eva's face, and she felt nothing but emptiness behind her. After a few excruciating minutes when Eva thought she was going to die for sure, they finally leveled off in the air. The gryphon's wing strokes slowed to a steady tempo, and instead of jolting, Eva felt a smooth rocking motion beneath her.

"Doing all right?" Andor yelled over Stormwind's whooshing wings.

"I — I think so!" Eva replied, hoping her voice sounded more confident than she felt.

"Good," the lord commander said. "Would you mind letting go a bit, then? I promise we won't drop you."

Eva wanted more than anything to tell him no, but instead she forced her arms to unclench a few inches. After a few more moments, she cracked open her eyes and found an expanse of blue all around them.

"Quite the view, isn't it?"

A quick glance over Stormwind's side at the miniature buildings, towers, and streets below sent Eva's head spinning. After a few moments and a couple of deep breaths, however, she ventured another look.

Gryfonesse sprawled out below them, its white marble shining like a gem in the midday sun. At their height, the crowded street traffic appeared to be a solid mass rather than individual citizens, wagons, and carts bustling up and down the avenues. Above the people, the king's banners rustled from turrets and walls, and even the palace's majesty seemed shrunken.

Andor whistled again, and Stormwind spread his wings, banking to the north. Below them, acres of fresh-plowed fields, pasture land, and orchards surrounded the city like a giant patchwork quilt. Eva looked to the east and saw nothing but rolling hills and woodlands stretching for miles and miles until they met the periwinkle horizon. In the face of such beauty and wonder, her fear gave way to awe.

Catching a thermal, Stormwind rose even higher, gliding like they were on a frozen pond. A silver glint showed the river twisting through the trees on the edge of the farmland. And then Stormwind turned again, and Eva saw the Gyr.

The home of the Windsworn loomed over Gryfonesse like a stern old man watching his grandchildren scurry about at his feet. A spear of raw, pale rock, the Gyr looked like it had been thrust from the earth to cut through the heavens. The snow in the valley had melted weeks ago, but Eva could see a hood of white across the Gyr's broken peak and other stubborn drifts tucked down into the mountain's craggy folds.

A few lonesome, bedraggled pine trees dotted the slopes, jutting out at odd angles from whatever patch of rock their roots could cling to. The first gryphons they saw circling and spiraling around the mountain looked like birds until they drew close enough to see the sunlight glinting on the multiple hues of their fur and feathers. Stormwind screamed, and Eva gritted her teeth against the sudden sound. Moments later, a series of faint cries carried back to them in greeting.

"Welcome to the Gyr," Andor said. "The most impregnable fortress in all of Altaris. Legend has it when the first Windsworn settled its peaks, they found a staircase carved into the side of the mountain leading all the way to the halls. The first thing they did was destroy the stair — the only way in or out is through the sky."

Eva's stomach clenched, realizing she'd only be able to leave the mountain through the same terrifying, heart-stopping transportation. The thought made her head spin, and all the fear rushed back at once. Eva clutched Andor in a death grip once more, heart hammering in her chest like Seppo working the forge. She squeezed her eyes shut again, only half hearing whatever Andor was saying.

"We'll show you how to care for your gryphon and get you settled in today," the lord commander said, either ignoring or oblivious of Eva's mounting terror. "Tomorrow morning you'll come before the Council."

Eva nodded in a daze, not even realizing Andor couldn't see her. The joy of the flight vanished, and she yearned to have her feet on solid ground — even if that meant the Gyr. Stormwind's smooth wing beats felt like a ship rocking on the sea, one pitch away from capsizing.

As if sensing her unease, Andor twisted in his seat. "All right back there?"

Eva shuddered, chilled to the bone despite her cloak. The brilliant blue sky and summer sun suddenly felt pale and cold. She pressed her eyes closed again and mumbled something in response.

"We're coming in to land," Andor said. "Hold tight!"

Stormwind dipped forward, and Eva's insides lurched. Torn between remaining oblivious to the empty expanse below her and wanting to see how much more she had to endure, Eva peeked out of one eye and saw the side of the Gyr rushing toward them. For a split second, she thought they were going to crash into the mountainside. At the last moment, however, a large shelf materialized, and Stormwind spread his wings to slow their descent.

As soon as the gryphon's talons touched down, Eva blew out the breath she'd been holding. Although she'd done nothing more than sit on the gryphon's back, she felt light-headed and breathless like she'd been running or working in the forge on a sweltering summer day. Her golden hair clung her face, damp with perspiration.

Andor slid from the saddle and held a hand to help her down. Eva took a cautious step, still swaying. "Are you okay?" the lord commander asked.

Eva felt the blood rush to her clammy face. "Y-yes." She took a deep breath and managed a weak smile.

"Everyone's first flight is a bit…unsettling," Andor said. "You did well."

The lord commander didn't seem like the kind of person who said something just to make a person feel better. Even so, unless not falling off was the only bar of achievement for a person's first gryphon flight, Eva felt she'd already failed her first test.

Eva followed Andor across the shelf toward a tall cavernous opening in the side of the rock. At the mouth of the opening a young girl waited at attention. She looked to be around Ivan's age but with her royal-blue uniform and the no-nonsense expression on her face, she seemed much older.

"Recruit Wynn," Andor said in a much louder and steelier voice than Eva had heard before.

The young girl thumped her fist across her chest. "Yes, Lord Commander!"

Eva swore she saw the hint of a smile behind Andor's beard. "This is Evelyn, our newest recruit. You will take her to the kitchens and then give her a tour of the Gyr. You'll find Sigrid has placed your chick in the Roost — Wynn will show you. Afterward, Recruit Wynn, please see to it that Eva is settled into her quarters within the garrison."

The girl gave a curt nod. "Yes, Lord Commander."

"I will send for you in the morning," Andor said to Eva. "We will talk before you meet the Council. Until then, try to make yourself at home. Your training begins tomorrow afternoon."

Eva nodded, but Andor continued to look at her. "Uh, yes, Lord Commander," she said, realizing what he was waiting for after a long pause.

Andor nodded. "Very good; until tomorrow then." With that, the lord commander left, swinging into Stormwind's saddle with an ease Eva doubted she'd ever accomplish. The gryphon reared and leaped back into the sky, leaving Eva alone with the Windsworn recruit.

"It's good to meet you," the girl said, offering a hand.

"Good to meet you. I'm Eva."

The young girl rolled her eyes and blew a strand of light brown hair out of her face with an exasperated sigh. "I know that, the lord commander just said so!"

Eva stared, taken back by the girl's abrupt change in behavior. But Wynn smiled and grabbed Eva by the hand, leading her into the cavern's depth.

"Come on, let me show you around!"

Chapter

 8

Wynn set off at a brisk pace, pulling Eva along after her. The tunnel sloped downward but was well lighted by a series of crystal lanterns along the walls. They gave off a warm, yellow glow that grew brighter the farther they traveled from the outside. After a few minutes walking, Eva looked back and found the sunlight had disappeared behind a bend.

"How do those work?" Eva asked, pointing to one of the lanterns.

"Magic, of course," the girl said like it was the most obvious thing in the world. "The Gyr used to be a fort of the Ancients — I thought everyone knew that. Some of the things they left behind still work, but don't ask me how. Most of it's useful, but you've got to be careful — there's tricks and traps hidden, too."

"Are they...dangerous?" By now, they were starting to pass people. When they saw Eva, many of them offered a kind hello, then stared until Wynn led her out of sight.

"Not really," the girl said, oblivious to the people's attention. She hadn't stopped talking since they'd entered the mountain. "Mostly, they'll just get you turned around, or stuck until someone else comes by to release the trap. You'll figure out where they are pretty quick, though."

Wynn took a turn to the right and continued deeper into the mountain. The tunnel widened enough that two horses and their riders could have ridden side by side without fear of hitting their heads on the smooth, straight ceiling above. Every so often, this main tunnel split off into a side passage or a door. Strange runes, similar to the ones tattooed on Ivan's body, were carved into the walls. Most could only be seen from the reflection of the lamps, but every so often Eva spied one flickering. What gave off the light, she had no idea.

The dull murmur of dozens of voices rose ahead of them, but Wynn steered Eva down a smaller side tunnel instead. "That's the Main Hall," the girl said, pointing in the direction they'd turned from. "It's where you'd normally eat, but I got told not to take you there. We aren't supposed to make a show. We'll go around back to the kitchens."

By the tone of her voice, Wynn almost sounded disappointed. Eva's stomach rumbled, reminding her she hadn't eaten all day. There hadn't been a chance to grab anything before leaving Soot's forge, and Eva felt pretty sure she wouldn't have been able to keep it down anyway. Now, the aromas wafting down the small passage made Eva's mouth water.

"Not bad, eh?"

Eva could only nod, sleepy and just a little bit sick after their meal. Delighted to meet the newest Windsworn recruit and the future rider of the red gryphon, the cooks heaped their plates with everything from thick dark bread and early season fruit out of the north to chilled ciders and grilled meat right off the skewer.

They continued alongside passages to avoid the majority of lunch traffic. After so many dips, rises, twists, and turns, Eva doubted she could even find her way back to the kitchens, let alone the shelf they'd landed on. Soon a new series of sounds filled the air: the dull thwack of wood on wood mingled with shouts and grunts. Without warning, the passage ahead opened up into a balcony overlooking an expansive area below.

Eva tried to hide her surprise. So far, everything she'd seen on

Wynn's tour made her think the inside of the mountain was all a series of tunnels and caves. But the training ground — Eva guessed that's what is was by the equipment and people drilling — opened up into an enormous cavern that could have fit Soot's cottage, forge, and yard in it with room to spare. Below, dozens of recruits sparred with one another, practiced their sword and axe strokes against straw dummies, wrestled, shot bows at padded targets against the wall, and much more.

"This is the Pit," Wynn said. "It's where we all train, no matter how long you've been here or what types of weapon you're assigned. You'll report here with me and the other fresh recruits tomorrow afternoon."

Wynn kept talking while Eva looked wide eyed over the grounds. In one corner, two boys hammered away at each other with wooden short swords in both hands. One lunged and missed, leaving the other an opening. The second boy cracked his opponent on the side of his head and jabbed him in the ribs before the instructor called a halt. Nobody seemed concerned as the boy fell to the ground in a ball, clutching the side of his head. Eva swallowed hard, stomach dropping.

A series of shouts below drew Eva's attention away from the injured boy to a large crowd forming on the far side of the Pit from them. The Windsworn recruits surrounded what looked to be a matchup of one against three. Before Eva could ask Wynn about the fairness of such a fight, a sharp whistle blew. The single fighter, wearing only leathers and a light cap, threw themselves at the other three. Although she couldn't tell at their distance, Eva didn't think any of the three landed a blow as the solo fighter picked them apart. In short order, each fell to the ground and, after one or two halfhearted attempts, stayed there. The crowd shouted, and the lone fighter raised their weapons in triumph.

"By thunder," Wynn said in a hushed voice. "I heard stories about her, but I didn't believe them until now."

"*Her?*" Eva asked in surprise. They'd seen plenty of women and girls in Windsworn attire throughout the day, but she found it hard to believe one had beaten three men with such ease.

"Yeah," Wynn continued. "I think her name's Sigrid. One of the lord commander's personal aides, a real hard ass."

Eva thought back to Sigrid's scowls and coldness and wondered what she could've done to cross the dark-haired rider. She made a mental note to stay away from Sigrid, especially in the Pit. The thought of standing across from her in the ring made Eva sick.

"Come on, no time to stop now."

Next, Wynn led her through the Great Archive, whose towering shelves held untold numbers of scrolls and books, the girl said, on anything and everything you could ever want to know about.

"They say it's the second-biggest library in all of Altaris — besides the Scriven, anyway."

Eva tried to linger, running her hands over the spines of several large tomes, but Wynn dragged her along, down more twisting and turning passages and caverns. She tried to keep track of them all: the armory, filled with weapons of every kind, shape, and size; the storerooms heaped with enough supplies, the quartermaster said, to feed the Gyr for a year; classrooms of recruits being lectured on history, battle strategy; and Eva's favorite, the baths — caverns dotted with natural pools of shallow water somehow heated by the mountain itself.

Zigzagging up a wide staircase cut into the stone, they climbed until Eva's legs burned with every step. At last, after what seemed like a thousand stairs, the path leveled into a tunnel that grew larger the farther they walked down it. Eventually, it opened up into a massive chamber even bigger than the Pit. Wynn called it the Roost, one of the highest points in the Gyr — where the gryphons ate and nested when not with their riders.

"I'll catch back up with you in a bit," Wynn said, already running off. "I've got to go see my chick in the nursery!"

Eva shouted after Wynn, but the recruit ignored her and she found herself alone. Unlike the rest of the mountain, the air here had a brisk chill. Across from her, the Roost ended in a gigantic shelf into open sky. Beyond that, Eva saw nothing but blue and a few sparse clouds in the distance.

The gryphons themselves rested on hundreds of natural pockets and ledges inside the cavern. These roosts and nests lined the walls all around them, continuing higher and higher until Eva stared straight up the hollow peak of the mountain. She saw gryphons of all sizes and shades of colors: gray, black, brown, white, tan, and every hue in between. Some slept, while others gnawed on quartered carcasses. The air buzzed with the sound of their calls and the rush of wings as the gryphons came and went without pause.

"Looking for a red one?"

Eva turned to find a woman with thick gray hair and a lined face walking toward her. She crossed into the open from a small side door built into the wall, holding Eva's chick in her arms. With trepidation, Eva reached out to take him and found the hatchling fast asleep, much to her relief.

"So, you're the one we've heard so much about," the older woman said with a slight bow. "I am Cassandra, the Gyr's roost master."

Eva took a liking to the woman at once as Cassandra walked her down the length of the Roost and explained her role. As she listened, Eva got the feeling the roost master's speech was well rehearsed, but Cassandra spoke in a way that suggested she'd never tire of it, or her position.

"We have over three hundred gryphons roosting at the Gyr at any given time," she said. "There are other Windsworn holdings across Rhylance, of course, but this mountain is the main headquarters and the largest. It is also the only breeding ground and hatchery in all of Altaris."

They passed dozens of younger Windsworn going about various chores such as pitching out piles and sticks and straw for the gryphons' nests, quartering fresh-killed animals for meals, or treating a variety of injuries from chipped talons to pulled muscles and broken feathers. When they returned to their starting position, Cassandra led Eva through side door she'd emerged from when they'd arrived. Inside, they found rows and rows of eggs in as many colors and patterns as there were gryphons outside. Farther back, a series of familiar, ear-splitting shrieks echoed from deeper within.

"Why don't you leave the eggs with their mothers?" Eva asked. It seemed cruel to separate the mothers from their brood.

"The eggs stay with the mothers until they are almost ready to hatch," Cassandra explained. "By that point, the chicks no longer require constant heat as they're fully grown inside the egg. The chicks develop a stronger bond with the rider if they are present during the hatching. Not every chick bonds with a rider right out of the egg, however."

Eva looked down at the bundle of dark red fuzz and fur still asleep in her tired arms and almost asked if sometimes the chicks made a mistake. But after seeing Cassandra's liking for the red gryphon and her passion in general, she thought better of it.

"Hey!" Wynn said, running up to join them from the tunnel leading to what Eva guessed was the nursery. She clutched a tiny gryphon with tawny feathers and brindled fur in her arms.

"Careful, Wynn," Cassandra said. "If you trip, you could hurt your hatchling."

Although she was only a few paces away, Wynn slowed to a walk. "Sorry, Roost Master." When she stopped, her gryphon chick climbed to perch on her shoulder, peeping and nipping at Wynn's hair. Eva felt a stab of jealousy as her own chick stirred. He probably would've bitten her ear off if she'd tried something like that.

The red gryphon woke growling, and Wynn led them to a bin full of chopped up pieces of meat. Eva fed the chick under the roost master's watchful eyes, careful of her fingers as he tore at each morsel she offered.

"You've got a lively one there," Cassandra said, chuckling. "He'll take a firm hand to raise, but being here in the Gyr now will make it easier."

"Maybe he'll learn some manners staying here," Eva said, flipping her hair back over her shoulder. Apparently full, the chick started nipping at her locks. When Eva's hair was out of reach, he pecked at her shirt and hissed.

"Oh, he won't stay here," Cassandra said. "Chicks stay with their riders in the barracks until they reach adolescence. *Then* he'll come to the Roost with the adult gryphons. It helps to build a stronger bond between gryphon and rider."

"Oh." Eva did her best to hide both the disappointment and apprehension she felt inside. That much bonding time sounded like a good way to lose half her fingers and toes.

"I'm here for whatever you need," Cassandra said in a way that sounded like the roost master was trying to reassure herself as much as Eva. "I'm sure it will take some getting used to for both of you — gryphons aren't simple *beasts* after all — they're as smart as humans, smarter in some ways. And that gryphon you have is one of a kind."

As Eva struggled to hold the squirming, pecking chick in her hands, Cassandra led them back out into the gigantic main cavern. "Take a look," the roost master said, gesturing at the scores of gryphons perched on the ledges. "You'll see whites, grays, blacks, browns, golds — even a few blue roans — but you won't find another red gryphon anywhere in Altaris. The birth of a red gryphon has always marked times of great change for our people. As his rider, you are tied to that same destiny."

When she finished, Cassandra stared at Eva like she was expecting some kind of grand, heroic speech. Eva coughed and looked at the ground. "I — I'll do my best."

Almost as if he sensed the uncomfortable moment, the red chick sank his beak into her arm. Eva yelled and dropped the baby gryphon, who scurried under a nearby straw wagon and stared out at them through angry yellow eyes.

"Sorry," Eva mumbled as she reached in to fish the chick out, jerking her hand back each time his tiny beak snapped at her. After several moments, she managed to distract him with one hand and scoop him up with the other. When she turned around, her face felt like she'd been stoking Soot's smelter all morning.

Cassandra looked anything but encouraging. "You...ah... seem to be off to a rough start," she said. Behind her, Eva heard Wynn snicker.

"He's... growing on me," Eva replied, wishing she could crawl under the straw wagon and hide herself. Several other riders were watching them from a distance, talking and pointing.

"Growing on you like a pox," Wynn muttered. Eva shot her a dirty look.

"Don't worry, my dear," Cassandra said. She patted Eva on the shoulder and then reached down to tickle the gryphon chick under his chin. Much to Eva's annoyance, the hatchling stretched out his neck and purred at the roost master's touch. "You're only one day in. It will come."

Somehow, Eva didn't think things would be that easy.

Wynn led Eva down a couple of levels and the tunnel widened into a cavern about half the size of the Roost with terraces carved into the rock on either side. Male and female riders of various ages congregated in a courtyard-like area below laughing and relaxing. On both sides, the balconies rose three stories high and lined the wall as far as Eva could see. When they came into sight, several new recruits around Wynn's age shouted and waved. Noticing Eva, the entire commons area began to talk in low voices, glancing at Eva until she focused on her feet. Excited by the noise, the gryphon chick struggled to free himself, but Eva held him tight. The last thing she needed was to embarrass herself in front of the entire Windsworn barracks on her first evening.

"Come on," Wynn said, tugging on her sleeve. "I'll show you the quarters the lord commander requested for you."

They went up a staircase to the left of the entrance and continued up to the top terrace. From up here, the hall looked much longer than Eva would have guessed. Doors lined the halls as they passed, some made of wood, while others looked to be carved from the stone itself. They continued away from the courtyard, their path lit by the same flickering crystal lamps, until Eva caught sight of sunlight in the bend ahead. Rounding a corner, she saw the source of the outside light: a wide, curved window carved out of the rock.

Eva shifted the hatchling in her arms and dared a glance outside. They were on the eastern-facing side of the Gyr now, and the pale, fading light illuminated the faint purple of the Windridge Mountains and surrounding wilderness a few miles away.

"You're lucky," Wynn said, jealousy plain in her voice. "All the new recruits get inside quarters throughout their first year."

Eva didn't know what to say, so she continued to stare out the window. None of the trees had sprouted leaves yet, leaving the mountain range dotted with dark spots of pines and pale gray bunches of barren aspens. In spite of everything that had happened over the past couple of days, she couldn't help but be taken with the view.

"Come on," Wynn said, tugging at her sleeve again. "I'd like to get back for the evening meal, you know!"

The young recruit led her down the hall past a couple more windows until they stopped in front of a thick wooden door. Wynn knocked and then swung it open, gesturing for Eva to go ahead of her.

Eva stepped in the room looking forward to meeting her new bunkmate... and stopped in her tracks, nearly dropping the chick in surprise. Propped against the wall on a cot in the far corner of the room, Sigrid looked up, brow furrowed in a deep frown. Her lips pulled back into a grimace, and her hawkish nose wrinkled like Eva smelled of something dead and rotten.

"Well, well, look what the gryphon dragged in."

Chapter 9

"Can't you keep that thing quiet?" Sigrid hissed for the dozenth time.

By now, it was early morning and gray light seeped through the small window between their bunks. Eva sat up in her bed, flustered and exhausted. Throughout the night, the chick had woken up almost every two hours, raising enough racket to wake the entire garrison. Eva had tried feeding him, but that only worked the first time. Afterward, nothing helped, and the chick screeched until he wore himself out and slept for a short while.

"I'm trying," Eva said. She stretched out a hand to stroke the hatchling's soft down. The baby gryphon snapped and her and let lose another wail.

"I don't care if it's the first storming gryphon born again," Sigrid seethed. "If you don't get him to shut up, I'll throw him out the window!"

Eva should've probably been offended or at least a little concerned by her roommate's threat, but she half entertained the idea herself as the chick darted under her bed. Fully dressed, Sigrid shot her a glare sharper than the two daggers at her hips and strode from the room, slamming the door behind her. Exasperated, Eva clenched her hands into fists and fought the urge to scream. She tried not to think that, in just a few short hours, she'd be appearing before the Windsworn Council, a prospect that would've been daunting enough even with a full night's rest.

Fortunately, the chick fell asleep again a few minutes later. Eva had just finished a hurried braid to hold back her long hair when someone knocked on her door. Opening it revealed Wynn holding a stack of blue tunics and pants in her arms. Her tawny gryphon bumbled around a pair of tall brown boots beside her feet.

"I'm supposed to escort you to the lord commander as soon as you're properly dressed," Wynn said, holding out the clothes. "Here; you'll need to be in uniform. I think these should fit."

Thanking Wynn, Eva closed the door and slipped into the uniform. The clothes fit well, a small mercy she was grateful for — the last thing she wanted to do was appear before the lord commander and Windsworn Council in too-short leggings or an extra large tunic. She already felt ridiculous enough.

All dressed, Eva slipped on the boots and opened the door. Wynn stood waiting, shifting from one foot to the other. "You ready yet?" the younger girl asked. "The lord commander doesn't like to be kept waiting."

Eva nodded and stepped out of her quarters. She had the door half-closed behind her when Wynn put a hand on the door to stop here. "Where's your gryphon? You can't leave him there alone!"

Berating herself, Eva went back in the room with some reluctance. After his all-night antics, the gryphon chick lay curled up at the foot of her bed, fast asleep. Using extreme care, Eva picked him up and cradled the gryphon in her arms without waking him. She tried not to imagine the ruckus the hatchling would cause when he came to and found himself in a strange place.

Eva followed Wynn down a new series of twisting, winding tunnels and staircases. There seemed no rhyme or reason to the Gyr's interior although every passage and staircase was shaped with perfect symmetry. In some spots, a staircase hewn in the rock melted away to a gentle slope. Tunnels ended in random chambers with no explanation or gradually shrank until only two or three people could pass through them side by side.

Riders of all ages stared in surprise as they passed, pointing to the still-sleeping red gryphon chick in Eva's arms. A few nodded or said hello but most looked at Eva like she'd grown a second head overnight. Wynn seemed to love the attention, smiling and waving to everyone. She'd say things like "Yeah, that's her!" or, to Eva's horror, "Make way for the red gryphon!" While the young girl blazed ahead, heralding their passage, Eva walked with her head down, hoping their destination wasn't much farther.

Without warning, they appeared at the edge of the Main Hall. It looked like most of the riders were done with their morning meal, but a few remained in small groups at several of the long tables, chatting among themselves. At the top of the hall, Eva noticed a balcony overlooking the tables below that she'd missed the night before.

"We're normally not allowed up here," Wynn said before they started up the stairs. "All of the officers' quarters are located back this way, plus the Council chamber."

When they reached the top of the stairs, Eva felt the eyes of everyone in the Main Hall on her back. She felt a wave of relief as they disappeared from the dais down a long passage lined with pillars. In between each column, Eva noticed tapestries interspersed between the columns and doors. The murals depicted a variety of Windsworn and their gryphons with plaques beneath each to identify them. Every now and then, Eva spotted a red gryphon and couldn't help but notice how brave and heroic their riders looked. Each one they passed made her stomach sink a little more.

They traveled about halfway down the hall without seeing anyone until Wynn came to a stop in front of a door inlaid with a pair of silver wings. Lifting the large knocker carved in the shape of a gryphon's head, she struck the door twice. Andor appeared a few moments later, and Wynn snapped to attention. Eva did her best to imitate the younger girl, but the result seemed awkward and ridiculous.

"Recruit Winifred, thank you for your assistance," Andor said. Eva looked sideways at Wynn, who grimaced, apparently not fond of what must've been her full name. "You are dismissed."

Wynn saluted, thumping her fist to her chest. "Good luck," she muttered under her breath as she passed Eva.

"Come in," Andor said.

He led Eva up a short spiral staircase into a spacious room with a large window across from the entrance. Charts and maps of all kinds covered the walls inside the lord commander's chambers. Eva recognized one depicting Rhylance, but most were of places she'd only heard in name or not at all. A stone table, seemingly carved out of the mountain itself, stood in the middle of the room and was stacked with books, scrolls, and more maps. Andor motioned for her to take a seat.

"Did Wynn show you around?"

Eva nodded. "Yes, she's been good company."

"Good," Andor said. "She looks up to you, you know."

At a loss for words, Eva nodded again, focusing on containing the struggling chick in her arms.

"You can set him down," Andor said. "There's nothing on the floor he'll hurt."

Relieved, Eva let the baby gryphon spring from her arms. He landed like a lopsided ball made of wool and scurried under the table at once.

"I trust that everything else is going well?" Andor asked.

For a moment, Eva considered saying something about being placed in the same quarters as Sigrid, but then she realized the lord commander likely had something to do with the arrangement in the first place. It didn't seem like a very good idea to start complaining on her first full day in the Gyr.

"Yes," she said, trying not to sound as lost as she felt. "It's just a bit…overwhelming."

"You'll get the hang of it," Andor assured her. "I know Soot, and if you lasted all those years with him, you'll do just fine here. But I want to stress that you'll receive no special treatment because of your circumstances. You've got almost five years of catching up to do."

"I understand," Eva said. When the lord commander put it that way, she didn't feel like she had a chance.

"My lord," Andor said. Eva looked at him, confused. "Our interactions until now have been somewhat…out of the ordinary, but now that you are a recruit, you will refer to me as either lord commander or my lord. Is that understood?"

"Yes, my lord," Eva said, unsettled by the sudden change in Andor's demeanor. His formality made her feel even more anxious.

"Very good," the lord commander said, offering her what Eva guessed was supposed to be an encouraging smile. It didn't help. "Let's not keep the Council waiting."

The hall ended in a pair of stone doors almost twice Eva's height. Two guards stood outside, each wearing gold-chased armor and sky-blue capes, a spear in one hand, ruby-hilted swords at their belts. When the lord commander approached, they both snapped to attention.

Fighting a growing panic, Eva followed Andor, doing her best to keep the hatchling from raising a racket in front of the Windsworn leadership. Late morning sunlight flooded through the windows, highlighting several men and women seated along the rounded outside wall of the chamber. As the lord commander took his seat in a chair carved with outstretched wings, the Windsworn Council studied Eva with a mixture of expressions.

The two seated on either side of Andor seemed especially intent. To the lord commander's left, a woman with sun-darkened skin and midnight hair looked at Eva, the hint of a smile playing on her lips. She sat easy in her chair, like a lioness sunning herself on a rock.

The man on Andor's right, however, seemed to be carved out of the mountain itself, down to his slate-gray hair, eyes, and well-groomed beard. A scar ran from the corner of his eye and nose across his cheek to the outside of his jawline. Eva glanced away, unnerved, and focused her attention on the lord commander.

"Welcome, Evelyn," he said. "Although we did not know who, the coming of the red gryphon and his rider have been long awaited."

"Let's not be hasty." It was the gray-haired man on Andor's let who spoke. His stern gaze cut into Eva like a knife. "The road to becoming full-fledged Windsworn is long. Many leave the mountain, never to return."

"I…" Eva swallowed hard and felt a sudden longing for the comforting light of her mother's Wonder stone. "I will do my best, I promise you." She realized how many people she'd already made that promise to over the past few days and hoped she wouldn't break it.

"Be careful what you promise, girl," the woman on Andor's right said. "We will hold you to it."

"My strong left and right wings," Andor said, nodding to the man and the woman. "Commanders Uthred and Celina."

The gryphon chick chose that moment to latch his front talons into Eva's arm. "W-well met," Eva said, trying to hide the pain. She shifted her arms and held back a gasp as the needle-sharp claws pulled free.

"You are afraid," Uthred said. "To become one with your gryphon, to become Windsworn, you must be fearless."

Although Eva didn't say anything, she felt certain if any of the riders in the room knew of her terror of heights, she'd be dismissed immediately. Had Andor noticed the day before? She didn't see how he couldn't have.

"No one is fearless, Uthred, not even you," Commander Celina said, never taking her eyes off Eva. As she spoke, she toyed with a forearm brace that looked more like stone than any metal Eva knew of. Celina's fingertips traced the runes carved into the brace's surface, considering her next words. "It's how we face those fears. Can you be brave, girl?"

"I —"

"She is too old," Uthred interrupted. "And built like a willow twig. You should have left her where you found her and brought the red gryphon to another rider, my lord."

Eva felt a spark of anger rise in her, but one look at Uthred's pale gaze quenched it like a hot blade in oil. She looked down at the gryphon chick, shifting him in her arms so his talons were pinned against her and her bare skin was out of reach of his beak.

"Eva has grown up working with one of the toughest men in Rhylance," Andor said in a loud voice, silencing several murmurs.

"I don't think I need to remind anyone here of Wayland's deeds or character. She will learn to hold her own."

At the mention of Soot's real name, Eva's fears momentarily faded. She would've given anything to ask Andor about her foster father's secretive past but knew now wasn't the time.

"Nevertheless," Uthred said, unmoved by Andor's argument. "We hold Council for a reason. I propose we vote to see if the girl stays."

Eva's stomach twisted, and her mouth went dry. *Vote?* Was Uthred trying to kick her out? Would the Council see Eva for the charlatan she was and send her home? Embarrassment, anger, and a small bit of hope swirled inside her as the Council fell into unrest.

"The girl has been *chosen!*"

"Uthred is right; she is too old to learn our ways. She will never be Windsworn!"

"Just look at her!"

"This is ridiculous! The gryphon has already bonded!"

The discontent grew into shouts, with Eva trapped in the middle of it all. The gryphon chick shrieked and flailed in Eva's grasp, upset at the noise. Tears welled in her eyes, and Eva wished she could melt into the floor.

"Silence!"

Andor rose from his chair, deep blue eyes daring someone to speak. "We will have order. A council this may be, but I am still Lord Commander of the Windsworn. Before anything is put to a vote, Eva would you like to say something?"

It was the last thing Eva expected or wanted. She swallowed, tongue feeling ten times too big in her bone-dry mouth. On one hand, this was her chance. With a few words, she could walk away from the Gyr, from Uthred, Sigrid, and the angry gryphon chick who'd overturned her world. A quiet life with Soot and Seppo waited, beckoning her back home.

Eva opened her mouth to tell them Uthred was right — there'd been some kind of terrible mistake. But as she did Eva felt something stir deep inside, like a tiny, flickering ember buried in ash. A feeling of defiance she'd never felt before. *Damn them all,* it whispered. *Prove them wrong.* She didn't know what hidden corner of her heart it came from, but she knew it wouldn't let her leave.

"Eva?" Andor asked again, raising his eyebrows. The gryphon chick chirped, breaking the silence.

Eva opened her mouth again and couldn't breathe, let alone speak. Words came out of her mouth, but she couldn't even tell what they were.

"Speak up, dear," Celina said. She looked amused, like she knew something the rest didn't and wasn't going to share. It seemed like the commander was making fun of her, but rather than upsetting Eva further, it fanned the tiny ember inside her until it glowed even brighter.

"I don't know why I was chosen," Eva said, raising her voice. "And no, I don't know what I'm doing. I can't swing a sword, and I don't know how to fly a gryphon. But I can work hard."

Andor nodded, and the room fell silent, leaving Eva no indication of how her words went over. "Let us consult with Captain Windholt," the lord commander said. "What is your decision?"

Eva turned to a gruff old man with hair shaved to a stubble. He wore a patch over one eye and gnawed on the tip of his drooping mustache.

"Why not," he growled at last. "Let's see what the girl's made of. Give her a chance, I say."

Andor nodded. "Captain Velinda?"

The seat to the old man's right held a middle-aged woman with a lean face and short hair so fair it almost looked white. She regarded Eva, fingertips pressed together beneath her chin, then looked down at the gryphon chick in her arms.

"Hmmm...no," the captain said in a slow, drawling voice. "I'm sorry, young lady, but I think not."

Equal parts inside Eva celebrated and were crushed at the same time. They continued to the next four, which tied the vote as it came to Uthred. Sensing her discomfort, the chick hissed, and Eva did her best to hold him away without looking too obvious.

"No," the gray-haired commander said at once. "This is no place for milk maidens — even if they can swing a hammer."

Andor frowned at Uthred. "I vote yes."

Eva glanced at Celina, hating the fact her fate was as the woman's mercy. The commander looked Eva up and down, for several gut-wrenching moments. "Come back to me," she said at last. "I have not yet decided."

Eva didn't think that would work out in her favor, but she tried to put on a brave face as the votes passed to the remaining six Windsworn. Two more women, faces marked with war paint, voted no but a dark-skinned man, and, somewhat to Eva's surprise, Cassandra, both voted yes. A man with long red hair bound in dozens of braids voted no, leaving only a woman with a shaved head and Celina.

"I hope you've made your mind up, Celina," the woman with the shaved head said. "Because I vote yes, which means we have a tie."

Eva's palms grew cold and trickles of sweat ran down her back and forehead, but she couldn't wipe it without setting down the red gryphon. By now, the chick had had more than enough of Eva holding him and fought with all his might until Eva relented and placed him on the floor to peck at her boots.

All eyes fell on Celina. Despite the added attention, she remained draped across her chair as if they were discussing the details of a summer picnic, not Eva's future with the Windsworn. To Eva, her beating heart sounded like a drum filling the entire chamber.

"Oh all right," Celina said at last, sitting up and waving a hand as if they'd all been asking her to play some sort of trivial game. "I vote yes."

Quiet mutters broke out across the Council. Uthred looked like he'd been forced to swallow a dagger, while Andor stared at Eva with the same concerned look he'd worn during the voting.

"It is decided, then," he said. "Eva will remain at the Gyr and undergo training to become full-fledged Windsworn. Eva, you are dismissed."

In a daze, Eva gathered up the gryphon chick and turned for the stone doors. As the other Council members began to talk among themselves, Celina's voice rose over the hubbub.

"Don't make me regret my decision, girl!"

Chapter

🦅 10 🦅

Wynn was waiting on the balcony at the end of the Officers' Hall. "How did it go?" she asked.

Although she would have rather talked about anything else, Eva told the girl about the Council and their vote.

"You're staying!" Wynn said at the end. Her enthusiasm made Eva feel a little better after the harrowing events. "And don't worry about Uthred — from what I hear he's a salty old bugger with everyone. Come on, we're going to be late for class!"

Eva followed Wynn across the Main Hall into a passage at the bottom of a narrow street. It rose several stories above them, orange-yellow lanterns illuminating so many windows that the whole chasm looked bright as daylight. Wynn went up a staircase to one side of the street and continued until she came to a large wooden door. She opened it and gestured Eva inside, following close behind.

Inside, Eva saw long rows of tables filled with recruits around Wynn's age, their attention focused on a large bald man with square spectacles perched on the end of a rather bulbous nose. When the door opened, the teacher looked up from whatever he'd been reading, followed by the rest of the class. Seeing Eva, they stared until the teacher gave an impatient cough.

"Ah yes," he said. "Glad you could make it. Eva, isn't it?"

Eva nodded. "Yes, sir."

"Portridge," the man said. "You may call me Instructor Portridge. Have a seat."

Feeling somewhat lost and naked in front of all the adolescents staring at her, Eva chose an open seat in the back corner and sat the gryphon chick down in front of her. He proceeded to leave several droppings right away, much to Eva's horror. Wynn took a seat next to her with her own chick. When she noticed the mess, the younger girl grimaced and scooted her chair away.

Eva grew a deep red — yet another first impression gone wrong. She looked around for something to clean the mess up with but found nothing. Instructor Portridge cleared his throat and stepped out from behind his podium, clearly aware of the issue. He produced a rag from somewhere and tossed it to Eva. "In the future, please leave your hatchlings in the nursery before coming to class."

A couple of students snickered until a stern look from Portridge silenced them. "Of course, sir," Eva said, looking at Wynn, who shrugged in silent apology. "I didn't know —"

The instructor cut her off with the wave of a thick hand. "Quite all right, quite all right — it is your first day after all. Wynn should have known better. Anyhow, back to the matter at hand — who can give me an account of the founding of Rhylance?"

About three quarters of the hands in the class shot up. Wynn, on the other hand, ducked her head, focusing on her gryphon chick. Portridge selected a mousy-haired boy near the middle, who stood up and clasped his hands behind his back.

"The Sorondar sailed across the Western Ocean almost four hundred years ago after a terrible plague. On their ships, they brought with them the last surviving gryphons and gryphon eggs from their homeland. When they reached Altaris, the two groups split, some staying on the coast to found Pandion while the gryphon riders continued inland and founded Rhylance."

Professor Portridge nodded along as the boy spoke, stroking his giant side whiskers. "Very good, very good. And who were the original inhabitants of the Rhylance Valley?"

71

This time, only a couple of hands raised, but Eva noticed the same boy who'd just answered had his arm stretched so high he was almost out of his seat. He looked to be one of the smallest in the class. "Let's give someone else a try, eh, Danny?" Portridge said to the boy before selecting a girl to his right. "Go ahead, my dear."

"The original inhabitants of the Rhylance Valley were the Scrawls," the girl said. "The Sorondarans fought with them to establish a kingdom here."

"Well done!" Portridge said. His gusto slid his spectacles to the very end of his mushroom nose. "Now, let's move on to the founding of the Gyr itself…"

Eva left the room, head buzzing. She'd learned some of the histories from books Soot brought her; only the nobility's children attended any formal schooling in the city. Given the opportunity, Eva devoured Portridge's lecture, eager to learn something new. She left the room with a couple of books she'd worked up the nerve to ask to borrow at the end of class.

"Don't know what you want all them for; you going to hit someone over the head with them?" Wynn asked, shaking her head.

"Don't you like to read?" Eva asked.

Wynn shrugged. "I'd rather practice with weapons."

They made their way back to the Roost to leave their chicks at the nursery for the remainder of the day's classes. Eva, trying to remember the way in her head as she followed Wynn, only got confused at a couple of turns. By now, the gryphon chick was hungry and restless. Eva gladly left him in Cassandra's care, who took the infuriated chick into her arms and seemed delighted when he tried to eat her finger. She tried not to hide her relief as they made their way back down to the many levels of the fortress, free at last of the little monster who'd plagued her over the past couple of days.

Eva's joy soon faded, however, when Wynn led them to the Pit for their next class.

Down on the main floor, Eva felt ridiculous as she lined up next to the other new recruits. Everyone else was at least four years younger than her, although watching a few of them warm up she didn't doubt any of them could outperform her with any weapon in the armory. Lost in her thoughts, she jumped when a loud voice erupted across the cavern.

"*Atten-shun!*"

Eva scurried into line with the rest and tried to imitate their pose. Tall even for her age, she stuck out like a sore thumb among the younger recruits.

Out of the corner of her eye, Eva saw a bear of man walking out of the smaller caves into the Pit, hands clasped behind his back like he was strolling through a garden. His brown hair was shaved to a stubble atop a block-shaped head. He didn't say anything as he approached, just stared at them through beady eyes, a look of distaste on his face as if the recruits gave off a foul odor. Eva dropped her eyes to the floor when he stopped in front of her and squared up to face the line of cadets.

"Good morning, magpies!" he said in the same booming voice. "My name is Drill Master Thaddeus Cross. Now, repeat after me: Good morning, Drill Master!"

"Good morning, Drill Master!"

"Excuse me?" Cross said, leaning forward on one leg and cupping a paw to his ear. "I didn't realize we were in the library. I said *Good Morning!*"

Eva flinched at Cross's bellowing but roared back with the rest. She stared straight ahead, over the drill master's shoulder at a rack of wooden staves against the opposite wall and tried to be as inconspicuous as she could while towering over the other recruits.

"And who do we have here?"

Drill Master Cross stepped forward until he was only a hand's breadth from Eva. Her stomach twisted like snakes, and she squeezed her hands together behind her back to keep them from shaking. Eva swallowed and tried to keep her face an empty mask.

"Excuse me," Cross said, hot breath on her face. "I believe I asked you a question. What is your name, Recruit?"

"Evelyn, sir," she managed without stammering.

"Evelyn, is it?" Cross said, teeth gritted like a bulldog. Eva could see every vein bulging in his face and beads of perspiration gathering on his forehead.

"Or Eva," she added when he didn't move. "I mostly go by Eva... sir."

"*And I mostly go by Drill Master, not sir!*" Cross bellowed, spraying spittle across her face. Eva stumbled backward.

"Y-y-yes, Drill Master!" Eva said in as loud a voice as she could muster.

Cross sniffed and stomped down the line, looking for his next victim. When she thought the drill master wasn't looking, Eva wiped her hands on the back of her pants and tried to still her pounding heart.

"You will learn today that I am not here to be your friend," Cross said, prowling up and down the line. Even without yelling, his voice echoed across the Pit. "I am here to teach you how to fight and kill, if necessary. And, storm willing, if any of you magpies are worth more than a pile of pigeon shit, I will train you into some of the fiercest fighting men and women in all of Altaris.

"You will be drilled in the sword, the bow, the spear, unarmed combat, and anything else that suits my fancy," Cross continued. He paced along their lines like a wolf outside a sheep barn, just waiting for his opening to strike. "You will sweat. You will bleed. You will vomit. You will break bones and pass beyond all bounds of exhaustion. And then you will do it again. Do you understand?"

"*Yes, Drill Master Cross!*" Eva's throat felt raw already, and she wondered if she'd sound as loud and rattling as Cross by the time she finished training.

Cross turned on his heel and spun to a stop right in front of Eva again. "Excellent. Now, let us begin. You there, Esther or whatever your name was. Let's see what prodigies are made of. Step forward."

Something told Eva it would be a big mistake to correct the drill master on her name. She stepped forward before he found another reason to bust her. Away from the line, she felt small and very alone like a rabbit beneath a circling hawk.

"We're going to go for a little run," Cross said. "Through what I like to call the Circuit of Stone. And then when we get back and have a sweat worked up, the real work begins. You take the lead behind me, Queen Magpie, and if I catch you slacking up there in the front, so help me. Now, move!"

For a large man, Cross possessed an unfortunate amount of speed and stamina. Eva and the rest of the class followed behind as the drill master led them out of the Pit into a series of twisting tunnels. Unlike the main passageways of the Gyr, these seemed far older and rougher, torn from the mountain innards. What's more, they had far fewer crystal lanterns, and Eva stumbled several times trying to keep up with the Cross, who set a punishing pace.

Although sweat soon poured from her, Eva's work at the forge demanded plenty of stamina. She pushed on without looking back to see how the rest fared. Cross kept going and going and still managed to have enough breath to curse them whenever Eva or anyone else lagged in the slightest. She didn't know how the younger recruits kept up — the run taxed her enough, and she had almost twice the stride as most of them. Down, down they went, stumbling and sliding on uneven stone and loose gravel. Eva had no clue where they were or how to get back to the upper levels, but after what she guessed was half an hour or so, Cross veered to his right and took them on another path leading up at a sharp slope.

By the time she recognized the Pit ahead, Eva's legs burned and her hair stuck against her skin in wet strands. Cross stopped when they reached their start position. Sweat darkened the front and back of his uniform, but Cross breathed like he'd taken a walk while the rest of them heaved and braced hands on knees, sucking air.

"No time for rest now, magpies!" Cross shouted moments later. "Drop to the ground."

Eva lowered her aching body to the cool stone floor, but as soon as her palms touched the ground Cross shouted for them to spring back up. And so it continued. Cross put them through all manner of drills and exercise until Eva slipped into a numb trance. As much as the drill master cursed and belittled the others, he heaped three times as much on Eva, the "Queen Magpie."

By the time Cross called a halt, the sunlight streaming through the cavern's opening had faded to a soft orange glow. Eva wiped the sweat from her face with the back of her equally sweaty hand and sucked a deep breath into her exhausted body.

"All right, magpies!" Cross had done at least half the exercises with them and looked like he could've gone for hours more if the mood took him. "You're dismissed! Be sure to hit the baths before you go to the Main Hall for dinner — don't want your stink ruining my meal, hear me?"

"Yes, Drill Master Cross," they said, voices dulled and weary.

"What!" the drill master shouted — by now, Eva doubted he'd ever whispered in his life. "Let me hear you!"

"Yes, Drill Master Cross!" their ragged, strained voices replied.

"That's better," Cross said. "Welcome to the Gyr, magpies!"

Chapter
✦ 11 ✦

Eva woke the next morning — and the next several mornings — sorer than she'd ever been swinging a hammer in Soot's forge. Although training with Cross only happened every other day, it was just enough time for Eva's tired and aching body to reach peak agony before being thrust back into countless drills, runs, courses, or whatever new hell the drill master dreamed up in their absence. When they weren't exercising their bodies, Cross put them through the same basic motions with wooden swords until Eva thought the boredom might kill her before the physical work did. With so many different weapons to learn, she didn't see how she'd ever improve, no matter how much they drilled.

Aside from sword work, they practiced archery, knife throwing, footwork with the spear and shield, wrestling, and every other martial skill imaginable. Eva soon found that although she had the strength and endurance to survive Cross's trainings, she lacked any sort of talent for the finer points of combat. To make matters worse, Cross insisted on pitting three to four of her younger classmates against her each time they fought. It more than made up for their differences in age and size, but nobody benefited.

Eva soon found showing any mercy to her opponents only encouraged Cross to push them harder. As a result, the younger recruits hated training with Eva even if it wasn't her fault. Eva felt bad until she observed the older Windsworn training. One time Sigrid broke a boy's nose and dislocated a girl's shoulder in the time it took Eva to cross from one side of the Pit overlook to the other. From that moment on, Eva counted her bruises and lumps a blessing.

To make matters worse, the gryphon chick only seemed to loathe Eva even more as he grew. Now he was the size of a large cat or small dog. Even with added strength from Cross's conditioning, Eva could hardly contain the chick in her arms anymore. He'd also started molting his down and enjoyed pulling it out all over Eva and Sigrid's quarters, not to mention shredding their bedding with his growing beak and talons.

Any hopes Eva had of Sigrid warming to her vanished after the first week. She sneered whenever Eva groaned and dropped on her bed after a long training sessions. Other than that, if Sigrid wasn't yelling at Eva for something she or the chick had done, the girl pretended like Eva didn't exist — even on the rare occasions they were in their quarters together for something other than sleeping.

But despite all that, there were things Eva enjoyed about the Gyr life. She loved her non-combat classes, the ones about diplomacy, the history of Altaris and the gryphon riders, and more. Her friendship with Wynn also grew. At dinner, the two of them usually sat apart from the other Windsworn recruits. The younger ones in Eva's class quickly grew resentful of the reluctant beatings she gave them, while Sigrid seemed to have scared the older ones into keeping their distance. That or word had spread that the red gryphon's future rider wasn't all she'd been cracked up to be.

There was one other person who made an effort to speak to Eva whenever their paths crossed: Tahl. Since he'd just become a full-fledged Windsworn like Sigrid, Eva rarely came across him in her daily activities. When she did, her face had a habit of reddening, even before he said hello. Most of the conversations began and ended with Eva muttering something slightly indiscernible, but even those few moments helped carry her through the punishing days with Cross, frustrating evenings with the red gryphon, and icy encounters with

Sigrid.

At the moment, Eva had more pressing problems to worry about than Cross, her chick, or even Sigrid. Today was their first class with the adult gryphons to learn the basics of flight. After weeks cleaning out old nests, caring for the various gryphon injuries and maladies, and long lectures, the dreaded day had arrived.

Now, to make matters worse, she'd gotten lost after taking what she thought was a shortcut from the library. Instead, Eva and the gryphon chick found themselves in an unfamiliar narrow tunnel. The red gryphon hissed in her arms as the cracked crystal lanterns flickered, casting an eerie light around them.

"I don't like it, either," Eva said, attempting to calm the chick with a pet on his mottled down and feather head. He responded by nipping at her hand, but by now Eva could anticipate such attacks and jerked it back.

When the tunnel split in two again, Eva paused and blew out a deep breath, trying to keep her emotions under control. On top of being lost and late for flight class — bad enough under the best circumstances — she told herself it wouldn't do to get worked up and wander into some trap room or pit. Closing her eyes, Eva counted in her head like she'd learned from the meditation classes then went with her gut feeling: the left tunnel.

Several turns and dozens of paces later, Eva noticed the smooth walls melt into the roughhewn rock that she'd only seen before in the lower parts of the Gyr, even though she knew she wasn't far from the Roost. The lanterns flickered and faded even more, but a pale blue light appeared ahead and grew as Eva approached. The air turned cold — colder even than the Roost, and Eva felt goose bumps spread up her arms. She'd just decided to turn around when a wild screech split the silence.

Eva bit back a scream of her own, and the gryphon chick leapt from her arms, scurrying toward the noise. For a long moment, Eva considered leaving him behind then, realizing she'd probably be thrown off the side of the mountain for doing so, gave chase.

"Get back here!"

In the dim light, Eva could barely see the red gryphon's tail as he whipped around another curve in the tunnel ahead of her. She growled and ran harder.

"Ha!" Rounding the corner on a burst of speed, Eva dove and stretched out to snag the gryphon chick. She hit the ground hard but held on tight as the hatchling kicked and fought to free himself. Undeterred, Eva yanked him closer, copper-colored wings buffeting her face. "Gotcha, you little monster!"

The hatchling went limp in her arms, and Eva felt a surge of relief. At the same time, the air above her felt close. Eva rolled over and found herself staring into the milky, sightless eyes of an ancient black gryphon.

Before Eva could make a sound, a spotted and wrinkled hand clapped over her mouth. An equally ancient man appeared above her, blocking Eva's site of the black gryphon. Holding a finger to his lips, he slowly slid his hand away and motioned for her to rise. As she did so, the blind gryphon jerked its head toward her, emitting a low hiss. Eva clamped her hand over the chick's beak as it started to answer.

Eva followed the old man around the edge of the chamber, hugging the rock wall until he brought them to a smaller cave, too small for the black gryphon to enter. The ancient gryphon's milky white eyes followed them and it clicked its beak and tapped its long, gnarled claws on the stone floor. Inside, Eva spotted a few half-ruined books surrounded by old leaves and bits of long-dead animals but not much else.

"My, my, what do we have here, eh?" the old man asked when Eva entered the small cave. "Don't get visitors very often, by the storm, we don't. Good thing you didn't eat them, eh, Basil?"

Eva guessed Basil was the gryphon's name because when it heard the old man it let out a croaky sound like it agreed with him.

"I-I'm sorry, sir," she said. "I didn't mean to intrude. I got lost on my way to the Roost."

The old man shook his head and held a finger to his lips. Wrinkles within wrinkles lined his face, and long, thin strands of white hair blew like wisps across his head. His eyes, though, were bright and green and sharp as any blade. Unlike every other Windsworn Eva had seen, the old man wore stained and faded black leathers.

"Best not speak too much, my dear," he said, grinning. His smile showed a sparse collection of cracked and yellowed teeth. "Basil doesn't take kindly to interruptions."

"Please," Eva said in a lower voice. "If you'll show me the way out, I'll leave you alone."

The old man cackled, and Eva felt a tingling run down her back. The gryphon chick tensed as well, burrowing against Eva in a rare show of fear. The old man's laughter died on his thin lips, and he almost looked hurt by Eva's reaction.

"Don't worry, dear, you're in safe hands with me and old Basil," he said, voice softening. "I am Lord Vyr!"

The way he said it made Eva think she ought to know the name. She racked her brain to recall a Lord Vyr from the long list of Windsworn in her history lessons but drew a blank. It didn't seem prudent or polite to say that, however.

"It's nice to meet you, my lord." She shifted the gryphon chick in her arms and saluted.

Lord Vyr gave another broken smile. "Ah! A girl with manners. Very good."

Still flustered and ready to be gone, Eva had no idea what to say.

"May I see?" he asked, holding his arms out. "The gryphon? The… red gryphon."

As rocky as their relationship was, Eva felt a sudden surge of protectiveness toward the little gryphon.

"I…I'd better keep him," she said. "He isn't the friendliest."

Lord Vyr chuckled and jerked a thumb toward the black gryphon pacing back and forth outside in the larger chamber. Eva caught sight of his milk-white eyes staring back at her as if it weren't blind at all. "I understand completely. Come, let me show you something."

The old man beckoned Eva over to a small stone table in the center of the cavern. A chill ran through her when she looked at its surface. It was carved with deep lines of ancient runes and had several dark brownish-red stains that looked like blood long dried.

"It's all here," Lord Vyr said, waving a hand over the table.

When he offered no further explanation, Eva venture a question. "All…what?"

"Everything!" the old man said, sounding irritated. "If you're smart enough to read it. A gryphon born once in a generation, to fight the iron storm and save us from the breaking wind."

The back of Eva's neck tingled and the gryphon chick fell still in her arms. "Is that the prophecy?" she asked.

"A part of it, yes."

Eva's heart quickened. Here she might be able to find her answers, find out if she truly belonged at the Gyr, if she was truly meant to be Windsworn.

"But," Eva said, staring at the table. "What does it mean? What does the prophecy say about the rider?"

"Huh?" Lord Vyr looked at her like she was the one mumbling nonsense.

"The rider of the red griffin."

Lord Vyr frowned and picked his nose. "The prophecy doesn't say anything about the rider."

Eva's heart sank. Lord Vyr must have noticed because he placed a hand on Eva's shoulder. She winced — it was the same one he'd just been inspecting his nose with.

"Isn't the rider just as important as the gryphon?" she asked.

The old man studied her for a long while and shook his head. "That's the trick! Only you can answer the questions you seek." He jabbed a finger into her breastbone, and Eva took a step back.

"That doesn't make much sense," she muttered.

Lord Vyr threw back his head and laughed until his cackles echoed throughout the cave. "Just like your father!"

Your father.

Eva's blood ran cold. "My father? How do you — did you know him?" It seemed impossible. How could Lord Vyr known Eva or anything about her past?

"Fear or greatness," the old man said instead. "I see them both pulling at you. Which will you choose?"

"Please!" Eva said, desperate for any bit of information he would give her. "Please, tell me what you know of my father!"

Instead, Lord Vyr pointed to a ragged tapestry hanging from the back of the cavern. "Behind there, you will find safe passage to the Roost. Take only left turns until you recognize where you are."

"I'm begging you," Eva said, tears welling in her eyes. "Please...I need to know."

With a surprisingly gentle touch, Lord Vyr raised her chin until their eyes met. "The truth cannot be found here with a blind old gryphon and crazy old man. Remember what I said — fear or greatness. You can only serve one. Now, it is time for you to go. Basil grows restless."

As he spoke, another blood-curdling screech reverberated through the chamber, and Eva felt a rush of wind as powerful black wings beat at the walls outside the small cave. Lord Vyr lifted the corner of the tapestry, exposing a tunnel just wide and tall enough for Eva to fit through.

"It would not be wise to return," Lord Vyr said. "But if you do, a jar of honey would not go amiss."

Eva nodded, unable to speak as her mind whirled with dozens of questions. Wiping the last tear from her face, she hefted the gryphon chick and ducked into the tunnel.

"Fear or greatness!" Lord Vyr's shout echoed after her long after the sound had faded in the dim light and dark stone. "Remember, Evelyn!"

It was only then Eva realized she'd never given the old man her name.

Chapter

12

Just as Lord Vyr promised, Eva soon found her way back to familiar paths and arrived at the Roost in short order. She walked into the open cavern and found Roost Master Cassandra at the far end of the chamber, a tan gryphon beside her, surrounded by the rest of Eva's class. When she saw Eva, Cassandra shot her a look of reproach but didn't break from her lecture to say anything. Wynn gave her a questioning look, but Eva shook her head.

"*Later*," she mouthed.

"Riding a gryphon is not at all like riding a horse," Cassandra said. "In flight, you move in all directions: left, right, up, down, sideways. You must be holding on at all times, or you will fall. Am I understood?"

"Yes, Roost Master," the class answered in a subdued voice that would've turned Drill Master Cross's face purple.

Cassandra pursed her lips together and looked over the recruits. "Good. I can stand here and talk until I die of old age, but the fastest way to learn is by doing. Wynn, why don't we have you go first?"

Wynn shot Eva an excited grin and pushed her way to the front of the group. She made to climb into the gryphon's saddle then and there, but the roost master grabbed her shoulder, stopping Wynn in her tracks

"Not so fast," Cassandra said. "As I said before, this is no common plow horse you're riding; this is a gryphon. They are not beasts of burden. Now, approach Gaius in the front."

Cassandra pivoted Wynn around until she stood in front of the big tan gryphon. Gaius watched her with golden eyes but didn't seem very interested in the young girl before him. Wynn took a cautious step forward, arms extended until her hands touched Gaius's beak. Eva couldn't help but stare at the wicked curve at the end of the gryphon's beak.

"Very good, Wynn," Cassandra said, "Now, you may step around his wing into the saddle. Go easy now!"

Gaius sank to the ground and spread his great wings, and Wynn stepped around to the space between the wing and the gryphon's feline torso. After a moment's hesitation, the young girl swung into the small saddle. When he felt Wynn settle on his back, Gaius rose, too. Wynn grinned and waved to everyone from her vantage point atop the gryphon.

Next, Cassandra stepped around the wings and cinched both of Wynn's legs down with straps and buckles attached to the stirrups. Wynn firmly in place, the roost master did a once-over on the gryphon's saddle and harness then stepped back.

"Yah!" Wynn shouted, flicking the reins. Gaius turned his mighty bird's head around and looked at the girl like he might a fly buzzing around him.

Cassandra frowned. "Gryphons are not our servants, Wynn, they are partners. If you wish to ever become Windsworn, you must learn to work with them, not command them. Now, try again."

Wynn blushed then reached forward and patted the gryphon's neck. "All right, Gaius, let's —"

Before she could finish, the gryphon leapt forward and launched himself into the air. Wynn's initial scream turned into a shout of excitement as the tan gryphon climbed higher and higher toward the crack of sky far above. Watching Wynn, Eva recalled her own trip on Stormwind, and her vision started reeling. She looked at the ground and squeezed her eyes shut. When she opened them again, Gaius swooped down and landed. The class erupted in cheers as Wynn waved to them from the gryphon's back.

"Very good," Cassandra said, looking satisfied but somewhat less enthused than the recruits. "Who's next?"

One by one, they went through the entire class until only Eva remained. With each student she saw successfully take off and land, her heart sank lower and lower. At last, no one else remained, and the roost master beckoned to Eva.

"All right, Evelyn," she said, smiling. "We saved the best for last. I imagine you can't wait until you're soaring on the back of that gryphon of yours, so we'd better get you trained up!"

The entire class turned to watch, and Eva wished she could melt into the stone floor. She swallowed and tried not to look as terrified as she felt at the prospect of another gryphon flight. Riding on the back of Stormwind with Andor controlling the creature had been bad enough, but now it would be just her and Gaius. Even the gryphon regarded her with his big amber eyes as if wondering what she was waiting for.

Cassandra beckoned to her. "Come on, girl, we haven't got all day!"

Eva took another step, mouth dry as her palms were damp. Lord Vyr's cryptic words echoed in her mind *Greatness or fear...greatness or fear*. At the moment, fear looked to have won the day. Still, she squeezed her shaking hands until her fingernails bit into her palms as she approached the gryphon.

Up close, the tan gryphon seemed even bigger than Stormwind, although Eva's fear could certainly have had something to do with Gaius's imposing size. Sickness rose in Eva's tangled stomach, and she knew she was going to throw up. She turned so she didn't get it on the gryphon when —

"Excuse me!" A voice echoed from across the Roost. Tahl's voice. Eva hadn't thought it was possible to feel worse until she realized she'd look a fool in front of him, too. As the class turned their attention to Tahl, Eva fought the urge to run and hide.

"My apologies, Roost Master," Tahl said, approaching them. Eva wondered how he walked like that: so graceful and sure. "I've come on an errand from Lord Commander Andor. He wishes to speak with Eva — immediately."

Minutes later, Eva walked beside Tahl, unable to believe her luck. Although disappointed, Cassandra had no choice but to release Eva before she could go for her first ride. Eva did her best not to look relieved as she joined Tahl and left the Roost.

Half of her wondered if the lord commander had decided to kick her out after all — Tahl didn't know why he'd been asked to summon Eva. The rest of Eva's attention focused on Tahl. He seemed to know everyone and had a smile and greeting no matter whom they passed. When they ran into younger Windsworn around their own age, Eva couldn't help but notice the knowing smirks the boys shot Tahl and the frowns she received from some of the girls.

"So, how do you like life in the Gyr?" Tahl asked when they reached a hall wide enough for them to walk side by side again.

"It's great," Eva lied. In truth, she thought about quitting and going home every other night, but something about Sigrid's dislike for her kept her going. She told herself every day she remained proved the other girl wrong.

"Good!" Tahl said. He seemed keen to listen, and Eva wished she had something more to say. "How is the chick doing?"

"He's...a handful sometimes," Eva said. Since she still had a full day of class ahead (assuming she wasn't being kicked out), Eva had left the chick in the Roost.

Tahl nodded. "Some are like that, but challenging gryphons can form the strongest bonds with their riders. I'm sure you two will warm to one another as time passes; it's just like any relationship."

In spite of her inner doubts, Eva could almost believe him. The thought was better than the alternative: that the red gryphon would one day be big enough to eat her. Eva forced the terrifying image from her mind and struggled to think of something else to say to keep the conversation going.

"So, what do you do, once you're a full-fledged Windsworn?" Eva asked.

"A lot of the same things as you," Tahl said, shaking his head. "The training never ends, but it does slow down a bit. Our time in the sky is spent doing patrols and that sort of thing. There's rumors that the Juarag are getting bolder on the eastern frontier, though, so that could liven things up around here."

"Oh." Eva couldn't think of anything intelligent to say about that — having spent her entire life in Gryfonesse she knew little about foreign affairs. A long silence stretched between them.

In the quiet, Eva noticed how close they were, close enough their hands bumped one another as they walked through some of the more congested or skinnier halls. She wondered what Tahl's hand would feel like. Growing up working the forge, she still remembered the first boy who'd commented on her calluses, burn scars, and blisters. Recalling the teasing, Eva bunched her hands into fists and hid them behind her back.

"Almost there," Tahl said. They entered the Main Hall and proceeded up the balcony. This time, two guards were posted outside of the lord commander's quarters instead of at the end of the hall in front of the Council chamber.

"Returning to the lord commander with Recruit Evelyn," Tahl said. Eva's insides fluttered when he said her name. The guards nodded, boredom plain on their faces, and gestured for them to proceed up the staircase

"It's a bit weird having guards everywhere," Tahl said when they'd circled out of sight.

"What do you mean?"

"Since the attack on Devana, it put the Council a bit on edge, I think. They insisted the lord commander post a guard outside his chamber. I mean, we're supposed to be untouchable up here. The fact that some Scrawl boy could just —"

"Ivan didn't kill her," Eva said. The edge in her voice surprised her. Tahl raised his hands as if to fend her off.

"I'm just saying," he said in a gentle tone. "If you don't think the Scrawl did it, then who?"

Before Eva could answer, they reached the top of the stairs and Andor stepped out to meet them. Dark circles highlighted an overall look of weariness on the lord commander's face.

"Thank you, Tahl," he said. "You are dismissed."

Tahl hesitated. "I was thinking…I mean, I can wait and escort Eva back to her quarters after you've finished talking with her, my lord?"

Eva welled with excitement, but Andor dashed any hopes of a second walk with a tired wave of his hand. "Thank you, but no need," he said. "I will make sure Eva can find her way back."

The young rider shrugged as if he didn't care either way, shattering Eva's joy from their trip. "As you wish, Lord Commander." Tahl saluted, and Eva watched him leave out of the corner of her eye before Andor waved her in.

"Please, come in."

Eva nodded, feeling tense as she crossed the room to the stone table. After the public dressing down with the rest of the Windsworn Council, she didn't find Andor as friendly and fatherly as when they'd first met.

"I'm sure you're busy with your training, so I won't keep you long," Andor said. He ran a hand over his sleep-lined face and through his hair, giving it a rumpled look quite unlike his regular tidy appearance. "I apologize for the incident in the Council chamber. I should have explained to you… things moved a bit different than I anticipated, and for that I ask your forgiveness."

"It's…" Eva trailed off. It wasn't okay, and she couldn't bring herself to tell him it was. "No apologies necessary, Lord Commander."

"I trust your training is going well?" Andor asked, apparently as eager to move on as Eva.

"There's a lot to take in," Eva said. "But I'm learning," she added, hoping she didn't sound too lost and hopeless.

Andor nodded. "Good, good. To business then: The Scrawl boy — Ivar or something, wasn't it? — the boy will be tried before the king in two days' time. As you can probably understand, the Scrawls are less than pleased that we've detained one of their own, but given the circumstances there wasn't anything else we could do. The situation is…delicate. We've built a solid alliance with the Scrawls over the last hundred years, but this incident has the possibility to put that in jeopardy."

"I think I understand," Eva said. She fidgeted on her chair, not sure where to look.

"Good," Andor said. "You enter the story, of course, when Ivan hid in your woodshed and Devana's egg hatched for you. Because of this you must testify at the Scrawl boy's trial."

"Ivan didn't do it, Lord Commander!" Eva blurted out. "I know he didn't! I — I can't explain it, but —"

Andor held up a hand, and Eva sucked in a deep breath, trembling from the outburst. "Eva, I need you to calm down," he said. "No one is asking you to condemn the boy. I only want you to tell the truth, as you saw it. That being said…the evidence against him is damning, to say the least. Even if he didn't kill Devana, he stole one of our eggs."

"I'll come," Eva said at once, surprising herself. She tried not to picture testifying before the entire court when another sickening thought filled her. "What…what will happen if the king believes Ivan killed Devana?"

Andor sighed and looked out his window. "The Scrawl boy will be sentenced to death."

Chapter

13

The day of the trial came, and the thought of speaking before the king's court loomed over Eva like a dark, swirling cloud about to burst. She'd told Wynn about her conversation with the lord commander. Now the younger girl sat beside her like a mother hen, pushing biscuits, oatmeal, bacon, and wheat cakes her way, although Eva didn't touch anything.

"You're going to starve if you don't have something!" Wynn said.

Eva shook her head. Her stomach felt like a bunch of writhing snakes, and she knew she wouldn't be able to hold anything down even if she had an appetite. Just when Eva thought Wynn would stuff something in her mouth, a guard appeared and tapped Eva on the shoulder.

"Time to go, Miss."

Eva followed the man to the lower shelf where she and Andor had landed. She was so wrapped up in the coming trial that Eva almost forgot about the flight down to Gryfonesse. It would be the first time she'd flown since her journey to the mountain. In the past two days, she'd done her best to avoid the Roost other than to drop off the red chick for care. So far, Cassandra hadn't had the chance to get her airborne.

When they came out of the passage, Andor was waiting along

with Celina, Uthred, and the rest of the Windsworn Council. Eva felt their eyes boring into her and focused on the ground just in front of her until she reached Andor and gave him a weak salute.

"All ready?" he asked.

Eva nodded, and the lord commander frowned.

"Do you feel okay, Eva?"

"Fine," she managed to say in a completely unconvincing tone.

When Stormwind leveled from his descent, Eva forced her eyes open and found they were skimming above the tops of the highest buildings in the city. Below, people looked up from their everyday business, shouting and pointing at the gryphons soaring above them in a perfect arrow-shaped formation. One look at the speeding ground sent Eva's head spinning, and she closed her eyes again. She felt Stormwind's wings shift, and when she looked again they were descending over the courtyard.

When they landed at last, Eva slid from the gryphon's back, grateful to be on solid ground once more. Lines of soldiers with polished armor, winged helms, and tall spears stood at attention. In the middle of them, before the palace doors, was the king of Rhylance.

While the rest of the Windsworn landed around them, Andor placed his hands on Eva's shoulders and stared at her with his pale, searching eyes. "I almost forgot. The king may seem a little…cold. Don't let this rattle you. It's nothing you've done, I promise. Just truthfully answer whatever questions you're asked, and everything will be fine."

Assembled together, the Windsworn walked down the rows of soldiers. Andor and Eva at the lead with Uthred and Celina behind, followed by the rest. As they drew closer, Eva couldn't help but notice the similarities between King Adelar and the lord commander.

They were of almost identical size and build with the same icy blue eyes set in hard, stern faces. Whereas Andor's graying blond hair came to his shoulders, the king's was cropped short. There could be no denying it — the two most powerful men in Rhylance had to be close relatives.

Eva realized how pale and sickly she must look despite the intricate braids she'd worked in her hair in anticipation of appearing before the king. Her legs felt like two bars of flimsy, red-hot iron straight out of the forge. As they approached, Eva focused her attention on the king's feet until Andor stopped and sank to one knee, Eva and the rest following suit.

"Arise, all of you."

The king stepped forward and drew Andor into a brief, rigid hug. A quick smile cracked through his hard countenance, and Eva thought she glimpsed a younger, happier man buried beneath the burdens of kingship. "It is good to see you, Brother," the king said.

When his eyes fell on Eva, however, any trace of pleasure dropped away faster than a heated blade placed in quenching oil. "And who is this?" the king asked the lord commander.

Andor seemed nervous, which made Eva even more on edge. "This is the girl I told you about, my King. The one Devana's egg hatched for."

King Adelar looked Eva over and, much like Uthred and Drill Master Cross, seemed to find her severely lacking in whatever he sought. "Indeed."

Without another word, the king continued down the line to Celina and Uthred like Eva wasn't there. Andor beckoned her to follow him inside.

"Did I do something wrong?" she asked the lord commander. Andor shook his head but offered no explanation.

Eva couldn't help but wonder if there was something he wasn't telling her, although she couldn't imagine what it might be. Inside the citadel, they passed down a long hall with statues of gryphons sitting between the marble pillars. Each bore a bronze nameplate, but Andor moved too fast for Eva to read them.

They soon entered the court itself, two massive doors wrought with gold, each carved with a wing. More winged-helm guards stood at attention as Andor and the rest of the Windsworn Council passed through.

Inside, the throne drew Eva's eyes at once — a massive thing carved from a single piece of light-colored wood, a pair of wings rising from either side. A half circle of tables was laid out at the bottom of the dais. There on the far left, Eva saw the delegation of Scrawl Elders waiting.

The pale men and women sat with their hands in their laps as if this were nothing more than a play preparing to begin. One or two leaned over and whispered something to their neighbors, but for the most part the Scrawls stared forward, silent. Although all of them wore long, dark forest-green robes, there was no hiding the rune tattoos covering almost every inch of visible skin on their bodies. Eva recalled Ivan's ability to stop Seppo dead in his tracks with a few words and a twist of his hands. How much power could a dozen Scrawl Elders wield, then?

Andor waited until the rest of the Windsworn had taken their seats across from the Scrawls before motioning for Eva. She walked behind the lord commander like he was a shield protecting her from the Elders. When they neared the tables, one of the Scrawls — a man with a braid of long white hair over his shoulder — stood and smiled in greeting.

"Well met, Lord Commander," he said, clasping his hands together and bowing.

"Well met, Master Vladim," Andor said, dipping his head. He put a hand on Eva's back and guided her forward. "This, as I'm sure you've heard, is our newest recruit at the Gyr. The one the red egg hatched for. Evelyn."

The old man smiled, and the blue ink on his face shifted and crinkled with his weathered skin. "It is an honor to meet you. I also thank you for the kindness you showed our young Ivan. We have had a chance to speak briefly to him before the trial, and he spoke well of you."

Eva blushed. "I — of course."

"I must apologize again for the trouble he has caused," Vladim continued. "Ivan is powerful but does not yet have full control of his powers. He can be headstrong, rash, and impatient as well. Had we done a better job teaching him patience, perhaps none of us would be here today."

"Be that as it may," Andor began. Before he could finish, however, a herald walked through the doors of the court.

"All rise for his royal highness King Adelar of Rhylance!"

When everyone was in their proper place, the man rapped his staff against the marble floor and stepped to the side. The king walked past in measured paces like a wolf on the prowl. When he seated himself at the throne, he looked as absolute and unmoving as the Gyr itself. He waved a hand, and the court took their seats

Chain clinked against the marble floor as Eva's head turned in time to see Ivan enter, escorted on either side by palace guards. Contrary to her fears, the Scrawl boy seemed well fed and rested — better off than Eva at any rate. A chain wrapping around his shoulders bound his arms and hands in front of him, but in a gesture of good faith nothing covered the boy's mouth. Even so, the two guards kept one hand on their sword hilts and looked ready to strike the young Scrawl down at a moment's notice.

Ivan glanced around the room and broke into a large smile when he saw Eva. Some of the Windsworn turned to her and frowned, quelling any thoughts Eva had of waving back. The guards led Ivan below the throne to the center of the circle of tables and then stepped back.

"Lord Commander Andor, will you explain the purpose of this court?" the king commanded.

"Of course, my King," Andor said, standing. "The Scrawl boy before you is accused of stealing an egg from the Gyr and murdering of one of our gryphons. The thief will be tried according to Sorondar law and if found guilty, sentenced to death."

The king looked at the Scrawl Elders with his gray-chipped eyes and motioned for Vladim to rise. "Rune Master Vladim. We have asked you to attend this court under the belief that the actions of your acolyte do not reflect those of the Scrawl people as a nation. Do you have anything to say before we begin?"

Vladim clasped his hands together and bowed once more. He walked out into the middle of the tables and stopped in front of Ivan without looking at the boy.

"The Scrawl Elders played no part in this travesty, your Highness," the rune master said. "Nor has our extensive searching since the event revealed further conspirators. My apprentice is young, headstrong, and often reckless with his developing powers. It is my belief that his theft of the egg was the result of overconfidence and misunderstanding of his abilities. As for the death of the gryphon mother, Ivan may be rash, but I do not believe he is a murderer."

Glancing down the line of Windsworn and at the nobles seated above, Eva didn't see any who agreed with the Scrawl Elder. Most looked ready to execute Ivan then and there.

"Thank you, Rune Master," the king said. He turned and gestured at the Windsworn. "Lord Commander Andor, please stand and give your account."

As he walked to the center of the court, Eva watched the lord commander. To her relief, the bloodthirsty look the rest of the Sorondarans had was absent from his face.

"My King, lords and ladies, visiting dignitaries, and fellow Windsworn," Andor said. "I have a sworn testimony from my right wing, who saw this young Scrawl fleeing the Roost. When he entered the nesting area, Uthred found the female gryphon Devana dead, her throat slashed."

"A grave crime, indeed," Vladim said, "But was there no witness of the murder itself?"

"What else was there to see?" Uthred asked. He rose and pointed to Ivan. "I saw this boy, fleeing from the Roost. There was no one else present."

Eva saw several Scrawl Elders break into angry mutters, frowning at Uthred. Vladim, without turning around, seemed to sense the tension among his peers but showed no emotion as he continued. "Be that as it may, there is still no explanation for how Ivan entered or left the mountain," the rune master said, spreading his arms wide. "There are many kennings and much power to be gleaned from the runes, but flight is not one of them, I assure you."

Now it was the Windsworn delegation's turn to cast angry looks across the court and grumble to one another. Even Andor scowled. "Are you suggesting that a Windsworn helped your apprentice in and out of the Gyr?"

"I only posed the question," Vladim replied. "It seems —"

Several shouts erupted from both sides, interrupting the rune master. The contention spread until the entire room shouted back and forth and several members of each party rose from their seats.

"Silence!" The king's voice broke through the din, and the court went quiet as everyone settled back into their places. He fixed his cold eyes on Ivan. "Let us hear from the boy."

Eva couldn't see Ivan's face, but the young Scrawl didn't seem tense or worried. Eva thought he must have been the only calm person in the room.

"My story remains the same, your Highness," Ivan said. He turned around, chains clinking with the motion, and looked between Andor and the Windsworn. "I didn't steal the egg to harm it. I was protecting it."

"Filthy liar!" More outrage burst from the Windsworn, but Adelar raised a hand and silenced them with a stern look.

"And what," the lord commander asked, "made you think the egg was in danger?"

"I saw it," Ivan said. For the first time, he seemed flustered, almost confused. "I can't explain it, but I had a vision — the egg would be destroyed if I didn't take it."

"I see," Andor said. Eva could tell at once he didn't believe the boy. "And how did you gain entrance into the Gyr? Did you climb the mountain?"

"I — I don't know, my lord."

"Did you fly on a gryphon?"

"I... I can't remember," Ivan said, brow furrowing. "There are... parts missing. I recall picking up the egg and then nothing until I was in the city."

Uthred snorted, loud enough for the entire court to hear.

"So, you would have us believe you stole the egg to protect it because of a vision?" King Adelar asked. "And yet you have no recollection of how you completed the act?"

A sheen of sweat appeared on Ivan's shaved head, and Eva realized just how young the Scrawl was. "Yes, your Highness," he said in a low voice.

A dreadful silence settled over the room. Even the Scrawl Elders looked incredulous after their acolyte's account.

"Where is the girl?" the king barked. Eva jumped in her seat and felt ice rushing through her limbs when she realized he meant her. King Adelar looked at her and waved. "Come up here, and tell us your part in this farce."

Trembling, Eva rose. As she walked around the tables, she clenched her hands together, fighting her trembling body. She felt naked in the middle of the court, and everyone's eyes fell on her like dozens of pinpricks. Reaching the base of the throne, she forced herself to look up at the king. Adelar's piercing eyes froze her to the spot.

"Well?" the king said. "Tell me your story."

Eva's tongue felt rougher than mountain stone. She opened her mouth twice, and no words came out. All the while the king stared at her, boring into her with his expression of disdain. After a moment, Andor walked up beside her. "Go on, Eva," he said.

Reassured by the lord commander's presence, like a shield from everyone's focus, Eva found her voice and related everything that had happened from the moment she found Ivan in the shed until the riders arrived and the red egg hatched. The king listened without comment, his gaze never shifting from her. As she spoke, Eva stared at his feet, afraid that if she looked up she would be unable to talk again.

"The Scrawl told you the egg was for you?" King Adelar asked. "He said he brought it to you and wouldn't leave until you took possession of it, is that correct?"

"Y-yes, your Highness," Eva said. "Several times."

Surprised murmurs broke out across the court and in the balcony above. The king leaned forward on the throne and looked into Eva's eyes. "This is the truth? Lying to the king is a crime punishable by execution."

"I-I swear, your Highness," Eva managed to say. Her body felt like it had been dunked in ice water, and she fought to breathe.

The king stared at her for several more moments without saying anything. Just when Eva thought she'd be sentenced to death right there in the court, he stood. "I would speak with the lord commander and rune master in my private chambers."

As the two men followed Adelar into a room behind the throne, the court broke out in dozens of conversations. Dazed, Eva found her way back to her chair and almost collapsed into it.

"Well done," Celina leaned over and said.

"Thank you, Commander," Eva mumbled. She felt exhausted, as tired as if she'd just finished a full day of training. The only thing she wanted was to crawl in bed, away from everyone. Celina, however, continued talking.

"The king is in a difficult position," the commander said. "The boy stole the egg, but he may very well have saved it — and there is no proof of murder."

"So, what's going to happen?" Eva asked. She looked across the room at Ivan, who stood on the edge of the Scrawl's tables while the Elders spoke among themselves. When he caught her eye, the boy grinned and waved. Eva had no idea how he could act like that given the fact that his life hung on the king's decision. She looked back at Celina. "You don't think — they won't kill Ivan, will they?"

Celina's hand strayed to the bracer on her forearm, and she ran her fingers across the dark metal. "I do not think so," she said at last. "The murder of a gryphon is a grievous thing, but not something the king would risk a war over."

Eva wasn't sure why Celina chose to talk to her when the rest of the Council sat around them, but it made her feel less alone in the daunting chamber. "So, you think he's telling the truth, too?" she asked.

The commander laughed, leaving Eva blushing and wishing she'd kept her mouth shut. "Someday you'll learn the truth isn't as simple as this or that," Celina said. "Sometimes, you've just got to settle for the middle ground."

Not wanting to look like an even bigger fool, Eva looked away without response, feigning interest in the tapestries behind the throne. One in particular caught her eye. It appeared to be a lineage of the kings and queens of Rhylance, back to the kingdom's founding, but there was a spot at the bottom that looked like it had been cut out. Eva almost asked Celina about it then stopped herself — she already felt ignorant enough.

Moments later, all thought of the tapestry left Eva's mind as King Adelar, Andor, and Vladim appeared. The lord commander and rune master wore subdued expressions. The king, Eva guessed, wore a permanent scowl. He sat on the throne and looked across both parties, eyes lingering for a moment on Eva as they passed over the Windsworn delegation.

"After much discussion," he said, "I have decided to let the Scrawl boy live."

Eva sighed, drained but relieved for Ivan. Around her, the Windsworn scowled at one another, but no one dared voice their displeasure to the king. For their part, the majority of the Scrawl Elders looked no different than if the king had decreed their acolyte would be put to death.

"However," the king added, cutting through the surprised whispers of the nobility in the gallery above the court, "until the murderer is discovered or the lord commander can be certain that there will be no further attacks, the rune master has agreed to leave his apprentice in the custody of the Windsworn. Both parties have agreed to these terms, and as such, I declare this matter resolved."

With that, King Adelar rose, waving a hand to dismiss everyone. Dozens of voices began speaking all at once until the throne room buzzed with conversation. Eva glanced at the throne and found the king staring at her, a strange, vacant expression on his face. She looked away at once but could still feel his gaze upon her as she filed out with the rest of the Windsworn, desperate to leave the palace. When the gryphon riders passed the Scrawls, most pretended not to notice the other, although Andor and Vladim exchanged curt nods.

Eva focused on the floor as she passed and was almost to the palace doors when Vladim called out to her.

"Miss Evelyn, could I have a moment of your time before you depart?"

Surprised, Eva looked over at Andor, who nodded. Although it was about the last thing she wanted to do, she turned around and forced a tiny smile on her face.

"I will be brief," the rune master said in a low voice. "I am in debt to you for your testimony today."

"I...I just told the truth, nothing special," Eva said, embarrassed.

Vladim smiled and shook his head. "Ah, but it is," he said. "You have saved the life of an innocent boy, one who is very precious to us. The gift of divining the future from the runes is among the rarest of gifts with our people – Ivan is the sole living member of our order with this power. I would caution you, however. Even if he had complete grasp of this ability, the future is still...uncertain. And fragmented."

The rune master cast his eyes around and lowered his voice. "As such, I feel I should warn you: I said this to the king and lord commander in private, but I believe there is something sinister at work in your mountain. Something none of us comprehend. Will you do something for me? Will you check in on Ivan whenever you can?"

"Oh," Eva said, still trying to process Vladim's warning. What did he mean, something sinister? "Of — of course."

The rune master smiled again and bowed. "As kind as you are beautiful. Until we meet again, please take care of yourself and your new charge. The birth of a red gryphon is no insignificant thing, even to my people."

"Uh...thank you," Eva said, unsure how to respond. She made an awkward goodbye and hurried to catch up with Andor.

Outside, the lord commander was already across the courtyard, preparing Stormwind for their return journey. She saw Ivan nearby with two other Windsworn securing him on the back of a gryphon, chains and all.

"I told you it would all work out!" he yelled to Eva. Before she could reply, the two Windsworn looked at her, their expressions saying they didn't think it had worked out that well at all.

"What did the rune master want?" Andor asked. When Eva

101

explained, she was surprised to see the lord commander nod in agreement.

"I think that would be good," he said. "Under guard at all times, of course. Just promise me one thing."

The lord commander placed his hands on Eva's shoulders, rooting her to the spot with his blue eyes, so very much like his brother's. "Promise me if Ivan says anything odd or acts strange in any way that you will let me know immediately. Understood?"

Eva nodded, wondering how a smith's assistant could find herself wrapped up in so many grand events and promises in such a short amount of time.

Chapter
14

By thunder, girl, what is your problem?"

Eva winced at Cross's shouting and paused her drill with Wynn. Single-handed, the younger girl had beaten her bigger, stronger opponent throughout the entire exercise, and it hadn't gone unnoticed by the drill master. Cross strode forward and yanked the wooden practice sword from Eva's hand, drawing the attention of everyone else drilling in the Pit.

"I-I don't understand, sir," Eva said, staring at the drill master's feet.

"Look at me when you speak, Queen Magpie!" Cross snarled. "Of course you don't understand. You don't comprehend even the basic, fundamental points of fighting. A sword in your hands is as useless as talons on a duck. Now pick it up and —"

"Drill Master Cross."

A moment before, Eva thought any reprieve would have been welcome — until she heard Uthred's cold voice echo down from the balcony.

"Commander Uthred, sir," Cross said, "Attention, Recruits!"

Eva and the rest rushed to form a line. Standing stock still, Eva's stomach clenched. Sigrid descended the stairs behind Uthred, face as cold and lifeless as the stone surrounding them.

The commander crossed the cavern with slow, measured steps, studying each recruit as he passed. Normally full of shouts and the clangor of battle, the Pit fell into complete silence. Eva felt her stomach tighten with every one of Uthred's footfalls as he approached her. Sigrid, at least, remained at the other end of the line.

When at last he reached her, Uthred stared at Eva like she'd forgotten to bathe in the past month. Eva stared ahead, focusing all her might on a rack of spears against the far wall.

"Well?" Uthred spoke in a low voice, but it still seemed to carry across the whole cavern.

Eva tried to swallow the knot of fear in her throat. The commander hadn't specifically addressed her, so maybe if she just —

"I am speaking to you, Recruit Evelyn," Uthred said.

"Y-yes, Commander!" Eva yelled back, voice breaking.

"The question," Uthred began as he started pacing up and down the line again, eying the younger cadets as he spoke, "is why you are not giving Drill Master Cross your fullest efforts? The question is why do you consistently fail to meet even a minimum of expectations? The question is why you are here at all?"

Eva's mind raced for an answer. Her heart pounded against her chest. "Commander, I —"

Uthred cut her off with a wave of his hand. "I do not require a verbal answer, girl. Instead, we shall let your practice weapon do the talking. Pick it up."

Eva stepped out of the line and retrieved her weapon with a shaking hand. When she turned around, she found everyone staring at her. Most, like Wynn, had wide-eyed looks as if they were as terrified as she was. Drill Master Cross, however, wore a nasty smile.

Uthred pointed to the training circle, marked by a ring of red paint on the stone ground. Eva stepped inside and waited, mind racing to guess what her punishment would be. Fear or greatness, girl. Every part of her body screamed at Eva to run. Instead, she resolved, this time would be different.

And then Uthred beckoned to Sigrid. Eva's insides went cold as the other girl picked up a training sword from the rack and stepped into the circle.

It was the first time Eva had ever seen her bunkmate smile. Under different conditions, it might have been pretty, but Eva had a hard time appreciating Sigrid's finer features, knowing what was coming next. Cross and the recruits gathered around, and Eva realized her humiliation would have an audience.

"Perhaps," Uthred said, "your poor efforts are the result of a lack of challenge? I spoke against placing you with the younger recruits, and it seems I was correct. Let's see how you fare against someone your own age and size. Begin!"

Sigrid sprang forward, and Eva raised her wooden sword just in time to meet the overhead swing. The shock raced through Eva's entire body, and she nearly lost her grip on her weapon. Showing no mercy, Sigrid advanced toward her with a series of blurring cuts that Eva struggled to deflect, let alone counter. In spite of Eva's forge muscles, each blow left her hand tingling even more as her grip weakened

Eva soon realized Sigrid was toying with her like a hawk circling a rabbit. The dark-haired girl pushed her all around the training circle, striking just slow enough for Eva to block the cut while preventing her from waging any counterattack.

They continued without pause, Sigrid's relentless drives pushing Eva right to the edge of the ring so that the onlookers were forced to jump back to avoid being hit. The burning spread from Eva's hands up into her arms and shoulders until the wooden sword felt heavier than Soot's forge hammer.

"Halt!"

Eva dropped her sword point at Uthred's command, hand numbs and lifeless. Sigrid leaned on her sword in a self-assured stance. The dark-haired girl still had that smug smile on her face, and Eva knew she had no hope of getting rid of it.

"Recruit Evelyn, Windsworn have to attack their opponents, too," Uthred said. Some of the class snickered at that, the ones who were first to team up against her when Cross ordered Eva to fight two or three of them at once. "This time, I want you to go on the offensive. Begin."

Eva brought her sword up in a guard as fast as she could manage, but Sigrid didn't attack this time. The other girl hung back at the edge of the training circle, daring Eva to come to her.

"I said attack!" Uthred shouted.

Mouth dry, hands slack, Eva swung a sideways cut at Sigrid. She almost didn't register the parry as Sigrid's counterattack struck her across the side of the head and knocked her to the ground.

"Again."

Eva tried to shake the dizziness from her head. Her vision swam, and the side of her face throbbed where Sigrid's wooden blade struck her. Somehow, she managed to stand and raise her practice sword.

"Again," Uthred commanded.

Sigrid remained on the far side of the ring, still smiling. This time, Eva advanced with caution, staying just outside of Sigrid's reach. After a couple of exchanges, Eva feinted a lunge and swung overhead. Sigrid saw through the trick with ease and parried. Before Eva could recover, Sigrid struck her across the arm and jabbed her in the ribs.

Eva folded in half, gasping for air, ribs burning like fire. An instant later, Sigrid struck her across the back, and Eva collapsed on the ground.

"Again," Uthred said. No one else made a sound.

Using her sword like a cane, Eva rose again, bent over like an old crone. She gritted her teeth and limped forward, one hand clutching injured ribs. She made a halfhearted jab and a few slices. Sigrid blocked them all with ease, striking Eva in return each time.

Lips curled in a silent snarl, Sigrid unleashed a fury of blows all over Eva's body. Each time, Eva blocked half a second too late. At last, Sigrid swept low and caught Eva behind the knee, knocking her to the ground yet again.

Through the haze of pain, Eva saw the other recruits muttering to one another, and even Cross wore a concerned expression on his face. Still, no one dared speak against the commander. Wynn rushed forward to help her up, but a wave from Uthred sent her out of the circle.

"Is this the best you can do after all these weeks?" Uthred said.

"The rider of the red gryphon? Again."

Tears ran down Eva's face, as much from frustration and embarrassment as pain. She ground her teeth together and stumbled before getting her feet beneath her on the second attempt. She tried to muster the courage and strength to attack once more, knowing full well what the outcome would be.

Through a half-swollen left eye, Eva saw Sigrid on the opposite side of the circle. The snarl was gone from the dark-haired girl's face, and she stared at Eva with a blank expression. When Eva took a faltering step forward, Sigrid looked at Uthred.

"Commander, I think —"

"I will let you know when the fight is over," Uthred said.

Eva took one wobbly step toward Sigrid and then another until they were just a sword's length apart. The other girl waited for Eva to make her move, eyes narrowed.

"The fight is not over," Uthred repeated.

Eva summoned the last of her strength into a wild blow. Sigrid sidestepped the attack with ease. The last thing Eva remembered was a blinding flash and searing pain through her head.

Chapter

15

Eva's eyes flickered open. Groaning, she closed them again, a dull, aching pain coursing through her from head to toe.

"You awake?"

It was Wynn's voice. Eva ventured a small peek again, and the younger girl's freckled face filled her vision. Her right eye opened wide, but the left seemed to be swollen shut.

Eva coughed, and her ribs flared with an angry reminder. Her fingertips felt soft, fuzzy blankets, and she realized she was in a bed. When or how she got there, Eva couldn't even begin to guess.

"Sigrid knocked you out," Wynn explained. "They brought you to the infirmary a few hours ago. You missed dinner, but I brought you some bread and stew if you want it."

Careful to move as little as possible, Eva shook her head. "Just a drink," she whispered. Her voice felt coarse and sounded like it came from the other end of a tunnel.

Wynn disappeared from Eva's line of sight and came back with a small cup. She helped Eva prop herself up on a pillow and held it while Eva took a few sips until she started coughing. The cough sent another wave of pain through her, and Eva winced, lowering herself back down.

"That was a rotten thing," Wynn said, nose wrinkling in disgust.

"You didn't deserve that."

"I don't belong here," Eva said, ignoring her friend. Tears welled in her good eye and splashed on the blankets.

"Don't say that," Wynn said. "You can't help it that you just started your training. Uthred and Cross, and Sigrid, they're all just jealous the egg hatched for you."

As much as she wanted to believe Wynn, Eva knew in her heart it wasn't true. Rather than arguing, she looked away, unable to roll over. After a few moments, she heard Wynn rise and felt a gentle hand touch her shoulder, then Eva was alone.

When she heard the door shut, a thin sob burst from Eva's lips. In the empty room, surrounded by gloom of the dim crystal lamps, she'd never felt more alone. She didn't belong. She wasn't, and would never be, Windsworn. With even darker thoughts swirling through her mind, Eva slipped away into a deep slumber.

Eva woke a second time and felt fingertips sliding through her hair. She flinched, still half-asleep, and opened her eyes. Sunlight streamed through a small window across the room from her. She knew she must be dreaming because Tahl's face was outlined in the glare.

Seeing her awake, he jerked his hand back. "I…uh." It was the first time Eva had ever seen him unsure. "I'm glad you're awake."

"Thanks," Eva muttered. Her initial excitement at Tahl's visit was quelled when she realized he must've known what happened, otherwise he wouldn't have been there. Realizing what she must look like, Eva fought the urge to pull her blankets over her head and hide until Tahl left. She ran a hand through the snarls and tangles in her hair, but Tahl took her wrist in a gentle grip.

"Relax," he said. "You got pretty beat up."

Eva felt her face flush. "Does everyone know?" she whispered, dreading the answer.

"No," Tahl said. Eva's hopes rose, only to be crushed by his next words. "But they probably will soon; it's hard to keep a secret in the Gyr. I…I found out last night and told the lord commander what happened."

"You didn't need to do that," Eva said, an unexplainable irritation rising in her. "I may be incapable of defending myself with a sword, but I don't need someone else to fight my battles for me."

She felt Tahl pull back in his chair, which only made her angrier. Angry at herself for snapping at him, angry for being awful at her training, and angry at everyone and everything that had placed her in the infirmary bed. "Sorry," she mumbled. "I just… it's been a long couple of days."

"The lord commander was furious," Tahl said. "Rumor has it he yelled at Commander Uthred in front of the whole Council."

Eva snorted, and the dried blood in her nose itched. "Maybe he's right. I just needed a beating, then I could be sent on my way."

Tahl's hand lighted on top of Eva's. "Don't say that."

"Why not?" Eva asked. "It's true. And now everyone knows it. Uthred and Sigrid made sure of that."

"It was a command from Uthred," Tahl said. Eva looked at him, and it must've been sharper than she thought because he pulled back his hand. "I mean, she…I spoke to her, and she felt…bad."

He trailed off, and Eva wondered if he was making it all up. Anger boiled inside of her.

"Oh good," she said. "I'm glad she feels *bad*. That makes everything just fine. She beat me to pieces, but that's okay because she feels *bad*."

"Eva —"

"Go away, Tahl," Eva said. "Maybe you should go see Sigrid. She feels *bad*."

She hated herself for saying it, but she'd reached the point where she didn't care what anyone in the storming mountain thought of her. Tahl wore a pained expression on his face as he stood and turned toward the infirmary door. Eva saw him pause as if he wanted to say something and almost said something herself, but then he was gone.

Soon after, the healer came to look over Eva's bandages and see how she was feeling. Eva answered her questions with terse answers and stared out the window, brooding, when the old woman finally left.

Morning passed into afternoon. While she slept, someone brought a tray of food. Eva sat up in her bed and picked at it but didn't feel much like eating or doing anything, for that matter.

Eva wondered why Andor hadn't come yet. Would he end this nonsense and dismiss her from the Gyr? He owed her that, at least — he'd caused all this. The lord commander yelling at Uthred made her feel about as good as Sigrid feeling *bad* she'd been his instrument of punishment.

Day passed into evening, and Eva slept off and on. Whatever balm the healer had applied on her bruises seemed to be wearing off. She hurt all over but found some comfort that no one had brought the gryphon chick to her. She told herself he'd probably already been given over to someone else's care.

The door opened, but it wasn't the healer. It wasn't Wynn or Tahl, either.

Celina walked across the room bearing a tray of food. She carried the tray at arm's length like a wild thing that might bite her. Depositing it on the table, she nodded for Eva to eat.

Eva muttered an insincere thanks and dug in, not caring about her poor manners or Celina watching her every move. She seemed pensive, almost thoughtful. When Eva finished and wiped the last of the food away, the commander studied her without a word.

When at last she spoke, Celina's voice cut through the silence like a blade. "What Uthred did to you was unfair and unjust. But life, if you haven't realized it yet, is unfair and unjust. You can sit here and feel sorry for yourself, or you can do something about it."

Eva wanted to tell her that was easy for her to say, that she'd never been humiliated in front of the entire Gyr, but instead she stared at her blankets.

"The lord commander wishes for me to begin training you in private, to help you catch up with the other recruits your age," Celina said.

"Oh, does he?" Eva said. The anger rose in her again, just as it had with Tahl. "He can't come here and tell me himself? His second in command ordered me beaten into unconsciousness, and he can't even come here and say he's sorry about that? Instead he sent you to give me more beatings, is that it?"

As soon as she'd finished speaking, Eva knew right away she'd gone too far. Celina clenched her jaw, eyes alight, and Eva flinched, expecting the woman to strike her.

Instead, Celina placed a gentle hand on Eva's shoulder. "I know it's not easy, Eva," she said. "Not only are you behind on years of training, but you're being judged at a higher standard than the rest. Believe it or not, I know what that's like."

"Really?" Eva asked. She found it hard to believe Celina had ever been anything but the best.

The commander nodded. "But none of that matters. The only thing you need to ask yourself is if you're going to give in or prove them wrong."

As soon as she'd finished, Celina stood. Without replying, Eva watched her walk across the floor. When the Celina reached the door, she paused.

"Your first lesson will begin in two days," the woman said without turning around. "Or you can let them win. You decide."

Chapter 16

Eva left the infirmary the next morning, before anyone else came to visit. Her left eye settled into a mottled blend of blue, purple, and brown, but the swelling had started to go down and she could open it. The split in her lip had scabbed over, in addition to the large lump on the side of her head from Sigrid's final blow. Her ribs, the healer informed her, weren't broken, even if it still hurt to breathe too deep.

Limping down side passages to avoid contact with as many people as possible, Eva made her way back to her quarters, bruises hidden beneath a cloak hood. When she opened the door and saw it was empty, a wave of relief washed over her. Sigrid's belongings were still in the room, however, so she hurried to gather a fresh uniform and headed down to the pools to clean herself up.

Beyond that, Eva didn't know what to do. She pondered Celina's words in the hours after the commander left but felt lost and unsure. Sigrid and Uthred had all but beaten the determination from her, and she felt hollow, empty. At the same time, she couldn't imagine giving up and going home to face Soot.

Since it was midday, she found herself all alone in the pools — everyone else either in training or on duty. Eva slid into the warm water and dipped her head underneath, enjoying the sensation of weightlessness and utter silence. When she resurfaced, she leaned back against the shelf of rock and blew out a deep breath as the water worked at the bruises and knots in her muscles.

Eva's hurt, anger, frustration, and embarrassment from the past few days drifted to the ceiling along with the small tendrils of mist rising in the cool, dim cavern. Eva lost track of time in her blissful isolation and didn't care if she made it to any of her classes. She closed her eyes, at peace in the absolute quiet of the cave.

Greatness or fear?

Like a fire flaring to life, the words rose in Eva's mind, cutting through her tranquility. For a long time, she stared at the shadowed ceiling above, torn between her choices. At long last, Eva pulled herself out of the pool. It wouldn't be easy, but she knew what she had to do.

When she reached the Roost, Eva spotted her class on the far side of the cavern. As she drew closer, they turned and stared until everyone was ignoring Cassandra's lecture. Trying to be as inconspicuous as possible, Eva joined Wynn in the back, burning from the dozens of eyes on her.

"Welcome back, dear," Cassandra said like Eva had been on leave and not beaten to a pulp. She snapped her fingers at the rest of the recruits, drawing some of their attention back to her. "Now, as I was saying, there are several indicators that a gryphon egg is close to hatching..."

The roost master uncovered a table beside her with several gryphon eggs of various colors nestled in baskets. As the rest of the class drew forward to get a better look, Wynn and Eva remained in the back.

"You look like —"

"I know," Eva said. Her mouth twisted into a half grin, half grimace that made her swollen face ache. "Don't I look pretty?"

"Sigrid ought to be horse whipped for that," Wynn whispered, bunching her hands into fists. "First her, then Uthred, then her again!"

"It's all right," Eva said. "I'll heal."

"I'll give her something to sneer about," Wynn continued, ignoring Eva.

The way she said it made Eva think it wasn't just an empty threat to make her feel better. "Don't try anything, Wynn," Eva said. "You'll end up like me or worse if you pick a fight with Sigrid."

Wynn looked at her with a mixture of surprise and annoyance. "Let it go? Look at you! By thunder, Eva, you're the biggest coward I know. When are you gonna stop letting people walk all over you?"

The younger girl's words hit Eva like a punch in the stomach. She opened her mouth, but no words came out and Wynn walked away to join the others, shaking her head.

For the rest of the class, Eva hung back, not caring about the striation patterns in the different colors of eggs or the various temperatures required during different stages of the chicks' growth inside them. A burning irritation settled inside her, especially whenever one of the recruits risked a glance her way to look at her bruises.

When class ended, she ignored Wynn, who held back to join her, and instead went to check on her gryphon chick. The prospect of looking after the hatchling didn't bring her any relief, but she'd already had enough of people for the day.

"He's been completely unruly while you've been gone," Cassandra said before excusing herself to check on some of the brood mothers. "Every time I turned around, he's fighting with the others — he doesn't seem to get along with anyone."

Alone, Eva made her way through the incubation cave into the smaller antechamber that served as a nursery for the gryphon chicks. Even with the other juvenile gryphons in the cavern, it didn't take long for Eva to find hers.

The red gryphon hunkered down in the far corner, wings spread over a chunk of meat. Three other chicks had him surrounded, working to steal it from Eva's chick. A black and a gray tried to circle around behind the red gryphon, but the corner forced them to come from the front.

Growing tired of the standoff, the third, a white hatchling, attacked. The red chick reared up on his hind paws, and his front talons met the white in midair, knocking it to the ground. In the moment their opponent diverted his attention, the black and gray pounced, and the red gryphon disappeared beneath them.

"Get off him!" Eva yelled rushing across the nursery. She backhanded the black and grabbed the gray's neck, tossing him aside. Seeing his allies defeated, the white chick scampered away. The other hatchlings gathered on the opposite side of the cave, hissing and chirping at the sudden outburst.

Free of his attackers, the red gryphon gave Eva a thankless look and turned his attention to the remaining bits of meat on his bone. Eva knelt down and reached out a hand to brush him across the top of his head. When she did, the chick snapped at her as if she were no different than the other hatchling trying to steal his prize. Eva frowned, irritated by the gryphon's lack of appreciation for rescuing him. She reached out again, and the chick's beak sank into the side of her hand.

Screaming in pain and anger, Eva swung her arm, launching the hatchling into the air. He landed in a clump of down and half-grown feathers a few feet away. Before he could recover, Eva dove on the gryphon, pinned him in her arms.

"What's wrong with you?" she yelled as the chick writhed in her arms, his yellow eyes furious. "You chose me! I didn't ask for this!"

The hatchling continued to struggle in her arms, but Eva held it firm, her shouts melting into frustrated sobs. After a few moments, Eva felt the chick's struggling cease. She opened her arms and let him go. Rather than returning to his bone, the red gryphon sat down on his haunches and stared at her, head cocked to the side. Neither girl nor gryphon moved.

After a long interlude, Eva stretched out her hand. Ignoring the pain from the hatchling's bite, she held her palm in front of his beak. The gryphon eyed it with suspicion but didn't strike. Encouraged, Eva stretched out her fingers and stroked his neck feathers.

Eva held her breath as the chick drew closer and sat down beside her. Eva's fingers ran down his back, and the gryphon arched his hind end like a cat when she scratched the base of his tail. She thought of the other hatchlings fighting her chick and her bout with Sigrid. The idea came to her that maybe they weren't different at all — a pair of outcasts driven together by a strange wind. And then it came to her.

"Fury," she said.

The gryphon looked at her.

"Fury," Eva repeated. "That's what I'm going to call you."

She thought back to all the moments she'd spent with the red gryphon until then and realized how the chick must have felt, being raised with no mother, different from the other hatchlings. If she was being honest with herself, Eva knew she hadn't been the best caretaker. Sure, she'd made sure the gryphon chick was well fed and looked after, but she'd never shown it any affection or love. She'd treated Fury just like any other part of her Windsworn training: something she went through the motions and did, without putting any heart into it.

"I'm sorry," she said. Shame filled the empty void left from her outburst. "I'll do better. But you're going to have to as well. You and I need to stick together — we're never going to make it here if we don't."

Fury chirped, and Eva stood then picked the gryphon chick up.

"Come on," she said. "Let's go show them what we're made of."

Chapter

🦅 17 🦅

T he problem," Celina said as Eva laced up her padded leather armor, "is that Cross teaches everyone to fight like a man, to fight like him. You are not a man, and you are not built like Cross. If you don't want to get yourself killed, you're going to have to learn to fight within your abilities."

"I'm not sure what that means," Eva said. Although she was eager to learn and prove her detractors — Uthred, Cross, and Sigrid — wrong, she didn't see how acting more like a lady would help her win any swordfights. It'd certainly never helped her while working in the forge.

"It means," Celina said, stepping forward to poke Eva in the chest with her wooden practice blade, "that you've got to be fast. Fast, agile, quick, and, most importantly, without mercy.

"They will doubt you," Celina continued, rubbing the dull gray bracer on her arm. "They will underestimate you. And if you let them, they will break you. To prove them wrong, you will train harder than any other Windsworn."

Eva swallowed. She thought she was quick and had a lean strength from swinging a hammer and pumping bellows, but merciless didn't fit the bill. Then she thought back to the humiliation Sigrid and Uthred subjected her to in the training ring and felt the embers of anger flare to life again. "Okay."

Celina gave a curt nod. "Good." She took the wooden practice blade from Eva's hand and replaced it with a heavy iron variant with blunted edges. Eva tried to raise the sword. It was far heavier than the wooden one, heavier even than the sharpened practice blades they worked the posts with in their exercises. The length of iron felt more like a forge hammer than a balanced weapon.

"How am I supposed to swing this?" Eva asked.

"You will find a way," Celina said. Without warning, she swung her sword in an overhead cut. Using all of her strength, Eva managed to raise the heavy sword just in time to deflect the blow aimed at her head. Celina took a step back, and Eva lowered her weapon until the tip touched the floor. Her arms were already beginning to burn.

"Never drop your guard," Celina shouted as she lunged forward. Eva sidestepped the stab and brought the heavy sword up to push the wooden tip of Celina's weapon away from her ribs. The twisting motion made her wince from her injuries, but this time she kept her weapon at the ready, even if it wavered in her grip.

Celina recovered faster than Eva could parry. She smiled again — the same grin of a fox who'd cornered a rabbit, like she'd given Eva in the Council chambers. "Better."

The older woman sprang at Eva again, and they traded a series of blows. Each time, Celina moved just slow enough for Eva to block the attack. Sweat poured from her, as much from the anxiety of being struck as from the exertion of the training.

After several intense moments, Eva's strength gave out. She raised the heavy blunted blade a fraction of a second too late. Celina's wooden sword came in like a blur and stopped less than a finger's width from Eva's neck. She tapped the blade against Eva's neck, and Eva twitched at the thought of how much it would have hurt.

"Dead."

Eva swallowed. Her arms felt like straps of metal that'd been cooking in the forge — hot, flimsy, and liable to fold in half.

Celina allowed Eva a handful of breaths and then brought her sword up, gesturing for Eva to do the same. "Again."

They repeated the process several times. Each time, Eva got slower and slower as the weight of the heavy iron blade set her arms, shoulder and back on fire. Each time, Celina's answer was the same:

"Again."

And so it continued until Eva could only manage to lift the point of the weighted weapon a couple of inches off the ground.

"Good," Celina said. "The first lesson is over. We continue tomorrow, at the same time."

Eva half dragged the sword over to the rack and hung it up. By now, the pain in her arms had subsided to a throbbing ache, and she couldn't close her fingers into a fist without her hands shaking. She walked across the small room and reached for the door to leave, until a thought struck her.

"Commander Celina?"

The older woman looked up from wiping the sweat from her face. "Yes?"

"Why did you vote for me to stay?"

For the first time, Eva saw a surprised look cross Celina's face. "I guess I saw a little bit of myself in you," she said, regaining her cool demeanor.

Comparing the two of them, Eva couldn't imagine two people more different. The disbelief must have shown on her face because Celina crossed the room and placed both her hands on Eva's shoulders.

"When I first came to the Gyr, I would have given anything to go home," she said. "I was small for my age. I spent two years getting picked on by the other recruits, beaten up in trainings, and I never felt more alone. But it made me tough, and I realized if I kept my head down and worked as hard as I could, I would prove everybody wrong about me."

"Just like you told me to do," Eva said.

"Exactly," Celina said. "And you know what happened?"

Eva shrugged. "You proved everyone wrong?"

Celina nodded. "I became the top of my class. Nobody would step into the training circle with me, not even the boys. I wasn't necessarily stronger or better, but I learned to be fast and I learned that I *wanted* it more than the others. When I saw you standing there all alone in the Council room, I wanted you to have the same chance."

Embarrassed, Eva ducked her head. "Thank you."

When she looked up, Celina had a small, sad smile on her face. Eva wasn't certain, but she thought she saw tears in the corners of the hardened woman's eyes. She turned Eva around and gave her a small push before she could tell for sure. "Go on, off you go."

The recruits filed out of the Main Hall after dinner, eager for an early evening off. Some sat out on the overlook and watched the sun set while others retreated to the library or commons. Many went straight to bed, eager for the extra sleep. Eva, on the other hand, excused herself from Wynn and took a winding path into the depths of the mountain to see Ivan.

Following Andor's directions he'd given her after the trial, Eva came around a sharp corner and found a guard standing attention outside of an iron-banded door. The man jerked out of what Eva suspected was a catnap but relaxed when he saw it was just her.

"I'm here to see Ivan," Eva said. Although Andor said he would let the guard know she would be visiting, Eva still felt nervous, like she was breaking some kind of rule.

The man nodded. "Of course. The lord commander said you might stop by from time to time. I'm afraid I'll have to lock you inside, Miss. If you need anything, I'll be right here. He's pretty quiet, though. Just reads most of the time."

In Eva's arms, Fury let out an impatient cry as the man started undoing the series of locks across the door. The security seemed a bit much to Eva, but she supposed it was better than a death sentence. She winced as the gryphon's talon slipped and nicked her.

Holding back a curse, Eva sat the growing chick on the ground — he still stumbled around and couldn't keep up with her strides but was now big enough that Eva couldn't carry him for long without a break. Since their moment in the nursery he still liked to test Eva every chance he got but seemed to have a respect and even fondness for her — as long as she kept him in line.

The door swung open, revealing Ivan sitting cross-legged in a chair on the opposite end of the chamber. The crystal lamps cast a warm glow over his shaved head and pale blue rune marks. When he looked up and recognized Eva, he grinned.

"You came!" the Scrawl boy said, shutting the book in his lap and hopping up to greet her. As Ivan neared them, Fury hissed and leaped at the boy. Luckily, Eva caught the hatchling just before he could sink his beak or talons into Ivan's robes.

"Fury!" Eva said. "Ivan is a friend."

The red gryphon didn't think so. When Eva let him go, the gryphon hopped onto a nearby shelf where he sat and stared at Ivan, yellow eyes gleaming in the dim light.

"Sorry about that," Eva said. "I don't know how, but he must remember that you stole him when he was in the egg."

"Fair enough," Ivan said, unperturbed by the gryphon's reaction. His eyes went wide, apparently noticing Eva's subsiding but still-visible injuries for the first time. "What happened to you?"

"I, uh," Eva said, looking away to hide her face. "I'd rather not talk about it right now."

"That's okay!" Ivan said. "I'm just glad I have someone to talk to. I mean, I don't mind reading books and all — they give me as many as I want, but it gets kind of lonely. I've almost run out of space to write on, too!"

For the first time, Eva noticed the rune chalk marks in the low light. The letters covered almost every open space of stone in the small room. Fury must have noticed it, too, because he hopped down from the shelf and hid behind Eva's feet, hissing. The strange letters caused the nape of Eva's neck to tingle, but Ivan still beamed at her.

"Umm, what are those for, Ivan?" she asked, not sure she wanted to know the answer.

"Oh, just practice," The boy said as if he'd been doing nothing more than whittling on a stick. "I've got to try and keep up on my studies."

He must have seen the doubtful look on Eva's face because he took her by the hand and led her to the only chair in the room. When

Eva sat down, Fury jumped into her lap, although he kept his eye on Ivan and his body remained tense.

"Don't worry," Ivan said. He climbed onto the bed nearby and folded his legs beneath him. "The runes don't hold any real power unless they're attached to something living."

Eva thought of Seppo. What Ivan said didn't make any sense. Seppo was just an empty shell of metal. Sure, he could move and think for himself and had a personality, but he had no blood, as far as Eva knew, no non-metal substance of any kind other than his eyes.

She said as much, and Ivan's face crinkled as if he'd been thinking about it for a long time. "I...don't know," he said. "Your golem is... something else entirely, but I don't know what. The runes he has marked on him are a far older alphabet than any I've ever seen. There are lots of things the Ancients learned to do with rune magic that we've lost, though."

"Like how to make Wonders?" Eva asked, thinking of her mother's glowing stone hidden back in her quarters.

Ivan nodded. "Right! We only know how to channel the power of the runes and kenning chants through something living. That's why we're all covered in ink!"

The topic of rune magic made Eva uneasy, so she decided to change the conversation. "I'm sorry I couldn't come sooner."

Ivan shrugged. "I'm sure you're busy. But I knew you would come tonight — I saw it. Besides, the Elders tell me it's very important for a Skrael to develop patience."

"S-Skrael?" Eva said, testing the strange word on her tongue.

"It's what we call ourselves in our own tongue," Ivan said. "When your ancestors came to Altaris, Scrawl was the best they could manage, I guess. We *do* write a lot, though, so it's fitting, if not entirely accurate.

Eva nodded, feeling very uneducated and unsure what else to say. "Wait," she said, realization dawning on her. "What do you mean, you knew I would come tonight?"

Ivan tapped a finger to his forehead. "I dreamed it, of course! The dreams kind of went away for a while after I found you, but now they've been coming back. I was worried, thinking they were gone for good, but —"

"Ivan," Eva began. She shifted in her seat, causing Fury to shoot her an annoyed glance as he settled back in on her lap. "I'm not sure these dreams are a good thing. From what I understood at the trial, they're not…normal, even for a Scrawl."

"But that's the exciting part!" Ivan said like he hadn't heard her. "I might be the first! And what's even stranger is that I can work the runes *within* my dreams! It seems so real!"

"Let's talk about something else," Eva said, growing more uncomfortable by the minute. As far as she could tell, these strange dreams were the reason Ivan was imprisoned in the first place and might have something to do with the death of Fury's mother. She didn't think Andor would appreciate her discussing the subject with the boy.

"Okay!" Ivan said. Eva couldn't believe someone who was locked inside a mountain without daylight could be so enthusiastic. "You want to tell me what happened to you?"

Eva's stomach twisted — it was bad enough that word had spread throughout the Gyr. She'd felt relieved knowing Ivan was probably the only person inside the whole mountain who didn't know. The Scrawl seemed to like Eva — respect her, even — and she didn't want to ruin that.

"You don't have to tell me," he said as if reading her thoughts.

"No, it's okay." Eva blew out a long breath and then related the story of her fight with Sigrid.

"I didn't like her very much," Ivan said, the runes on his forehead bunching as he frowned. "And I liked that Uthred guy even less. I get a bad feeling whenever he's around."

Eva nodded, embarrassed but also relieved she could share the story with someone without being judged. Someone who just cared about who she was, not the implications it meant to her training, or Fury's raising. Before either of them could say anything else, a knock came at the door.

"Time's up, Miss," the guardsman said from outside the room.

"We're making a change of watch. I'm afraid you'll have to go now."

"Can't you stay a few more minutes?" Ivan asked. In that moment, he seemed very much like the boy of twelve summers he was instead of the self-assured Scrawl he tried to be the rest of the time.

"Sorry," Eva said, standing up and gathering Fury in her arms. "I promise I'll come visit as much as I can, although I don't know how much free time I'm going to have with my additional lessons."

"I'm sure I'll know before you will when the next time is," Ivan said, winking. Eva gave a thin smile, still uncomfortable at the idea. "Yeah…we'll see."

"Goodbye, Fury," Ivan said. He reached a hand toward the hatchling, who hissed again and snapped his beak.

"Sorry," Eva said. "He doesn't behave very well. Maybe next time he'll warm up to you."

"I hope so!" Ivan said. "See you soon, Eva."

He was still smiling and waving as the door closed.

Chapter 18

Eva opened the door to her quarters and froze. Sigrid sat honing her sword on the edge of her bed. It was the first time Eva had seen her since being released from the infirmary. She didn't know if Sigrid was sleeping somewhere else or merely coming in and leaving while Eva slept. The dark-haired girl's sudden appearance caused Eva's heart to jump into her throat and twisted her stomach into cold, writhing knots.

Sigrid's head spun toward her. Eva stood rooted to the spot. The girl certainly didn't look like she felt bad for what happened, and with a real sword in her hand Eva didn't want to be anywhere near Sigrid. She turned to leave.

"Wait!"

Eva turned, body tense. Sigrid sat the sword down on the bed beside her. She cleared her throat and seemed to find an intense interest in the floor at her feet. "Why don't you... come in."

Eva glanced up and down the hallway but saw no one in either direction. Preparing for the worst, she sat on her bed, across from Sigrid. Fury hopped from her arms and down on the floor to his basket-nest at the foot of Eva's bed.

Sigrid glanced at Eva and winced. The cuts on her face were scabbed over, and her black eye had turned now a nasty brownish green, although most of the swelling was gone. Sigrid cleared her throat.

"I...didn't mean —"

"You seemed to be enjoying yourself in the moment," Eva said. She didn't know what she wanted from Sigrid, but it sure wasn't a half-baked apology. Her hands clenched her blankets, and she stared at Sigrid, ready for whatever might come next.

A pained look crossed Sigrid's face before she sank into her regular scowl. "Uthred commanded me to fight you. I won't lie; I wanted to beat you in front of everyone, but —"

"But what?"

"Uthred's the lord commander's left wing, the third-highest officer in the Windsworn," Sigrid hissed. "If I'd refused, he'd probably have thrown me out of the Gyr."

"Oh right," Eva said, her voice rising. "Almost killing me was a much better choice. What did I ever do to you, anyway?"

Sigrid leaped off her bed and stood in front of Eva, both of her hands tightened into fists. Eva flinched but didn't move or look away.

"You don't know anything!" Sigrid yelled. "You're just a spoiled blacksmith's daughter who doesn't want to be here in the first place."

"Go on," Eva said. She felt the anger die in her, frozen by cold hate. "Hit me again if it'll make you feel better."

Sigrid balled her hands into fists, and Eva braced herself for the blow. Fury leaped on the bed beside Eva and crouched down, hissing. Sigrid's face spasmed, and she stormed out of their quarters, banging the door shut behind her. Eva did nothing for several moments. Her hammering heart seemed to fill the room. After several deep breaths, she started to calm down and felt drained — more exhausted than she'd ever been working the forge with Soot.

Without bothering to slip out of her uniform, Eva rolled over and pulled the blankets around her. She tossed and turned for almost an hour until, frustrated, she leaned under bed and yanked out her chest of belongings. At the bottom, she found her cloak and unwrapped the Wonder from its fold.

Light illuminated the room, and Eva felt the familiar warm glow fill her. Fury leaped out of his basket onto the foot of Eva's bed, staring at the stone.

"It's okay, Fury," Eva said, beckoning him closer. The juvenile gryphon crept forward and stretched out to touch the stone with the tip of his beak.

Eva smiled, watching the gryphon's reaction. After a couple of long moments, he seemed to decide the light posed no threat and lay down next to Eva. She stared into the stone's depths for a long time, watching the swirls of blue, pink, gold, and white until her eyes began to droop. Lying down once more, she clutched the stone tight to her. Just before sleep overtook her, she felt Fury curl up against her as well, his warm little body as reassuring as the stone in the colossal, empty mountain.

"Enough!"

Eva blew a bead of sweat away from a loose strand of hair and stepped back. Although she was soaked with sweat and her muscles burned, she smiled. Over the past several weeks she'd fought with bow, sword, knife, and spear under Celina's meticulous instruction. Most nights, Eva wolfed down her dinner and crawled into bed, savoring a few hours' sleep before starting all over again with regular class the next morning. Like an iron ingot hammered against the anvil, Celina shaped her into a warrior with each practice bout.

Now when they fought, a regular blunted sword felt light as a feather in Eva's hand, slicing the air almost with a mind of its own. She'd yet to come close to beating Celina, but in the past couple of weeks she'd landed a couple of blows. The small victories filled her with pride when she thought back to the helpless girl who'd been humiliated.

"You are a quick learner when your heart is in it," Celina said in between breaths. "I'll wager none of Cross's students would volunteer to put themselves in the training circle against you now!"

Not that any of them knew it, though. Celina conducted all of Eva's weapons training, and Eva liked it that way. She relished the idea of being the girl everyone underestimated, even as her skill continued to grow.

"Thank you, Commander," Eva said, placing her weapon on the rack and reaching for a nearby towel to wipe off her face. Celina did the same and handed her a water flask. Eva drank deep, feeling a warm satisfaction similar to the triumph of shaping a piece just right under Soot's watchful eye in the forge. She hadn't experienced it much since coming to the Gyr. Even though the Gyr's smaller birds of prey — hawks and falcons — brought her regular letters from Soot, she still missed home.

After their fight, Sigrid started keeping regular hours in their shared quarters, although she and Eva only spoke to each other when it was absolutely necessary, meaning hardly at all. They'd worked out a sort of silent schedule, so the only time they came across each other was to sleep at night. It didn't make for the most pleasant conditions, even with Fury around and Wynn's company throughout the day

Of Tahl, Eva saw very little. Whenever she happened to sight him, a group of admirers had him hemmed in or he was so far down a bustling passageway that Eva had no hope of reaching him. Their exchange in the infirmary bothered Eva, especially because she couldn't find a chance to apologize. The thought that Tahl cared enough to look in on her after the fight led to more than a few hours tossing and turning. Eva tortured herself wishing she could go back and do something different.

Celina waved to the door when Eva lingered. "Off to class, then."

"I've got time for one more bout," Eva said, a small, mischievous smile on her face.

Celina laughed. "As much as I hate to admit it, you can recover a lot faster than I, Eva," she said. "If I'm going to give you a run tomorrow, I'd better save my strength."

Eva thought there was more behind the statement than Celina wanted to let on. Although she didn't dare mention anything, the commander's complexion had taken on a pale hue, and her face looked hollow and stretched against her prominent facial bones. The dark circles beneath Celina's eyes finished the effect. Even so, she'd yet to lose her usual vigor when Eva trained with her.

Celina unbuckled her padded training leathers, drawing Eva's eyes to the slate-colored bracer on Celina's wrist. In all their time training she'd never seen the older woman take it off. Although it didn't seem to pinch her skin, it fit snug and never moved no matter how intense Celina sparred.

"Commander," Eva said, "why do you always wear that arm guard?"

Celina held it up into the sunlight streaming through a small window slit. The bracer soaked in the light, giving no reflection. Eva noticed a series of strange runes carved in spiraling lines around it.

"This bracer is very dear to me," she said. "A trophy won on a journey I took long ago. It is a Wonder, a relic of the Ancients who once dwelled across Altaris."

Eva's eyes remained on the bracer while Celina spoke. When she finished, Eva opened her mouth to tell her about the white stone but stopped. Unlike the commander, she kept her stone secret and safe in the chest in her quarters. Even Wynn didn't know about it and, although Eva trusted Celina, it felt wrong to tell even her. "You found it?" she asked instead.

Celina nodded. "In the far east on a very long and dangerous exploration."

Eva's mind filled with scenes of faraway lands and forgotten ruins. No one talked much about the lands east of Rhylance. The Endless Plains met the eastern slopes of the Windridge Mountains, but beyond them she'd learned very little in her lectures with Portridge and visits to the library.

"Why did you go east?" Eva asked. As far as she knew, there weren't any cities or civilizations in eastern Altaris. The Juarag inhabited the Endless Plains, but the only interaction they made with Rhylance was through raiding parties.

Celina looked surprised. "Surely you know about the Great Eastern Exploration?"

The way the commander said it made Eva feel embarrassed she

didn't, but she shook her head anyway. "Should I?"

"I don't believe," Celina said shaking her head. "Soot was one of the members of our party! That's where Seppo came from. He never told you?"

Eva's jaw dropped. "Soot?" She had a hard time believing the home-loving blacksmith had ever taken part in any grand adventures. "He never said anything about it. Please, tell me more!"

Celina hesitated, and Eva knew she'd said something wrong. "Another time, my dear," the commander said "I promise. The tale is too long to tell at the moment. Now, get to your next class!"

Eva protested, but Celina shooed her out the chamber, shutting the door behind her. Walking down the hall at a slow pace, Eva's mind wandered as much as her feet. On her way to class, Eva resolved to send Soot a letter, or ask him in person if he didn't respond. For such a large place, the Gyr sure didn't hold very many answers.

Chapter 19

Eva awoke with a start, chest heaving, sweat running down her face. She'd been having a nightmare — something about a golem made of shadows chasing her through the halls of the Gyr. She took several deep breaths and looked over to see Sigrid asleep in her bed. All was calm and quiet.

As she tried to return to sleep, Eva's mind drifted to Celina's revelation about Soot. Contrary to her promise, Celina refused to speak of the expedition the next time they met. Eva's incessant asking had made her so mad, the commander sent Eva running stairs in an abandoned hallway for almost an hour after their sparring.

After that, Eva didn't want to risk irritating Celina further. She pored over books in the library and worked up the courage to ask Portridge after class one day, but neither paper nor instructor offered much more.

"It was an exploratory journey to the eastern coast of Altaris almost twenty years ago," Portridge had told her. "The group encountered hostile Juarag and various other savage tribes in the eastern woodlands. Other than a few trinkets and ruins, nothing of note was discovered."

Eva forced thoughts of the Eastern Expedition out of her thoughts in an effort to quiet her mind and go back to sleep. Rolling over, she found Fury's spot at the foot of her bed empty. In recent days, he'd taken to sleeping there more than in his basket. Eva didn't think of it and stretched out her legs, trying to get comfortable. But a nagging feeling refused to let her rest.

Annoyed and exhausted, she sat up again and leaned forward to look at the basket nest at the foot of her bed. Terror struck her. Fury wasn't there. A quick inspection of the small room confirmed Eva's worst fears: somehow, the red gryphon had disappeared.

Eva looked around, unsure what to do. For a moment, she thought about waking Sigrid, but they still weren't speaking to one another. The last thing she wanted was Sigrid to know she'd somehow lost her gryphon in the middle of the night. Instead, Eva dressed quietly and cracked the door of their quarters open. Behind her, Sigrid snorted, sprawled out on her bed. Eva waited until her snores began again then slipped out the door.

In the hallway, Eva ventured several whispered calls. When Fury didn't answer, she walked several paces in both directions, finding no trace of the gryphon. With no idea what to do, Eva returned to her door, fighting the panic rising inside her.

After several deep breaths, she tried to calm her racing mind. How could Fury have escaped the room, let alone shut the door behind him? A second thought struck her: What if the person who'd killed Devana had returned for her chick?

Eva slipped back into her room — Sigrid continued snoring away — and belted on her small recruit's knife, the only weapon she had. She turned to leave then paused and returned to her chest. Covering the stone's light with her cloak, Eva withdrew her Wonder. If there was ever a time she need calm and courage, this was it.

Back outside, Eva hurried to the end of the hallway and then paused when it split. She had no clue where to go next.

"Think, girl," she told herself. Somehow, someone had managed to steal Fury practically out from underneath Eva — all without the gryphon making a noise. But where had they gone? Eva had no idea.

Minutes ticked away, and Eva grew anxious, standing at the split in the hallway. Time was running out. She had to make a decision, but how?

And then it hit her. "Ivan," Eva muttered, turning down the tunnel that led to the lower levels. She didn't place much faith in the Scrawl's visions, but right now anything was better than standing in the hall.

She'd never been out of her quarters this late before. The lamps cast long, flickering shadows across the walls, making the stone dance. Silence reigned. Each time Eva took a step, the scuff of her boots echoed down the passage, further highlighting her aloneness.

Two wrong turns later, Eva found the hall leading to Ivan's chamber. A couple of turns away, she paused. She had no idea if a guard was posted outside the door around the clock or not. If there was, Eva didn't have a clue what she would tell him to let her in. She considered turning around when voices drifted down a nearby side passage.

"I've got things under control."

A bolt of fear raced through Eva — it sounded like Uthred. She strained her ears to hear whom he was talking to.

"Hardly think so…keeping an eye on things." Eva couldn't be sure, but she thought it was a woman's voice, possibly Celina. What the two commanders would be doing in the halls at this hour, Eva couldn't imagine. She held her breath as Uthred started speaking again

"Strange things…Catacombs."

Eva hesitated then took a couple of steps down the side passage.

"Wonder why you're skulking around at night," Eva heard Celina say. "From the boy."

The boy. They had to be talking about Ivan. Eva ventured another couple of steps forward, heart thudding in her chest.

"Ridiculous," Uthred said. "You'd best watch yourself, Celina."

The voices ceased, and a set of footsteps faded in the opposite direction while the other pair — Uthred's, Eva guessed by the heavy footfalls — grew louder, and closer.

Panicking, Eva ducked down another side hall and ran. The thought of what Uthred might do to her if he caught Eva out of her quarters in the middle of the night spurred her onward. After switching directions several times, she slowed to catch her breath. As soon as she did, Eva heard footsteps again, much closer than before.

Eva shrank against the wall, hugging the shadows. A moment later Uthred appeared at the fork in the tunnel a few dozen paces away. The commander paused for a long moment and stared toward her. Remembering her scouting training, Eva remained motionless even after Uthred looked away and glanced back. After another long pause, Uthred hurried off in the other direction. Eva let out a long sigh before realizing the direction Uthred was headed: to Ivan's cell.

Creeping forward as fast as she could without making a sound, Eva followed after the Windsworn commander. When she peeked around the corner of the hall leading to Ivan's cell, however, she found it empty. Eva waited several long moments, and when no one appeared, she hurried forward as fast as she could in silence.

A faint muttering sound, guttural and unintelligible, grew louder as Eva approached. The sound grew louder as she approached the door. No guard stood on duty, and it hung ajar. The deep chanting sound came from within.

Torn between running away and checking on her friend, Eva gritted her teeth and inched forward. A blanket of dread engulfed her, and it took every last bit of willpower she had to bring her shaking hand to the door and push it open.

Ivan sat on his knees in the middle of the chamber, facing the opposite wall. Horrified, Eva realized the chanting came from the Scrawl. Every instinct in Eva's body screamed at her to run. Mouth dry, she forced herself to take a step forward.

"Ivan?" she whispered, so quiet she barely heard herself over the boy's chant.

He didn't answer. Eva took another step.

"Ivan?" This time she spoke louder, but still no response.

Clenching her hands into fists to stop the shaking, Eva walked around the Scrawl's side. Ivan stared ahead like he couldn't see or hear her. While his lips moved, forming the awful, strange language, the rest of his body remained completely still.

"Ivan?"

A scream tore from Eva's lips when she looked into the Scrawl's face. Ivan stared at the far wall, chanting in a deep voice that wasn't his own, oblivious to her presence. But worst of all were his eyes. They glowed a deep amber like twin coals smoldering. Terror seized Eva, and she stumbled backward, crashing to the ground.

Eva scrambled to regain her footing, and her Wonder stone swung free from beneath her shirt. Golden light blazed forth, lighting the room like midday. Ivan groaned and slumped on his side, silent. Although her heart pounded in her chest, Eva paused. When the boy rolled over and looked at her, his eyes were normal once again.

"Fury," he said in a hoarse voice. "Trouble...the Roost. Hurry!"

Leaping to her feet, Eva stuffed the Wonder stone back out of sight, sprinting out of the room. Not bothering what noise she made or whom she came across, Eva ran like she'd never run before, hurtling down the Gyr's corridors.

A new feeling rose through her terror and panic, tugging at her heart like an invisible string.

Fury.

She couldn't say how, but she knew the gryphon was in danger now, would have even without Ivan's warning. The sensation drove her onward, overcoming her agonizing gasps for air and burning legs. Fury was in danger, somehow calling out to her for help. Desperate, reckless strength flooded Eva's limbs, and she tore up the stairs faster than before.

When Eva reached the Roost at last, the gryphons were astir, screeching and beating their wings in a wild cacophony. Through it all, Eva heard a person shouting from the direction of the landing on the opposite end of the cavern. The same instinct told Eva Fury would be there, too. Stumbling, Eva forced her legs to keep moving. Each breath she drew felt like daggers stabbing at her throat and chest.

Nearing the edge of the landing where the rock dropped off into a cliff, Eva spotted a small figure hopping up and down — Fury. Before Eva could express her relief at finding her gryphon unharmed, another shout rose, from over the edge of the rock.

"Where are you!" Eva shouted as she dropped onto her belly and crawled forward to look over into the darkness.

"Down here — I can't hold on much longer!"

It was Sigrid. Peering over the ledge, she looked down and saw the dark-haired girl clinging to the side of the rock. A large brown gryphon hovered in the empty space in front of Sigrid, its stressful screams rising into the night. Eva guessed it was Sigrid's. Eva's blood ran cold as she stared into the abyss. She rolled over onto her back and shut her eyes to stop the world from spinning.

Taking a deep breath, she looked down again. "It's Eva!" she shouted. "Hold on; I'll find something to pull you up with!"

A muffled curse rose up from Sigrid's position. "Hurry!" the girl yelled in a panicked voice.

Eva ran back to the wall where all the gryphons' saddles and harnesses were stored. She looked around wildly but saw nothing that was long enough or strong enough to reach all the way down to Sigrid. At last, she spotted a rope that looked like it might be long enough. Rushing back to the ledge, she heard Sigrid yell again.

When she reached the edge, Eva dropped to her belly and tossed the end of the rope over. Sigrid's eyes, wide and full of fear, met hers. The rope ended a couple of feet short of Sigrid's reach.

"Too short," Sigrid said with her usual venom. "Is that the best you could do?"

"That's all there was!"

She pulled the rope up, mind racing. Maybe she could tie something on the end or —

"I'm slipping!"

The answer came to Eva. There was only one option left.

Since the first day of flight training, she'd been on the back of a gryphon three times, once with Andor to go to the trial, and the second and third when she ran out of excuses and Cassandra practically hauled her onto the back of a training gryphon. Each time had been just as bad as the previous, leaving her light-headed and sick.

"Send your gryphon up!" Eva yelled, hardly believing her own words. "I can't reach you from up here!"

"Sven, go!"

The gryphon hesitated, reluctant to leave its rider in her precarious position. Sven could do no good down there by himself — if Sigrid fell, she'd likely slide down the wall, too close for the gryphon to grab until she struck something and careened out into the darkness.

"Sven!" Eva shouted. "I can help!"

At last, the brown gryphon tore himself away from his rider. Sven rose with an anxious cry and landed beside her. Without thinking, Eva swung onto his back. Sven wore no saddle, no legs straps, or any other means for Eva to secure herself to the gryphon in the open air. Using the rope, she tied a quick loop around Sven's neck and twisted the remainder of rope around her left arm. Trying not to think about falling, Eva nudged the gryphon with her heel, and Sven launched off the ledge.

They burst into the open night, and Eva spotted Sigrid below, still clinging to the mountainside. As soon as they were clear of the rock, Sven wheeled around and dropped in as close as he could beneath his rider.

Eva shivered as much from fear as the cool night air. Due to Sven's size, a large gap remained between them and Sigrid, more than plenty of room for her to fall past them. Eva wondered if Sven could grab Sigrid with his talons but feared the sudden shift in weight would send all three of them plummeting to their deaths.

"Sigrid, you're going to have to jump," Eva said, voice cracking. "We can't get any closer!"

"Storm that!" Sigrid yelled back. "You'll drop me!"

In spite of her fear, Eva's temper erupted. "Then fall and die!" she snapped. "I'm not going to get myself killed because you won't trust me! *Jump, damn you!*"

Almost as fast as Eva finished speaking, Sigrid kicked off from the cliff. For a moment, Eva saw the girl hurtling toward them. She stretched out as far as she could, the rope wrapped around her left arm anchoring her to Sven.

As Sigrid struck her gryphon's wing, her hand met Eva's. Knocked off balance by Sigrid's landing, Sven careened sideways, and they spun out of control. Screaming as the rope bit deep into her arm, Eva heaved with all her strength, and Sigrid managed to kick her leg up over the gryphon's back behind Eva.

With the weight of his passengers balanced, Sven spread his wings and pulled out of the free fall. Feeling the gryphon level out, Eva almost collapsed across the back of his neck. They'd done it.

"By the sky, I never want to do that again!" Sigrid yelled in her ear.

Eva nodded and burst into manic, sobbing laughter. Sigrid joined in, and they howled like lunatics until Sven touched down inside the Roost.

Eva half slid, half fell from the gryphon's back. As soon as she fell to the solid ground, a ball of fur and feathers struck her in the side. Wrapping one arm around Fury, Eva rolled onto her back, elated and exhausted.

Then she heard the footsteps running toward them.

Chapter 20

As Eva pulled herself to her feet and reached for her knife, Uthred and Celina appeared out of the darkness. Fury hissed and hunkered down at Eva's legs. A simultaneous wave of relief and unease gripped Eva, and she was thankful for Celina's presence after what she'd heard from Uthred in the halls below.

"What happened?" Uthred demanded. His hand gripped his sword hilt, and he looked ready to draw it at the slightest provocation.

"I-I heard screaming, Commander," Eva said, still shaky from the wild flight. "When I got here, Sigrid was hanging from the rocks. Sven and I were able to rescue her."

"And how did you hear her screaming if you were in your quarters?" If Uthred seemed impressed by Eva's feat, he showed no sign.

Eva swallowed hard, Uthred's dark eyes boring into her as she struggled to answer with at least part of the truth. "I woke up, and Fury was gone," she said. "I came looking for him, and that's when I heard her."

"You lost your gryphon?" Uthred looked like he couldn't decide whether to be incredulous or furious. "If so, how did the chick get out of your room?"

"I-I don't know," Eva said, dropping her head to avoid the commander's glare. "He was just…gone."

Before Uthred could grill Eva further, Celina cut in. "Sigrid! What do you have to say about this? What happened?"

"I woke up, and Eva and her gryphon weren't there," Sigrid said. "I came looking for them in the Roost. When I got here, something had upset the gryphons. I couldn't see the roost master anywhere, and then I spotted Fury by the cliffs. When I ran to him, a blast of wind hit me, and I fell over the edge."

Sigrid paused and looked at Eva, almost unbelieving. "If Eva hadn't come, I'd probably be dead."

Celina and Uthred looked at one another.

"I'll take a look around," Uthred said, drawing his sword.

Celina nodded. "Eva, Sigrid, come with me. The lord commander must hear of this at once."

Eva gathered Fury in her arms. The chick trembled in her arms, and she realized how much worse the night could have ended. She glanced at Sigrid, but the other girl looked straight ahead as they walked.

A group of riders and recruits was gathering at the entrance of the Roost. Celina sent a pair of older riders who'd had enough sense to arm themselves to go assist Uthred and ordered the rest away.

"Everyone, back to your quarters!" Celina snapped. "The lord commander will address everyone in the Main Hall in the morning. Now go!" The Gyr's second-in-command left no room for argument. Looking over the shoulders and muttering among themselves, the group filed out.

"Where in the sky is Cassandra?" Eva heard Celina mutter.

While the four of them continued to Andor's quarters, Eva tried to wrap her mind around the events of the past few hours. There hadn't been an attack since she'd arrived at the Gyr. How had Fury gotten out of their quarters? No one could have taken him against his will — the gryphon's noise would've woken them.

Part of Eva wondered if Sigrid wasn't telling the whole truth, but she found it hard to believe the girl was involved. Who would throw themselves off a cliff just to look innocent? Without a doubt, she'd been asleep when Eva left — no one could fake snoring like that.

None of it made sense, and Eva felt even more dazed trying to sort it all out. When they arrived at the lord commander's door Celina raised her hand to knock, but before she could the door swung open, revealing a disheveled Andor, cinching on his sword belt with one hand.

"Celina!" he said, surprised. When the lord commander saw Eva and Sigrid, he frowned. "What's going on? I just had an officer tell me there was some sort of attack in the Roost."

"We can shed some light on the rumors, Lord Commander," Celina said, gesturing to the two girls. "Sigrid was attacked, but Eva arrived in time to prevent anything worse happening. Uthred and I happened to hear the gryphons raising an alarm — he's looking for any sign of the attackers now. I thought it best to bring the girls to you immediately."

Eva looked at Celina, waiting for her to mention something about catching Uthred in the hallway, but the woman was finished. Andor beckoned Eva and Sigrid inside. "I would like to speak to these two in private. Please remain outside my door to escort them back to their quarters when I am finished. I don't want anyone roaming the halls alone."

Eva and Sigrid followed the lord commander into his chambers, and Eva flinched as the door shut behind them. Andor motioned to the high-backed chairs around his parchment-strewn table and sat down across from them. His eyes passed over both of them.

"Tell me what happened."

As Eva then Sigrid related their portion of the night's events, Andor's face remained stern but otherwise unchanging. Once again, Eva omitted the portion of her story involving Celina, Uthred, and Ivan. Eva knew Ivan couldn't have been responsible for the attack. He would have had to pass by Eva — invisible and faster than a person could run — somewhere in the passageways to get to Sigrid first. She also knew any mention of the Scrawl would likely condemn him regardless of any testimony she could make for his innocence.

"I will ask this only once," Andor said when they'd concluded. "I am aware of the recent... happening between you. If this was in any

142

way a continuation on that from either of you, this is your last chance to tell me. Anything that comes to light later will not go well."

Eva and Sigrid looked at each other, bewildered. "No, Lord Commander," they both said.

"Eva saved my life," Sigrid said. Eva's head whipped sideways, stunned by the admission. Sigrid glanced at her and continued with some reluctance. "I...I'd probably be smashed to pieces at the bottom of the mountain if it wasn't for her."

Andor nodded. "If nothing else, perhaps a camaraderie will come out of this night."

Embarrassed, Eva focused on the piles of reports and maps on the table. "It's not a big deal," she muttered. "Sigrid would have done the same thing if it were the other way around." At least, she hoped Sigrid wouldn't have let her fall to a gruesome death.

"Your actions tonight were worthy of the Windsworn," Andor said. Eva could tell by his voice, it was the biggest compliment he could've given her. The lord commander opened his mouth but then seemed to think of something else. "Sigrid, why did you look for Eva in the Roost first?"

"When I left the barracks, I saw someone headed in that direction," Sigrid said. "They were wearing a cloak and looked to be about Eva's size. I followed them, but when they entered the Roost, they were gone. That's when I saw Fury."

Andor stroked his short beard and stared past them at the wall. "And Eva, that wasn't you? Why didn't you check the nursery in the Roost first?"

Eva opened her mouth, desperately trying to come up with a believable story. "No," she said, buying some time. "It wasn't me. I thought there might be a chance that if Fury somehow got out on his own he might head to the kitchens. He eats all the time lately."

She knew how unconvincing she sounded, but if Andor suspected anything, he didn't show it. Sigrid, on the other hand, stared at her like she'd just told them gryphons could fly and they were supposed to be surprised.

"Sigrid, I would like to talk to Eva alone for a moment," Andor said. "Please wait outside with Commander Celina; we won't be long."

Eva felt her stomach clench and her heart race as Sigrid rose, saluted, and left. Andor waited for the door to close before speaking again.

"Eva, I wanted to ask you in private if there was anything you wanted to add?" The lord commander studied Eva with his deep blue eyes. She fidgeted with her hands, and she stared at Fury curled up by the embers in the fireplace.

"Nothing, sir," Eva said "I'm sorry that Fury got out of our room. I don't know how it could've happened. I didn't hear anything, and —"

"Come now, Eva," Andor said. For a moment, Eva was afraid he knew everything and was going to call her bluff. "We both know Fury didn't escape on his own. And for him to be taken without a sound..."

The lord commander broke off and walked to the fireplace. He knelt down and stroked the feathers on top of Fury's head, staring at the red gryphon.

"The name's a little unconventional, but it fits," Andor said. Finished petting the gryphon chick, he stood and looked at Eva. "There is something at work here that I don't understand. You must be extra careful, Eva. Someone wants your gryphon. Until we find out why or who they are, I don't want you going anywhere without at least one other person with you at all times. Do you understand —"

An urgent knock cut him off.

"Lord Commander, I'm sorry to interrupt." It was Celina's voice. The Gyr's second in command sounded almost frantic. "It's Roost Master Cassandra. She was attacked as well."

Andor rushed to the door and pulled it open. The dark rings under Celina's eyes looked even more pronounced. Behind her, Sigrid stared past them, stunned.

"How bad is she?" Andor asked.

"Uthred believes she will recover in time," Celina said. "Although she took quite the blow to the head. She awakened long enough to

144

say someone struck her from behind, although she has no idea who her attacker was."

Eva's stomach sickened. She knew she needed to tell the lord commander about Uthred and Ivan but couldn't work up the nerve now that she'd already lied to him, especially in front of Celina and Sigrid.

"Please escort Eva and Sigrid back to their quarters," Andor said to Celina. "Have a guard posted outside of their room until morning. I must go speak with Uthred."

Celina said nothing as they walked back to the barracks. To Eva, every flickering shadow looked like an attacker waiting to ambush them. By the time they made it to their quarters, her heart pounded almost as fast as it had earlier when she'd almost been caught by Uthred and found Ivan entranced.

"I will wait here until the guard arrives," Celina said. "Get some rest; you've both had a trying night."

Reassured by Celina's presence, Eva thanked the commander with Sigrid before closing the door behind them. Eva wished it had a lock and realized the irony of wanting to be trapped *inside* a room with Sigrid. She convinced herself no one would dare attack tonight, not with the entire mountain roused from sleep and Celina standing watch.

Alone together for the first time since the cliff, Eva and Sigrid slipped into bed in silence. An awkward silence engulfed the room. Since the fight in the training circle they'd established a cold but working relationship. Now, Eva didn't know what to make of it. She knew, however, things would never be the same as they had been when both girls had gone to bed the previous evening.

Like nothing had happened, Fury lay down beside Eva and fell asleep at once. Wide awake, Eva stared at the stone ceiling, going over every detail of the night. Even with his head start on her, she didn't see how Uthred could have made it to the Roost and back out before Eva got there. He'd clearly met up with Celina at some point that didn't arouse her suspicion. How much did Andor know about Uthred's behavior? Celina didn't seem like the kind to keep that from her commander. As Eva continued to work at the complex knot of what-ifs, Sigrid broke the silence.

"Eva? You awake?"

It took several moments for Eva to decide not to pretend to be asleep. "Yeah."

"I…" Sigrid began, followed by a long pause. She cleared her throat. "I was wrong about you. I'm sorry."

Eva blinked and felt tears running down the corner of her face.

"You saved my life tonight," Sigrid continued, her own voice choking up. "I know I probably can't ever make up for all the things —"

"You're welcome," Eva said. She'd heard all that mattered. A smile spread across her face, and despite the night's harrowing events, Eva felt a weight lifted from her chest. She took a deep, freeing breath. "Goodnight, Sigrid."

Chapter

21

The following days passed by slowly, mired in fear and unease that engulfed the entire mountain. Although the Gyr hadn't entirely felt like home to Eva, she'd grown to enjoy the constant echoes of chatter and laughter resounding through the halls. In the days after the attack, a heavy, oppressive silence settled in its place. The youngest recruits traveled everywhere in small groups, and the older Windsworn walked armed through the halls.

Each morning, Eva awoke wondering if the mysterious assailant still stalked the Gyr's passages at night, if she would go to breakfast and hear news of another victim. The worst were the nights when fear plagued her and she stared at the door of her and Sigrid's quarters, expecting it to creak open at any moment. It made it hard to concentrate in class, and even Celina acted troubled during their bouts.

Whatever malady affected her seemed to be growing worse. Her face took on the hue of dirty dishwater, and her black hair hung lank around it. Even so, her tutor still moved with the grace and strength of a panther when they fought, and Eva had yet to best her.

Cassandra soon returned to her duties as the roost master, none the worse for wear aside from the shrinking lump on back of her head. In between lecturing them on gryphon breeding cycles and flight patterns, however, she'd often stop all of a sudden and say something like: "Attacked in my own Roost; to think of it!"

Eva wasn't sure if it was Andor's orders or Cassandra's wish, but at least two guards in full kit always patrolled the Roost night and day. Seeing the armed men and women only worsened the effect, a constant reminder of the ongoing nature inside the Gyr. More than once, Eva caught sight of a guard or two trailing her as well, which only made her more anxious.

The one positive from the ordeal was Sigrid. Whatever ill will and bad blood had stood between them evaporated after the night in the Roost. Drawn together by a near-miss with death, the experience led to an unexpected yet growing friendship. With Wynn added in, they made a strange trio of misfits.

When news of the attack spread the following morning, Eva thought for certain Tahl would have come to ask if she was okay. After a week went by and she saw no sign of the boy, she sank into a slump and told herself she was a fool for thinking he'd ever cared about her. The depressing mood lasted until Sigrid mentioned offhand at dinner one night that Tahl had been with a Wing on a scouting mission. Eva couldn't help but renew her hope, waiting for him to return.

Since the incident, visiting Ivan seemed out of the question. Eva heard nothing about the Scrawl afterward and chose to take it as sign that he hadn't been implicated. When nothing more happened, she convinced herself more and more she'd done the right thing by not telling Andor.

Caught up with training, studies, and recent events, Eva forgot all about her birthday until a note from Soot arrived via falcon in the barracks. She hadn't mentioned the attack, but it seemed word had spread into the capital. Between the two, Eva's foster father demanded she come visit.

"I can take you on Sven," Sigrid offered when Eva told her about the letter. "We'll just have to get leave."

Eva's heart sank. Given the current state of caution in the Gyr, she doubted Andor would let her out of the mountain when he didn't even want her walking around alone. To her surprise, however, the lord commander agreed at once when Eva and Sigrid asked.

"I think it's a great idea," he said. "Besides, if I didn't let you go, Soot would knock down the mountain on all of us! Just one condition."

"Yes?" Eva asked.

Andor nodded to Fury. "Leave him here with Cassandra. Given his knack for getting into trouble, I don't want Fury loose in the city."

Eva laughed and agreed at once. When she left Fury with the roost master, however, she felt an unexpected pang of loneliness as Sven rose into the air and Fury called after her on the ground below.

"You're like a mother hen," Sigrid said over her shoulder. "He'll be fine — don't let it ruin your afternoon!"

Sven soared out of the cavern into open sky, and missing Fury soon became the least of Eva's worries. Since she'd rescued Sigrid, flying didn't terrify her, but a strong unease still filled her. As the mountain shrank behind them and the city grew below, Eva risked a glance down. The sight of the white buildings hundreds of feet below didn't send her head spinning...as long as she didn't look for too long.

Instead of having Sigrid take her directly to Soot's forge, Eva directed the girl to set her down outside the gate nearest to the Craftsman District.

"I grew up in the city," she said when Sigrid asked why. "I want to walk down a street that doesn't have a stone ceiling over me and enjoy the open air!"

Sigrid's nose wrinkled as they descended. "You mean that stench? The capital *stinks!*"

Eva laughed as a whiff from the tanning vats caught them on the breeze. She took a deep breath, inhaling the myriad of smells that defined her childhood. When Sven landed, Eva couldn't wait to walk down the old, familiar streets.

"I'll see you at the forge in a couple of hours!" she shouted to Sigrid as they took back off again.

Walking down the streets, Eva waved at familiar faces but didn't stop to chat. She enjoyed the familiar sights and sounds of the Craftsman District but hurried to Soot's forge, eager to spend as much time with Seppo and the old smith as possible. When her home drew in sight, however, it wasn't the sight of her foster father that greeted her.

A half-dozen palace guards stood around a carriage in the yard, two more guarding the door. When Eva approached, the entrance to her house, they stepped in front of her.

"Sorry, Miss, no one's allowed inside," one said.

"What do you mean no one's allowed inside?" Eva asked "Is something wrong? This is my home!"

The guard shook his head. "Nothing wrong, Miss. The king has asked for a private conversation with Master Wayland."

Eva gaped at the man. "The…king?"

Before the guard could respond, the door opened and Adelar himself stepped out. Bewildered, Eva sank down on one knee and dropped her head the ground. She felt a hand touch her shoulder. "There's no need for that here," the king said.

"I apologize, Sire," Eva said, the words running together. "I came to visit Soot on leave for the afternoon. I didn't know —"

Adelar cut her off with a wave. "There's nothing to apologize for. I…" he stared at Eva. After several moments, she dropped her gaze to the ground, uncomfortable. "I hear your studies are going well?"

"Yes," Eva said, cringing at the thought of what the king might have heard about her tenure with the Windsworn so far. "Very well, Sire."

"Good."

Neither of them spoke. After another long pause, Adelar cleared his throat. "I was just on my way. Enjoy your visit with your…with Soot."

Eva bowed as the king passed, pausing at the door to watch his retinue fall in behind him on the way to the carriage.

"That's something you don't see every day, huh?"

Spinning around at the sound of Soot's voice, Eva rushed through the doorway into the old smith's arms. "Soot!"

Eva's foster father gave a rare laugh as he patted her on the back, hard enough to jar Eva's vision. "By the wind, it's good to see you, girl!" He held her back at arm's length, examining Eva up and down.

She didn't know if Andor had mentioned her sparring match with Sigrid, but by now the bruises and cuts were gone. "You sure look lean and mean."

"What was the king doing here, Soot?" Eva asked as the carriage pulled out into the street and the guard fell in behind on their horses.

The old smith looked up and watch the royal succession leave. His brows furrowed for a moment before he noticed Eva watching. "Oh that? Just a visit — let's go find Seppo. We've got something to show you."

Eva opened her mouth to object, but Soot led her by the arm out to the forge. She could hear Seppo pounding away at the anvil. A wave of longing overcame her and — for a moment, at least — Eva forgot all about the king's visit, taken back by the sound of hammer striking hot metal.

"Hey, you rust bucket!" Soot shouted over the din. "We've got a visitor!"

Seppo's helmeted head turned their direction, and his round blue eyes seemed to glow bright when he spotted Eva beside Soot. Tossing his hammer aside, the golem bounded toward them, crossing the distance in less than three steps and swept Eva off her feet.

"Put me down, you big hunk of iron!" Eva shouted, laughing. After a few more tosses, Seppo relented and studied her much as Soot had just done, gauntleted hands on his hips.

"It is good to see you, Mistress Evelyn," he said, metallic voice ringing.

"It's good to see you, too, Seppo," Eva said, still smiling. "What do you have to show me?"

"Wait there," Soot said. He entered the forge and came back with a long wooden box closed with a silver clasp. It was about as long as Eva's arm and just wider than her hand.

"Happy birthday," Soot said, holding it out to her. "I was going to see if Andor would let you go for a day sometime to give it to you, but it looks like you beat me to it."

Eva swallowed a lump in her throat and looked down at the box to blink away a tear. Loosening the clasp, she lifted the lid and gasped.

It was a sword, the most beautiful weapon Eva had ever seen. The polished blade rippled like water in the sunlight, its hilt inlaid with silver and fashioned into a pair of wings. A talon clutching a round blue stone sat in the end of the pommel. Her hands fit just right on the grip as she lifted it out of the case.

It felt like holding a breeze — true master's work. When she held the sword up to the light, Eva saw a small letter etched into the base of the blade. A chill ran through her as she recognized Soot's maker's rune.

"I hope you never have to use it," Soot said, "but if you do, it will serve you well."

"It's beautiful," Eva said in a hushed voice, eyes locked on the waves of metal in the blade, the product of countless folds.

"Aye, it's not bad work," Soot said. Eva caught the pride in his voice.

Eva lowered the blade and looked at the smith, confused. "But you don't make weapons; you've told me that a hundred times!"

Which was true. Eva couldn't count the number of men and women who'd approached Soot over the years, requesting a sword, knife, or some other weapon. Each time, her foster father told them no, regardless of the price they offered. In most cases, it was more than they could make in a year forging scythe blades, plows, and other farm implements.

"We create things that help life grow, not take it away," Soot told Eva every time she grew frustrated watching another lucrative client walk away. Over the years she'd come to understand a little better what the old smith meant, but Eva suspected there were deeper reasons involved that Soot refused to bring to light.

"It's the best thing Seppo and I could do to protect you," Soot said as Eva laid the sword back inside the box, noticing the scabbard and belt inside as well.

"It might be a sword, but it's the most amazing thing I've ever seen," Eva said, embracing Soot and Seppo again. She meant every word, although the thought of using the weapon in battle terrified her.

They returned to the house, and Soot seated Eva down at the table, grilling her on everything that'd happened since she'd left for the Gyr. Again, Eva omitted the part about her fight with Sigrid. She also didn't tell Soot about her encounter with Ivan the night of the attacks, although the smith knew most of that from Andor, it seemed.

"Be careful, Eva," Soot said, brow furrowing. "Andor's right — there's something going on up there, and I don't like it one bit."

Eva saw her opportunity to the steer the conversation in her favor and seized it. "Speaking of things going on," she said, "Why did the king just happen to come pay you a visit?"

Soot cleared his throat and found a sudden interest in the roof. "I told you, just a visit. He...he wanted me to make him a new helmet."

"You don't make arms or armor for anyone," Eva said, nodding to her sword, sitting on the table. "I thought this was an exception?"

"Well, you don't just tell the king no, do you?" Soot said, looking everywhere but where Eva sat.

Eva fought her rising frustration, knowing already Soot wouldn't tell her anything. Instead, she decided to try another tactic. "I heard you took part in the Great Eastern Expedition; how come you never told me that?"

Beads of sweat gathered on the old smith's forehead, but from anxiety or anger, Eva couldn't tell. "Who told you that?" he asked.

"Oh, a little bird," Eva responded, glancing away.

"I highly doubt a little bird told her," Seppo chimed in from the window where he'd been listening. "At least, I've never met one that talks."

Soot shot a sideways look of disgust at the golem. "It's a figure of speech."

"Answer the question!" Eva said.

Soot folded his arms, frowning. "We went exploring to the east, nearly died a dozen times, and came back with nothing to show for it."

"Excuse me!" Seppo said, indignant. "What do you mean, nothing to show for it? You found *me!*"

Soot rolled his eyes. "And nothing to show for it but a walking, talking tin bucket that never shuts up."

"Are you talking about me again?"

Eva shot Seppo an exasperated look of her own. "If that's all there is to tell, how come you never mentioned it to me before?"

"Because I left that life behind," Soot said. "Trust me, Eva, it's better not to get involved in grand journeys and honorable causes. People get hurt, and the next thing you know you're raising their child, and —"

Soot's eyes went wide, realizing what he'd said, and silence engulfed the room.

"What," Eva said, trying to control her breathing, "does that mean?"

"You shouldn't have said that, Soot," Seppo said from the window. "You should not have said that."

"What do my parents have to do with the Great Eastern Exploration?" Eva continued. "You told me they died when Juarag raiders attacked their homestead."

Soot stared at her for a long time. "I...I'm not the one who can answer that, Eva."

Eva opened her mouth but had no idea what to say. Nothing made sense. Before she could form any kind of response, a knock came at the door. and Sigrid poked her head in. "Am I interrupting something?"

Furious, hurt, and confused, Eva stood and turned for the door. "No," she said. "I was ready to leave, anyway."

"Eva, wait," Soot said, walking toward her.

Eva shook her head. "Don't. If you cared about me, you'd tell me the truth. What is going on?"

Soot swallowed. "It's not...I can't."

"Goodbye, Soot," Eva said. Before the smith could say anything else, she pushed past Sigrid and hurried toward Sven.

"Eva, wait!"

Tears falling, Eva refused to turn around. She waited at Sven's side until Sigrid approached, holding her sword in its scabbard.

"He wanted me to bring this," Sigrid said in a quiet voice.

"Leave it here," Eva said.

"Eva —"

"I said leave it here!"

Ignoring her, Sigrid slid the weapon through the straps on the side of her saddle and secured it into place before climbing onto Sven's back. She stretched out her hand for Eva, who almost ran away. Instead, she let Sigrid pull her, numb and empty, into the saddle.

Chapter
22

Summer faded into fall. On the mountainside, the scattered scrub oak trees painted the dull gray rock they clung to with vibrant tones of yellow, orange, and crimson. Below the Gyr, the white marble of Gryfonesse stood like an island surrounded by seas of golden fields and painted woodland.

Although the days were warm, mornings in the Roost proved frigid. Oftentimes, a layer of frost covered the cavern rim. Drill Master Cross, Portridge, Cassandra, and the rest drilled and lectured them at a punishing pace. Almost before Eva realized, the first hints of winter found their way in the Gyr. In no time at all, the fledgling recruits would begin their trials.

Since her visit with Soot, Eva had done everything to learn all she could about the Great Eastern Exploration. As before, though, her efforts produced few results. None of the books in the library had any account of the event, and when she asked Instructor Portridge or Celina about it, she got the same answer as before. That was when she even saw Celina. Her sickness growing, the commander had canceled a number of their trainings, and Eva worried if the woman would ever recover.

She'd also thought about asking Andor, but the lord commander couldn't ever be reached when Eva tried. Whether he was avoiding her or just swamped as stories of even more Juarag raids came from the frontier, Eva didn't know. Regardless, weeks passed, leaving Eva no closer to uncovering the answers she sought.

After yet another failed attempt to gain an audience with Andor, Eva made her way down back to the barracks, choosing to skip the larger, busier passages. Word had spread — Eva guessed thanks to Wynn's gossiping among the new recruits — about Eva's role in saving Sigrid during the night of the attacks. That combined with the rumors of her private training with Celina and the anomaly of Fury made it hard to get anywhere inside the Gyr without a dozen different people stopping to make small talk.

"Eva?"

Eva groaned as a voiced called out behind her. But when she turned around to see who it was, she squeaked in surprise. It was Tahl. He jogged to catch up, smiling. Although Eva hadn't seen him since the attacks in the Roost, the familiar weightless, spinning sensation filled her.

"Got someone meeting you down an empty side tunnel?" It sounded like Tahl was joking, but Eva fancied she heard a touch of jealousy in his voice. Or had she imagined it?

She told herself not to be an idiot. The golden boy of the Gyr didn't worry about who an awkward girl like Eva was seeing when he could have any girl in the mountain.

"Ha." Eva gave a weak laugh. "No...just wanted some quiet."

Tahl nodded and stepped closer. Eva's mouth went dry as a desert "I'm glad you're doing okay. I've been worried."

Eva's felt her stomach leap. Worried? About what? Worried about her?

"You...were?" Somehow, he'd gotten even closer. She could smell him — well-oiled leather and fresh pine. Eva wondered what he bathed with to make him smell like that, and then her brain stopped wondering about anything except his face. He had the stubble of a beard showing, and his lips...

"Very much," Tahl said in a low voice. He was so close Fury hissed and started pecking at his boots, but neither he nor Eva noticed.

"Me, too," Eva said. It sounded like her voice was coming from another person. She was worried? That didn't make any sense.

Tahl gave a short laugh. "I just said that," he murmured, leaning forward. Eva felt her throat tighten and thought she might collapse.

She could feel Tahl's breath on her face and closed her eyes. Eva's heart pounded so hard she knew he had to hear it. She shivered a little thinking about —

"*There* you are!"

Even after the beating Sigrid gave her, Eva still never had the urge to kill someone before. When Wynn's voice burst down the passageway, however, she knew what it must feel like. She and Tahl broke apart, and Eva wondered if there'd even been a finger's width between their lips before the interruption.

Wynn stomped down the hall, oblivious to what she'd just done. Eva and Tahl glanced around the passageway, keen to look at anything but one another. Eva felt the butterflies die in her stomach, as sure as if they'd all been swatted out of the air by a broom.

"I've been looking all over for you!" Wynn said. When she recognized Tahl, she nodded her head. "Oh hey. Anyway, we've got to go! We've got a scouting training in less than an hour, and sky take it if I'm going to sit through that on an empty stomach."

The young girl grabbed Eva's hand and pulled her in the other direction. With a final hiss at Tahl, Fury turned and followed the girls. As Wynn dragged her away, Eva twisted to look over her shoulder at Tahl. He rolled his eyes, and Eva bit back a laugh.

"See you soon!" he yelled after them.

When they reached the edge of the Main Hall, Eva freed herself from Wynn and made up an excuse about needing something out of her quarters before training. Wynn looked at her like she was mad for skipping out on a meal, but the younger girl's own hunger allowed Eva to slip away. It was a long shot, but one last place remained where she might find answers. But first, she needed some honey.

Fortunately, the cooks were more than accommodating. Jar in hand, Eva wound her way upward, trying to remember the path she'd taken to reach Lord Vyr. The passageways soon grew less packed with people, then empty. After a couple of wrong turns and several backtracks, Eva thought she recognized some familiar features. The cold, stale air and dust-covered lanterns confirmed her direction.

Fury followed close behind. He'd grown to the size of a hound and almost knocked Eva over every time he tried to leap into her arms for a ride. The gryphon's fuzzy red down was long gone as well, replaced by copper- and crimson-colored feathers that shone like burnished metal. Fury's front talons had hardened into razor-sharp points, but he still bumbled around with teenage clumsiness. Several of Eva's uniforms had been shredded as a result.

At the end of the long hall leading to Vyr's chamber, Fury stopped. Eva looked back and beckoned, but the gryphon shook his head and cowered down in an unusual show of timidness. Fury's hesitation gave Eva pause as well. She recalled the blind gryphon and the old man's unsettling behavior and looked back in the direction they'd came.

"I know you're there, girl," a voice echoed down the hall. "Might as well come here."

Eva glanced at Fury, who let out a small cry but followed behind her into the chamber. She held back at the entrance when she spotted the great blind gryphon sitting on his haunches across the cavern from her.

"Well, don't just stand there!" Lord Vyr said in an impatient tone. "Basil won't bother you now that he's got your scent."

Unconvinced, Eva edged along the rock wall toward Vyr. The old man sat down a large black tome he'd evidently been reading and looked at her, brows raised. "Did you bring the honey?"

Eva nodded and held the jar out. The old man's eyes lit up, and he took it from her with both hands. Prying the lid off, he dipped a withered hand straight into the pot and licked the golden goo from his fingers as it ran down his hand into his already matted beard. Eva did her best to hide her disgust.

"Yes?" Lord Vyr said, smacking his lips.

"Yes what?" Eva asked, perplexed.

Lord Vyr waved his honeyed hand, flinging sticky everywhere. "Why are you here, that's what!" he snapped. "I don't have all day, girl, spit it out!"

Eva looked around, wondering what else the old man could possibly have to do. She didn't think it would be very smart to say that, though. "I wanted to ask you a question."

"Perhaps I have an answer," Lord Vyr said. "This *is* good honey."

Eva considered her next words carefully and decided to build up to her most pressing question. "What's in the Catacombs?"

Lord Vyr sat down his honeypot, and Eva wondered if she'd already gone too far. "The Gyr is an ancient fortress, and even the lord commander does not know all of its secrets," he said. "Who can say what lurks in the dark below, what remnants of the Ancients dwell forgotten in the shadow?"

"But you know," Eva pressed.

Lord Vyr shook his head. "Even I am not that old, child. But I have been around a very long time, and nothing like these attacks has ever happened in the mountain. There is something…stirring. I feel it in my bones."

Eva remained silent, soaking in the old man's words. The light seemed to fade in the cavern, and an ominous feeling permeated the stale air. Eva wondered if she should tell Lord Vyr about Ivan but once again held back.

Who knew how often the old man and Andor spoke? They had to communicate on some level — what if Lord Vyr told Andor about the Scrawl? With no other leads, she knew Ivan would be the prime suspect, worse still, might be held responsible. The chance of the boy receiving a second trial didn't seem likely.

"Stay away from the Catacombs," Lord Vyr said, staring her down with his rheumy eyes. "And keep close watch on the red gryphon."

Across the room, Basil hissed as if agreeing with his rider. For a moment, Eva almost gave in to the urge pulling at her to leave, but desperation gave her courage. "I have one more question," she said.

Lord Vyr picked up his jar again. "Bah! You ask too many questions for a girl so young, but the company is not unappreciated." He smiled at her with his yellowed teeth, but it came off as more of a leer.

Taking a deep breath, Eva tried to focus as the old man took another handful of his prize and smeared it all over his lips and beard. "Did you know my father?"

Lord Vyr paused, honey-covered fist halfway to his mouth. "Indeed I did."

Eva felt a rush of excitement and tried to sort through the dozens of questions begging to be asked. "How did he die?"

"He was headstrong and proud," Lord Vyr said. "But dead? Not to my knowledge."

Chapter

23

In the days that followed, Eva thought she might go mad. Despite Lord Vyr's shattering revelation, he refused to say more. She'd pressed as far as she dared, but in the end it did no good.

Desperate, Eva wrote Soot a letter, begging for anything he would tell her, her earlier anger at him forgotten. Whether he was trying to figure out how to respond or just ignoring her, Eva didn't know. Each night, she stared at the ceiling, wide awake, wondering. If her father was truly alive, where could he be; *what* could he be doing? Who was he? Why had he left her? The questions plagued Eva until she thought she might go mad if they were left unanswered.

Celina hadn't resumed their training, either, and was absent from the Main Hall at mealtimes. Eva started to wonder if Uthred might be poisoning her. With nowhere else to turn, Eva knew where she had to go next. Even so, the thought raised goose bumps on her arms, thinking of their last encounter. She needed to see Ivan again.

How proved to be more difficult than Eva could have imagined. She'd wandered by Ivan's chamber a handful of times, looking for an opportunity. The guards were friendly enough and let her talk to Ivan through the door, but they didn't allow her in the room again, nor did they give them any privacy. And the questions Eva needed to ask couldn't be asked in front of an audience. On the plus side, he seemed completely normal each time she visited. If he had any recollection of their meeting the night of the attacks, Ivan gave no sign.

For days, she thought of all the possible ways to get a few minutes alone with Ivan. Each idea proved more impossible and ridiculous than the last. Whenever Eva caught sight of Uthred within the mountain, it only made Eva's task more urgent. She needed more proof.

Eva considered telling Wynn or Sigrid but decided against it. Although willing, Wynn seemed more likely to tell the whole mountain than be of any real help. Eva doubted Sigrid would believe her about Uthred, and a small part of her wondered if Sigrid might even go to the commander if Eva disclosed her suspicions.

After much thought, Eva realized she'd have to work alone — and probably at night. The thought of wandering around the dark halls of the Gyr made her break out in goose bumps, but she didn't see any other way. Plus, she noticed only one guard stood on duty at night. Dealing with one person instead of two, Eva told herself, doubled her chances of success.

Another week passed, and Eva struggled to come up with any solutions in between her busy schedule. To stay in practice while Celina — hopefully — recovered, Eva approached Sigrid. In the few times they'd sparred, Sigrid won almost every time. Almost. Even Sigrid couldn't believe Eva's progress, and she couldn't wait to show Cross the results of her grueling work.

"You're going to do fine," Sigrid said.

Eva thought Sigrid probably believed in her more than Eva did herself, but she didn't say anything. The day of Cross's portion of the trial came out of nowhere. Eva spent the morning frazzled and sick, but as soon as the bells rang out in the Main Hall and the fledgling recruits headed for the Pit, a calm, almost hollow feeling overcame her.

"What, do you want a medal or something, Queen Magpie?" Cross asked when Eva finished their run well ahead of the younger students. He'd gone slightly — *slightly* — easier on her since the sparring match with Sigrid and Uthred, but not by much. "Get over there, and get ready to step into the circle."

While Eva strapped on her padded practice armor and selected her training weapons from the rack, the rest of the recruits filed in. Soon, the entire class stood around, just as they had the last time Eva entered the circle. She vowed this time would be different.

"All right, magpies," Cross barked. He strode up and down their line, much as he had the first day of training. "I've watched you stumble around and make fools of yourselves for almost half a year. Now it's time to see if you've learned anything."

The drill master's eyes fell on Eva. "Why don't you go first, Queen Magpie? I've got a special treat for you."

He whistled, and Sigrid stepped out of the shadows, dressed in training gear and armed with two practice blades. She shot Eva an apologetic look. They were long past the beating, but seeing Sigrid standing there just like before made Eva's stomach churn. She pushed the fear down and remembered that this fight was a chance to prove herself.

Eva stepped into the ring and tried to pretend it was just another bout with Celina in the privacy of their training room. The younger students parted to make way for Sigrid, but this time her face held none of the malice it had during their first fight. If anything, she looked…nervous.

The recruits closed back around, filling the training circle. Cross stood on the edge, between Eva and Sigrid. "Begin," he said.

Eva didn't hesitate. Just as Celina had hammered into her over and over for the past months, she seized her moment. She threw herself at Sigrid, who jerked back in surprise but managed to block her overhead cut. They traded a few blows back and forth, but Eva felt tense and stiff. She realized she was gritting her teeth with every strike and forced her body to relax.

They moved inside the ring like two dancers twirling and whirling together and apart. Everything melted away except for the point of Eva's and Sigrid's weapons. Eva felt a surge of satisfaction and confidence just like getting into rhythm with hammer and anvil. Sigrid seemed to slow, and Eva found herself a fraction of a moment ahead of the other girl. Sigrid stabbed with her shorter sword, and Eva sidestepped. Eva's long blade caught Sigrid's as it came down, and the tip of her wooden short sword jabbed Sigrid's midriff.

Both fighters broke apart, panting and grinning.

"A touch to Queen Magpie," Cross said in a low growl. Eva wasn't sure if he was disappointed or trying to hide approval. "I see you've learned which end of a sword is the pointy end. But let's —"

"Drill Master Cross!" Eva and the rest of the class looked up to the balcony and saw Uthred. Eva felt real fear again, wondering what could have brought the commander to the training area.

"There has been another attack," Uthred said. "Please escort your recruits to the Main Hall at once. Everyone should be armed with at least a practice weapon. Post guards in the front and the back and stay together."

The recruits and their fledgling gryphons began to panic, but Cross brought them to order with a shout. The group gathered in a tight formation with Cross at the head and Sigrid in back. Clutching their practice weapons, eyes wide with fear, they started for the Main Hall. Eva stayed in the back with Sigrid and kept Fury in sight at all times. A feeling of dread loomed over her. She wondered whom had been attacked and if she was partly responsible. She'd been too complacent, she knew.

The Main Hall buzzed with scores of recruits and Windsworn of all ages. Armed guards stood at the entrances in full armor, hands on their swords. Eva felt the fear in the air as strong as the dozens of concerned voices all talking at once. Andor appeared on the overlook, but it took several moments for everyone to settle down enough for him to be heard.

"There has been another attack," he said, voice carrying across the chamber. "This time, a recruit has been killed."

The hall broke into chaotic shouts of outrage. Several riders shook their weapons in the air, demanding the entire Gyr be checked level by level until the culprit was caught.

Andor raised his hands, but it took several minutes of the other Windsworn officers shouting to quiet everyone enough for the lord commander to be heard again.

"Until further notice, I order everyone, both recruits and Windsworn, to travel everywhere inside the mountain in groups of two or more. It would also be wise to go armed whenever you leave your quarters and to make sure your rooms are secured before retiring at night. Patrols are being formed to search the mountain as we speak. Please return to your garrisons until further notice."

Eva wasn't sure the crowd would disperse — most seemed keen to begin a manhunt right then and there. Eventually reason won out, and people began to exit. Sticking close to Sigrid and Wynn, Eva joined the throng and worried about losing Fury all the way back to the barracks.

Once in their quarters, Sigrid shrugged off her padded practice gear and put on her leather and mail Windsworn attire. "I've got to take part in patrols," she said to the two of them, sliding numerous knives into her belt. "Whatever you do, stay here and don't leave without a group."

Eva nodded, still in shock. Wynn, on the other hand, buried her face in her hands and started sobbing.

"It's going to be okay," Eva said, rushing to her side and wrapping her arm around her.

"N-no, you don't understand," Wynn said voice thick from crying. "I heard them in the hall. The person who d-died was Danny!"

Wynn wailed even louder, and Eva's stomach dropped. Danny, the small boy who could answer every question in class, who'd worshiped the ground Wynn walked on even though she wanted nothing to do with him.

"I was s-so mean to him, and he was always nice!" she howled, the words almost impossible to make out.

Eva pulled Wynn tighter, sick to her stomach. Wynn buried her face in Eva's shoulder, still sobbing. After a few quiet moments passed, Sigrid glanced at Eva and nodded her head down at Wynn. Eva gave the younger girl a gentle squeeze, and she pulled back, wiping the tears away from her swollen eyes.

"Sorry, Wynn, but I need to take you back to your quarters before I go on patrol," Sigrid said. "They'll be doing roll, and we don't want you reported missing."

"Okay," Wynn said in a small voice. Eva rose with her and gave the younger girl a long hug. The girl's responding squeeze was limp, which didn't make Eva feel any better.

"I'll come stay with you until Sigrid's back," Eva told her. "I can't stay alone anyway while she's gone."

Sigrid caught her look and nodded. "That's a good plan."

Unlike the full Windsworn, the fledgling recruits stayed in a long hall with bunk beds lining both sides. The news that Danny was the victim had spread, and all the young girls were shaken, huddled together with their gryphons in small groups. Eva stayed by Wynn's bedside as the girl cried herself to sleep. Sometime around midnight, Sigrid returned, and they went back to their own quarters. Although Sigrid was fully armed, Eva jumped at every shadow and spent the whole journey looking over her back, unnerved.

She'd tried to piece together the attack from everything she knew. Had Ivan been involved, possessed again by whatever dark power held him in its sway the night of the previous attack? Based on what Sigrid told Eva from her briefing, it seemed almost impossible Uthred had killed Danny himself, in person. Even so, Eva still knew he had to have been involved. Danny's body, Sigrid told her, had been found in the lower levels near the Catacombs.

"Looks like he lost his way on the way to training or something," Sigrid said as they reached their door. "Must have come across something he wasn't supposed to see, poor little bugger."

"And you didn't find anything?" Eva asked.

Sigrid shook her head. "Nope, and neither did anyone else, although most of the older riders are still looking." Her eyes fell to the ground, and she kicked her boots against the rock. "Eva, there's something else."

"What?" Eva asked, afraid to know the answer.

"It's your Scrawl friend," Sigrid said. "The guards said he started acting strange right before they found the body — chanting and muttering and stuff. Rumor has it the dead boy's forehead had the Scrawl rune for death carved into it. There's a lot of the veterans pointing the blame at him. The lord commander kept them from doing anything drastic for now, but it's not looking good."

Eva bit her lip. This was it. For better or worse, she couldn't keep this thing to herself anymore. It might be Ivan's only chance.

"Sigrid, I need to tell you something."

Eva related the full account of what happened the night Fury went missing, including overhearing Celina and Uthred talking and finding Ivan in a trance. Sigrid listened without interruption until Eva finished.

"And you haven't told anyone?" Sigrid said.

Eva blushed. "No…I didn't have any real proof, and if I said something based on what I did know, I thought they'd blame Ivan."

"But what if Ivan is to blame?" Sigrid said. "Look, I know you think he's just a kid, but he's not. It sounds like he can do some serious rune magic when the mood takes him."

"Ivan's innocent," Eva said, voice raising. "Someone or something is using him. You didn't see how he was when the light from my Wonder brought him out of it. It was like two different people. I just need the chance to talk to him without anyone standing guard."

Sigrid looked at her like she was crazy.

"Please," Eva said. "I need your help."

Eva didn't say anything, but it passed unspoken between them. *And you owe me for what you did.*

Sigrid ran her hands through her tousled black hair and blew out a deep sigh. "Storm it all," she said. "I'll do it."

Chapter 24

They clung to the shadows, using Sigrid's knowledge of the patrol routes to creep down to the lower levels unseen. As they neared Ivan's room, Eva reflected on how well the plan was working so far. She'd started to think the biggest problem would be Fury — they'd locked him in their quarters before leaving, but no matter how Eva tried to calm him, he threw an ear-splitting tantrum as soon as the door closed.

"Damned thing almost took my hand off!" Sigrid muttered. She held up her right hand, showing Eva the bleeding cut.

"Sorry," Eva said. "He's...free spirited?"

"I don't care what any prophecy says, he's a vicious little beast," Sigrid said. "I wouldn't trade Sven for that demon even if you made me lord commander!"

Eva felt a twang of irritation. Fury wasn't *that* bad anymore — most of the time. "Can we focus?" she hissed. Bending forward, she peeked out of the crevice they'd hidden themselves in. Ivan's room was only a few turns and a couple of dozen paces away. "I still don't know how we're going to get past the guards."

"I've got an idea," Sigrid said. "But it won't leave you much time, so cut the small talk."

Eva shot her a questioning glance.

"I can tell the guards I saw something on the lower levels and need their help," Sigrid said. "It's the best I can think of."

"We can't do that!" Eva said. "If they find out you're lying, who knows what will happen?"

"The only way I'll get caught is if you're still there when I get back," Sigrid said. "So, make sure you keep it quick. I can't guarantee much."

Eva nodded and sucked in a deep breath. "Okay. Let's do it."

They snuck closer until they were in the same corridor as Ivan's room. Eva peeked around the corner and saw two guards. She pulled back around and nodded to Sigrid.

"Remember, be fast," Sigrid said.

Without waiting for Eva's reply, Sigrid sprinted around the corner toward the pair. Not daring to look, Eva remained out of sight as Sigrid told her story.

"Quick, I need your help!" she said. "I just saw someone running down toward the Catacombs. I called out, but they didn't stop. It might be the killer!"

Eva heard the skepticism in the guards as they replied. "We didn't see anyone go past."

"They went down one of the side tunnels," Sigrid said. Her flustered act impressed Eva. "Hurry!"

Sigrid must have looked desperate or the guards were tired of missing out on the action because a moment later Eva heard armor rustling and hurried footsteps. She ducked around the end of the corridor and pressed against the stone wall. Sigrid and the two guards ran the opposite direction, deeper into the mountain.

As soon as they disappeared, Eva ran for Ivan's door. "Ivan! It's me, Eva!"

She pressed her ear to the thick door but didn't hear any chanting from inside. A faint rustling sound drew nearer, and Ivan appeared behind the bars cut into the door.

"Eva!" he said in surprise. "What are you doing here?"

"I don't have much time," Eva said. "Do you know what's going on?"

"There was some shouting and then the lord commander came by, but he wouldn't tell me anything," Ivan said. "What's happening?"

Eva hesitated, searching for the right words. "Ivan…" she said. "A boy was killed and…and someone carved a Scrawl death rune into his forehead."

The dark, swirling markings tattooed on Ivan's face stood out in stark contrast to his paling face. "But…how could that be? Who would…It can't be a Scrawl; it can't!"

"Ivan, I came to see you a while ago, the night of the first attack," Eva said. "I could hear you inside, making some weird chanting noise…do you remember that?"

Eva studied Ivan's face, looking for any sign of deception, but the boy looked genuinely bewildered. "I don't know what you're talking about," he said. "But Eva…I'm afraid something is happening to me. The dreams I'm having lately, they're terrible. I'm in this cavern with a big archway, and someone is chanting in a language I don't understand. These runes catch fire and they're burning me, but I can't get away. I want to run, but I can't move! And sometimes I forget what I've been doing for hours at a time. Eva, I'm scared! What if I'm going insane?"

Eva's heart dropped. It was about the worst thing the Scrawl boy could have said. "I'll think of some way to help you, Ivan. But I have to know — you have to promise me that you're not part of this."

"I promise," the boy said. "I haven't hurt anyone!"

"I don't know when I'll be able to talk to you again," Eva said. "But you've got to —"

"What is this?" Uthred's voice echoed through the empty tunnel.

Eva turned around slowly, placing a shaking hand on her sword. The commander blocked the only way out with two guards, who held a struggling Sigrid between them. She was disarmed, hands bound behind her back.

"I think we've found our traitors."

"You're making a mistake!" Sigrid shouted, rattling the cell bars. "Someone else is going to die if you don't let us talk to the lord commander!"

But no one could hear her. After disarming and binding Eva, Uthred had them placed in the Gyr's dungeons in a secluded, forgotten part of the mountain. The cells were square stone rooms with a thick iron-banded door that had a tiny opening set with bars inside. The place was dank and damp as any dungeon had a right to be, buried in the middle of the mountain where even rumor of sunlight didn't exist.

While Sigrid continued to pound on the door, Eva slumped against the far wall. Fortunately, they hadn't found her Wonder, and she withdrew it but found little reassurance in its soft glow. Sigrid noticed the light and turned around, eyes wide.

"What in the sky is that?" she asked, backing up to the opposite wall.

"It used to be my mother's," Eva said. "I usually keep it hidden."

"It's a Wonder," Sigrid said. Rather than amazed or impressed, she sounded suspicious. "What does it do?"

"Just makes light," Eva said.

"Magic's magic," Sigrid said. "You sure it doesn't do anything else?"

"It's fine, I promise," Eva said. Shooting the Wonder stone one last scowl, Sigrid resumed pacing in front of the door like a caged animal.

"I'm sorry," Eva said after a long stretch of silence passed between them. "I shouldn't have dragged you into this."

"You did what you thought was right," Sigrid said, stopping her pacing long enough to shrug. "Nothing wrong with that."

Eva swallowed, fighting back the rush of emotions and fatigue that threatened to break her. "It doesn't matter," she said in a thick voice. "All I did was get us both in trouble."

Who knew how long they'd be left down here? Surely, Andor would at least get their side of the story, wouldn't he? In the meantime, Uthred was free to roam the halls. Eva's stomach turned thinking about Fury alone and unprotected.

"You're a lot tougher than you look, you know?" Sigrid said from across the cell.

"Thanks, I guess?" Eva said.

"No, I mean it." Sigrid hesitated then sat down beside her. Eva could tell she was struggling to say more. "I was jealous of you, when the red egg hatched for you. After all the work I did to become Windsworn, I didn't think it was fair you just got to show up here. So, no matter what happens, don't feel sorry. This is the least I could do."

"Thanks for helping me," Eva said. "And for being my friend."

Sigrid nodded and ducked her face down. Eva looked away as a sniff echoed in the dimly lit cell. They huddled together, shivering in the cold. Neither spoke. Eva didn't know when, but she must have dozed off. Sometime later, Sigrid shook her awake.

"Someone's coming!" Sigrid said.

Sure enough, footsteps echoed through the chamber. Eva rushed to tuck her Wonder beneath her uniform, and the light faded. They pulled themselves to their feet, stiff from lying on the cold stone ground.

"Hey!" Sigrid yelled, rushing to the door. "Get us the storm out of here!"

The footsteps stopped outside their cell. Eva looked through the little window in the top of the door and saw Tahl peering at them.

"What are you doing here?" Sigrid asked. "What's going on? Let us out!"

The boy shushed them, glancing around as Sigrid's shouts echoed throughout the dungeon.

"Will you keep it down?" he said in a low voice. "Nobody knows I'm here. The lord commander has left the Gyr; there's been a massive Juarag raid out on the frontier, the biggest in years. Most of the riders have gone with him — there's mostly just elders and recruits in the mountain now."

"But what about the attacks?" Sigrid asked. "How could everyone just leave?"

"That's what everyone left is doing — searching," Tahl said. "They say Celina is worse, maybe on her deathbed. Uthred is in charge. He doubled the guard on the Scrawl boy. There's some who think the

Scrawls are in league with the Juarag, that it's all some big scheme."

"Can you get us out?" Sigrid asked.

Tahl shook his head. "I can see about getting you some food, but you might be here a couple of days. Uthred told everyone you were trying to help the Scrawl boy escape; is that true?"

"No!" Eva said. "Ivan is innocent! Uthred is the one who needs to be stopped."

Tahl looked at her, confused. "Stop him from doing what?"

"Eva thinks he's the one behind the attacks," Sigrid said. "Which I said was —"

"No," Tahl said. "Commander Uthred is one of the most decorated and honored riders in all of the Windsworn."

Once again, Eva recounted overhearing Uthred and Celina in the tunnels.

"You don't have to believe me," Eva said when she'd finished. "Just get us out, and stay out of my way. I've got to get back to Fury before something happens."

Tahl looked taken aback, but Eva was too cold, tired, and hungry to care what he thought.

"None of this makes any sense," Tahl said.

"Please," Eva said, locking eyes with him.

"Do you believe all this?" Tahl asked Sigrid.

"Well…" Sigrid hesitated and looked at Eva. "I don't know exactly what's going on, but yes."

In spite of the dire situation, Eva beamed at the other girl.

"I'll be back as soon as I can," Tahl said.

As soon as he'd gone, Sigrid turned to Eva. "What are you planning on doing if we get out of here?"

"We've got to get a message to the lord commander," Eva said. "I'm a fool for not telling him in the first place — I just hope it isn't too late now."

"It doesn't look good," Sigrid said. "I mean, if it was Uthred, what's stopping him now?"

Chapter
🦅 25 🦅

The hours stretched by while they waited for Tahl to return. To their surprise, the guards brought them a hot meal of stew and bread but delivered it at swordpoint after they'd forced them back against the far wall. Eva and Sigrid devoured it like starving gryphons as soon as they'd left.

Once the food was gone, they tried to get some sleep, but every time Eva closed her eyes all she could think of was Fury and Ivan. The thoughts and scenes her imagination conjured up nearly drove her crazy before she heard voices echoing down the chamber later that night.

"Ow! Will you watch where you're going?"

"And will you be quiet before we're thrown in a cell, too?"

Somewhere outside, a gryphon hissed as well, and Eva held out hope they'd found Fury. Tahl and Wynn's bickering carried down the passageway outside, and Eva felt a ray of hope through their dank confinement. Moments later, Tahl appeared at the door.

"We've got to hurry," he said. "We found a secret passage through the back, but the guards might have heard us when we shifted the stone door covering it back into place."

"We *found* a secret passage?" Eva couldn't see her, Wynn's voice rose from the other side of the door, indignant. "We didn't find a secret passage, golden boy, I showed it to you."

Tahl sighed. "Yes, of course. Can you keep it down?"

Eva wondered how Wynn knew about a secret passage into the dungeons but decided that given the circumstances it would be better to ask later. Moments later, the door swung open, and a flash of red burst through the door, straight for Eva.

"Fury!" Eva said, trying to keep her voice down. The gryphon purred, rubbing his head against her knee. "I missed you too, boy."

Tahl and Wynn stood in the doorway, a large sack between them on the ground.

"Your weapons," Tahl said, untying the bag.

Eva buckled on her knife and short sword while Sigrid gathered her collection of knives and axes.

"Let's go," Eva said, rushing for the door. But Tahl blocked her path. "Tahl, look out! We've got to get a message to Andor."

"Eva, it's too late for that," he said, dropping his eyes to the ground. "Something happened while I was gone."

Eva's stomach twisted, and her heart felt like lead. "Oh no," she whispered. "Ivan. They didn't…"

Tahl shook his head. "They didn't kill him, not yet, anyway. But he escaped from his cell — burned down the door like it was kindling and overpowered all the guards. They tracked him to the Catacombs but haven't found him yet. If they do, he'll likely be killed on sight."

"No," Eva said. "No, no, no. There must be some mistake. Uthred —"

"Commander Uthred searched the lower levels with everyone else," Tahl said. "The Scrawl's gone, Eva. He deceived you."

"No," Eva said again, undeterred. "You don't understand; there's something else going on here — I've just got to find him."

"And how are you gonna do that?" Sigrid said, hands on her hips. "If no one else could find him, what chance do we have?"

Eva paused. It was true. She had no idea where Ivan would have gone. Her mind raced through their conversations…and then it hit her.

"I know where Ivan went," Eva said. "Or at least an idea. When

I talked to him last night, he told me he'd been seeing a cavern with a big arch in his dream — I'd bet anything it's somewhere in the Catacombs! If we find that cavern, we'll find Ivan!"

"Well, let's go, then," Wynn said as if that settled it.

Eva grabbed her shoulder before the younger girl could walk away. "Wynn, you can't come."

"The storm I can't!" Wynn said in a loud voice. The others cringed as it echoed throughout the dungeons. "You aren't going to leave me behind after I rescued you."

"Helped rescue," Tahl said. Wynn's eyes narrowed, but Eva stepped between them before the younger girl could hit him. "And besides," he continued, "this is treason!"

"Wynn, I need you to get a message to the lord commander and Soot," she said. "This is just as important as what we're doing. They need to know what's happened. Can you do that for me?"

The young girl hesitated a moment and then reluctantly shook her head. "Fine...but I want full credit for helping out with this, you hear me?"

Eva let out a dry laugh. "If I'm wrong, you won't want anyone to know you had anything to do with this, but it's a deal. Now hurry!"

Wynn took off down the passage, leaving Eva, Fury, Sigrid, and Tahl in the cell.

"You don't have to come," Eva told them. She tried not to think about wandering in the pitch black of the Catacombs with only Fury by her side. "You're already both going to be in enough trouble."

"Don't be stupid," Sigrid said. "Of course we're coming. Right, Tahl?"

Tahl looked away. "Well...ow!" He rubbed his shoulder, and Sigrid raised her fists, prepared to punch him again.

"You're either coming, or I'll knock you out and lock you in here," Sigrid said.

Tahl hesitated, and for a moment Eva thought Sigrid would follow through with her promise. "Fine!" he said at last. "But if we get court-martialed, don't say I didn't warn you."

Using Wynn's secret tunnel, they made it out of the dungeons and down to the lower levels without running into anyone else. When they reached the bottom of the storehouse floors, Eva stopped. The immaculately carved tunnels gave way to raw slabs of jagged rock, marking the beginning of the Catacombs.

"Are they still searching?" Eva whispered to Tahl.

He nodded. "Let me go first, a little ahead. If they catch me, you two can still make a run for it, and I can pretend like I'm delivering a message or something."

They agreed, and Tahl took the lead, traveling by the light of a shuttered crystal lantern he'd procured along the way. After only a couple of levels, however, it sputtered out, leaving them in darkness.

"Great," Sigrid hissed. "How are we supposed to see a storming thing down here? If we don't run into a patrol, we'll probably fall down some pit and break our necks!"

"They aren't just lying around everywhere, you know," Tahl said. "I was lucky enough to find one at all!"

"Oh for crying out loud," Eva said, pulling the Wonder out from beneath her uniform. It cast a dim light ahead, just as good as the crystal lantern. "Can we keep moving?"

Tahl shot Sigrid a questioning glance, but she shook her head. Now in the front, Eva led the way with no idea which way to go. It was the deepest she'd ever been in the mountain, and the chill of the dark seeped through her uniform. The passage narrowed until they had to walk single file: Fury, then Eva and Sigrid with Tahl in the back. All of a sudden, Fury stopped, causing them all to crash into one another.

Sigrid cursed. "What'd you stop for?"

"It's Fury," Eva said. The gryphon raised his beak into the air as if sniffing the air. He let out a low hiss and, without warning, sprang away into the darkness.

"Fury!" Eva, Sigrid, and Tahl ran after him. After a few dozen paces they came around a bend and were met with a three-way fork in the road.

"Storming little monster!" Sigrid said. "Eva, which way did he go?"

Eva had no clue, but she closed her eyes and tried to summon the same connection she'd felt with Fury the night of the attack. Nothing came to mind.

"I...I don't know," she said after a long moment. At the same time, voices echoed up the tunnel to the right, growing louder.

"Well, you'd better figure it out!" Sigrid hissed. "We're about to have company!"

Eva gritted her teeth, heart pounding in her ears. She had no sense of the direction Fury had taken. Straight or left? The voices grew louder, and the first flicker of light reflected around a bend.

"Eva!" Sigrid said. "Just pick one!"

"Hold on!" Eva's eyes flickered back and forth between the path, and now she could hear footsteps accompanying the voices. "Ahh..."

"No time, pick!" Tahl whispered.

Eva took a deep breath and pointed an uncertain hand straight ahead. "This way."

They sprinted down the middle tunnel, several sharp bends hiding their light from the patrol approaching the split in the tunnels. The voices of the patrol faded in the background, but they saw no sign of Fury. Eva started to second-guess herself and thought about turning back. At the same time, the path slanted downward, and she stepped, tripped, then fell headfirst.

Unable to stop, Eva tumbled down the slope, banging into the rock walls. Sigrid and Tahl crashed behind her, but after several yards the path leveled out again and they all rolled to a stop. As soon as they did, a large stone rolled across the tunnel, blocking the way they'd come.

"Storm it all," Sigrid moaned as they struggled to their feet. "I've had about enough of wandering around in this sky-forsaken hole!"

While Tahl tried to budge the stone slab, Eva untangled the Wonder stone from around her neck, grateful it hadn't chipped or broken. The light revealed a small, round cavern, the path continuing just ahead of them.

"This isn't going anywhere," Tahl said, smacking the rock with his hand. "Guess we're committed."

On one hand, she felt relieved they couldn't be followed. One the other, she realized, it also meant no help would be able to reach them. They were on their own.

They passed around a sharp bend and saw an orange light just ahead, glowing like coals in a forge. Eva tucked her Wonder inside her tunic, guided by the fiery gleam. The tunnel opened into a large cavern, and she saw Fury ahead, sitting and staring up at an enormous archway built against the far wall.

Eva shuddered and knew without a doubt they'd found the cavern from Ivan's dream. Illuminated by a series of raw crystals set in nooks in the wall, the runes carved into the arch loomed jagged and harsh. Eva's skin crawled, and she tore her eyes away. When she walked to Fury's side, however, he acted like she wasn't even there, staring up at the carvings.

Sigrid made a short search of the chamber and swore. "Dead end. We're stuck."

In spite of the ominous feeling it gave her, the arch pulled Eva's eyes back to it. Soon they were all standing in a line, staring at the wall.

"I wonder if it's some kind of altar." Tahl said in a hushed voice.

"Storming magic," Sigrid said in the same disgusted voice she'd used when Eva first showed her the Wonder stone. "Let me take a look."

Both Eva and Tahl turned to look at her, surprised. "Some of the characters look like the runes the Bersi use."

"Sigrid's Bersi," Tahl said, seeing Eva's confused look. "They're a small southern tribe, distant cousins to the Scrawls."

Eva stared at her. Despite Sigrid's hawkish features and raven-colored hair, she'd always assumed the girl was Sorondaran. There were a few recruits from some of the other cultures across western Altaris, but they were a rarity and Eva had only seen a handful in all the months she'd been living in the Gyr.

"If you tell anyone, I swear I'll punch your lights out," Sigrid said, still staring at the runes. Although her concentration was fixed on the wall, Eva still took a step back.

"It's sort of a secret," Tahl explained. "Only myself, the lord commander, and a few others know."

"Your secret's safe with me," Eva said in what she hoped was a convincing voice. But Sigrid wasn't listening. She peered closed at each rune, mumbling things under her breath, and she traced the outline, brow furrowed in concentration.

"Bring me some light," Sigrid said, waving her hand for Eva to step closer.

Eva pulled out the Wonder's chain from beneath her tunic and held the stone up as high as she could. As soon as the pale light touched the rock, the rune markings started to shine. Soon, the entire arch glowed like a blade just pulled from the fire and the entire chamber shone like the noonday sun. Pulled from his apparent trance, Fury hissed and backed away, the humans following suit.

Like blood leaking from a wound, the light spread from the rune carvings out across the wall within the arch. Glowing spiderweb cracks appeared in the rock. The webs of light spread faster and faster until the stone cracked and snapped, crumbling to the ground.

"We've got to get out," Tahl said, grabbing Eva by the arm. "The chamber's collapsing!"

"Wait!" Eva said, pulling her arm back. The last chunk of rock fell away, and the dust settled, revealing a passage on the other side. A second later the orange glow flickered out, leaving them in the light of Eva's Wonder.

No one moved or spoke. Grit and dust filled the air, and Eva coughed, breaking their stunned silence. Undaunted, Sigrid stepped through the opening.

"What are we waiting for?"

Chapter

26

The glow of the Wonder stone cast long shadows down the passage, and dust shone in the stale, still air. More ancient runes were carved into both sides of the rock tunnel. Eva tried not to look at them. She sensed a dark presence exuding from them, untold years of malice and hate bearing down on her. Their meaning seemed clear: *You should not be here. The Windsworn hold no sway in this part of the mountain.*

They continued downward at a slight slope for a few more minutes until Sigrid stopped abruptly and threw up a hand to hold Eva back.

"What is it?" Eva said, peering ahead of them into the gloom. It looked like the corridor widened into a large room.

"I'm not sure," Sigrid said, examining both sides of the tunnel. "Just a hunch, but…"

Tired of waiting, Fury pushed past Eva's and Sigrid's legs and bounded across the threshold of the larger chamber.

"Fury, no!" Eva snatched at his tail, but it was too late. As soon as the gryphon's rear paws touch the stone floor at the end of the tunnel, a loud click sounded followed by rock grinding on rock.

"Get down!" Sigrid leaped back, driving Eva to the ground with her. Eva felt a whoosh of stale air and looked up. A massive stone hammer swung down from the ceiling, cleaving the air where Eva and Sigrid had stood a moment before. It took several passes before its momentum played out and the hammer hung in the center of the chamber entrance, harmless.

They three of them rose, and Eva shuddered at the thought of what the hammer would have done had it connected with any of them. She scowled at Fury, who sat unharmed on the other side of the entranceway, head cocked to the side, waiting for them.

"He's going to get us all killed," Sigrid muttered.

"All right?" Tahl asked, face ashen.

Eva nodded. Her heart continued to race, and a tremble ran through her body.

"From now on, nobody goes in front of me unless I say so," Sigrid said. She pointed an accusing finger at Fury. "Understood?"

The gryphon rolled his head in exasperation but waited and fell in behind Eva when she passed. The chamber was cut into a many-sided geometric shape. On the wall opposite were three tunnels. Each had a different rune carved above the entrance.

"Hold on," Sigrid said, holding up her hand for them to stop. "Before I get smashed to a pulp, why don't you all stay back while I take a look at things?" She walked within an arm's reach of each entrance but made sure no part of her body passed the threshold.

"What do they say?" Tahl asked after she'd studied them in silence for several minutes.

"This language is all jumbled," Sigrid muttering, shaking her head. "It's old — far older than the runes any of the southern cultures use. I can only make out about a third of the words. From what I can tell, two passages lead to death, while the third continues deeper to something called the Heart of the Mountain."

"So, how do we figure out which is which?" Eva asked.

"I don't know, send that crazy gryphon of yours through and see what happens!" Sigrid snapped. Glancing at Fury, Eva decided to let Sigrid work things out on her own.

Muttering under her breath, Sigrid stared at the three tunnels for another long stretch. Eva grew more anxious with each passing minute — they didn't have time for this. She looked at Tahl, who cleared his throat.

"Couldn't we just throw something through each one and see what happens?" he asked.

Sigrid turned around and rolled her eyes. "Oh thanks, golden boy," she said. "Why hadn't I thought of that?"

She knelt down in front of the middle tunnel and pointed to a large square block cut into the rock. "That's a pressure plate, just like the one Fury stepped on that made the hammer swing down. If you step on the wrong ones, something very bad will happen."

"Then can't we just jump over it?" Eva asked, although she was pretty sure she already knew the answer.

Sigrid shook her head and pointed deeper down the tunnel. "There's plates going back farther than you can jump. More than likely, whichever one you step on first will trigger something else nasty. You might get pulped by another hammer, impaled on a spear that shoots out of the wall, dropped into a pit…take your pick."

"So, what do we do, then?" Eva asked, growing more frustrated. "Sit here until we die of old age or until we go insane and each walk through a tunnel to see who doesn't meet a nasty ending?"

Sigrid's eyes narrowed, but as she opened her mouth to retort, understanding dawned on her face. "That's it!"

Eva glanced back at Tahl, who shrugged. "I think she's lost it."

"No, idiots, listen," Sigrid said, motioning to them to come closer. "That's what we have to do — all three of us will step on a plate at the same time!"

Eva looked at Tahl again — he seemed just as reluctant as her to step on any more plates after what had just happened. "Are you sure, Sigrid? Last time we did that, a giant hammer almost squished us."

Sigrid nodded and pointed to the runes. "I'm sure… mostly. The trick will be to step at the same time. And whatever you do, don't move until I say we're clear. Eva, you take the left. Tahl, middle. I'll take the right."

As the other two took their positions, Eva looked back at Fury. "Don't. Move."

The gryphon cocked his head to the side and chirped before lying

184

down.

"Okay," Sigrid said. "On my count."

"One."

"Two."

"Three."

Eva held her breath and stepped onto the plate. As soon as both feet touch the square stone, she squeezed her eyes shut, bracing for something horrible.

"Hold very still." Sigrid said.

Eva felt a rumbling in the ground and clenched her teeth, willing her body to stay on the pressure plate instead of running away like every fiber of her screamed to do. The rumbling grew louder, and she could feel the ground beneath her quaking. She started to panic. What if the pressure plates dropped out from beneath them? What if something fell out of the ceiling above her?

"HOLD!" Sigrid yelled.

A boom like thunder reverberated through the chamber, knocking all three of them off their feet. When Eva looked up, a large slab of stone had fallen in front of her, sealing off the passage. To her right, Sigrid's tunnel was blocked as well, but Tahl's remained clear.

"I thought I said nobody move?" Sigrid said, climbing to her feet and dusting herself off.

They all shared a nervous laugh, then Sigrid led the way again. The tunnel beyond the chamber was just wide enough for them to fit single file. But Sigrid refused to carry the Wonder, although she remained in the lead. Tahl's shoulders brushed against the walls, and his head almost touched the ceiling. Just as Eva started to feel claustrophobic, they came to another open room again, this one about half the size of the first. A small square table sat in the center.

Motioning for the others to hang back, Sigrid took a cautious step forward, then another. When she made it to the table, she turned and beckoned them to follow. Joining Sigrid, Eva saw three of the four corners had a rune cut into them. The fourth was blank.

"What do we do?" Eva wondered. She looked around the room but couldn't see any pitfalls. The walls were solid rock, without any way out save for the way they'd come in.

"It's some kind of puzzle," Tahl said. "I think the table will spin if we push hard enough."

To illustrate his point, he braced himself and shoved at one corner, and the table shifted a few inches before Sigrid yanked him back.

"*Don't. Touch. Anything,*" she hissed. "There are consequences to everything we do down here!"

"Sorry," Tahl muttered.

Sigrid shook her head, swearing under her breath, and traced the runes on the table with her finger. After a moment, she looked up at the wall. Using her arm, she wiped away the grime and cobwebs, revealing a larger version of one of the runes on the table. She dusted off two other spots on the wall and found runes matching the other two on the table's corners.

Eva looked down at the table then up at the runes carved into the wall. They were one off from matching their positions.

"So, we just line them up?" she asked

"Looks that way," Sigrid said. "But I've got a bad feeling there's more to it."

They fell silent as the dark-haired girl tapped a finger on the table, glancing back and forth from the table to the walls.

"Okay," she said at last. "Right now, the blank space faces the way we came in, and all the other runes are off one to the right. So, by that logic, if we turn the table to the left, two of the runes will line up. Which means there's no way for all three runes to line up."

Eva felt a sinking feeling as she realized the puzzle was more complicated than they'd first thought. Even so, she was impressed — until then Sigrid hadn't seemed like much of a thinker — unless you counted thinking about bashing someone with a sword. She knew already they could have never made it without the other girl.

"Maybe…" Eva said, her voice trailing off as she tried to untangle her thoughts. "What if there's more than one other passage out of here? What if each rotation opens another passageway?"

"Not a bad thought," Sigrid said. "The only problem is I'm not sure which way we want to go. I'm also not sure what will happen if we just start spinning things around."

She stared at the table and the walls, and then her eyes widened as they fell to the floor. "Of course!"

Eva and Tahl looked at each other as the girl dropped to the ground and started sweeping at it furiously with her uniform sleeve. "Don't just stand there like a pile of pigeon droppings, get down here and help me!"

Eva and Tahl knelt down and started wiping. Their efforts revealed circles upon circles of runes coming out from the square table like ripples in a pond. When they'd finished, thick black dust covered Eva from head to toe. Looking at the circles within circles of runes made her head spin.

"Well, this just got a whole lot harder," Tahl said.

Sigrid started walking around the table, following one circle after another.

"What does it say?" Eva asked.

"It's all in riddles," Sigrid said. "*The left is the right if the sunlight you seek* — that's one line. In between that it's just a bunch of jumbled letters. Here's another one — *Thrice to the right leads to the heart, but twice past the first leads only to dark.* What in the sky?"

Eva repeated the lines under her breath. "I think I've got it!" she said. "*The left is the right if sunlight you seek* — one turn to the left will reveal a passage out of the mountain."

"And thrice to the right, that must lead deeper into the mountain — to the Heart," Tahl added.

Sigrid nodded. "It's the last one that's got me worried. "*Twice past the first leads only to dark.* Sounds like we want to avoid that one, but I don't know which one the first one is…"

She heaved a sigh and ran her fingers through her disheveled braids and spiky hair. "All right," she said at last, "Three times to the right it is. Nice knowing you all if I'm wrong."

Tahl braced his legs and heaved. Ever so slowly, the table started to turn. Each time it passed over one of the sides, it made a loud clicking noise. At the same time, different circles on the floor started spinning toward the left. Eva and Fury jumped onto the platform beneath the table, the only part of the floor that wasn't turning. As the bands began their slow rotation Sigrid's eyes raced to read the runes.

"Wait!" she shouted, waving her hands. "It's not the —"

The stone beneath Sigrid shattered, and she screamed, disappearing into darkness.

Chapter

✹ 27 ✹

Eva rushed to the edge of the hole Sigrid had fallen through, heart racing. Complete darkness met her. Even with the Wonder, there was no way of seeing how far Sigrid had fallen — or was still falling.

Tahl dropped down next to Eva. "SIGRID!" he screamed into the hole. "I didn't know," he muttered. "I didn't —"

"By thunder, will you shut up?" A strained, irritated voice drifted up to them from somewhere in the darkness.

"Sigrid!" Eva yelled. "Are you okay?"

"No, I'm not storming okay," Sigrid answered. She didn't sound too far away, but Eva had no idea how they were going to get her out. "Pretty sure my leg's broken. Dammit all, I'm a fool. The lines in the floor were talking about the floor, not the table. The table was just the key to the alphabet."

"Don't worry about that," Tahl said. "How far down are you?"

"Oh, I can see the two of you," Sigrid said, "Probably about — aahhh — twice your height down. Got lucky. I think I fell on a platform of some kind. Doesn't seem to be anything around me, though."

"What are we going to do?" Eva asked Tahl. "We don't have any rope."

"You're going to finish the puzzle that's what!" Sigrid yelled up at them. "Because I'm sure as storm not going to die down here!"

"But what if we mess up again?" Tahl said. "Who knows what will happen?"

"You're not going to mess up because I know what to do now," Sigrid said. "How many times did you turn the table to the right?"

Tahl glanced up at the table. "Two."

"Okay," Sigrid said. "Turn it five slots back to the left. That will move the outer ring to the right three times, which is what we wanted in the first place."

"But what about you?" Eva said. "If Tahl rotates the table and you get covered up, how are we going to get to you?"

"I don't know." She sounded grim.

"Then we're not doing it," Eva said. "We'll figure out how to get you out first, and —"

"There's no storming way to get me out without finishing the pattern!" Sigrid yelled. "Gahh — damned leg. Either do it, or we'll all die down here!"

Eva looked at Tahl. "I don't know what else to do," he said. "I could lower you down to her, but then you'd both be stuck.

"All right," Eva said, fighting back a rising sickness in her stomach. "Turn the table. I'll keep an eye on her.

Lying on the solid circle of stone around the table, Eva stared down as Tahl set his feet once more and started pushing in the opposite direction. The first turn rotated Sigrid's hole to the right, just like she'd predicted.

One more push, and Tahl brought the table back to its original place.

"Whatever you do, don't go back the other direction," Sigrid shouted. "I don't want to find out what 'twice past the first leads only to dark' means."

Tahl sucked in a deep breath and set his weight against the table again. The inner and middle bands rotated in opposite directions, each covering a piece of Sigrid's hole.

"Don't stop, don't stop!" Sigrid sounded frantic. "There's a whole bunch of counterbalanced pillars down here — if the table rests too long in the wrong place, they're going to fall! Finish the rotation!"

The entire room started to shake and rumble. Tahl heaved, and the table moved once more...then stopped. He pushed harder, teeth gritting and veins straining in his neck and head but to no avail. The table remained firm, one turn short.

"PUSH, DAMN YOU!" Sigrid screamed.

Fury cried in alarm as bits of rock fell from the ceiling. Eva threw herself at another corner of the table, but it held firm.

"PUSH! THE PILLARS ARE FALLING!"

Eva strained with every muscle in her body. The table moved a fraction, or did she imagine it? Her entire world seemed to be shaking, rising, and falling.

And then it gave way, clicking into the final spot.

The rumbling stopped at once. Eva and Tahl collapsed to the ground, panting.

Eva looked around and saw holes throughout the rings, gaping pits leading to emptiness below. She sucked in a breath of air and shouted for Sigrid.

"I'm here; I'm fine." Sigrid's voice rose from the opposite side of the chamber where she'd first fallen. "There's a staircase cut into the stone."

Eva and Tahl followed the sound of her voice until they found the top of the stairs. They picked their way down the stairs to where Sigrid lay on a small platform surrounded by a bottomless chasm. When they reached her side, Eva and Tahl each took an arm and lifted her up. Together, they staggered up the steps like a drunken five-legged creature. At the top, Fury rushed to their sides, and the three started laughing.

"We did it," Sigrid said. "We storming did it!"

"You did it!" Eva said. "That was amazing!"

"Not too amazing," Sigrid said, grimacing. "You're going to have to go on without me."

"We can't leave you here," Eva said. "What if we can't make it back to you?"

"Then I'll crawl out of here on my own and take all the credit!"

Sigrid said. She tried to frown, but a smile cracked her dirty, sweat-streaked face. "I'll only slow you down."

"I'll leave Fury here with you," Eva said.

Sigrid shook her head. "You're wasting time."

"She's right," Tahl said, taking Eva gently by the arm. "Come on; we can't be far."

"We'll see you again," Eva said, not sure if she was trying to reassure Sigrid or herself.

Sigrid nodded. "Be careful."

Eva, Tahl, and Fury crossed the chamber, sidestepping the holes in the floor until they reached the new tunnel. Tightening her grip on the Wonder stone, Eva led the way.

The new passageway was wide enough for Eva and Tahl to walk side by side, Fury trailing close behind them. They continued in a straight line until Eva imagined she saw a light growing ahead. It grew stronger, revealing an end to the tunnel, bathed in orange light. They reached the threshold and stopped. If they'd learned one thing, it was to double check before they walked anywhere in the Catacombs.

Eva squinted into the next chamber. It was a stone's throw wide with a narrow bridge running down the middle. A sheer, yawning abyss waited on either side. Eva had a feeling it was a lot deeper than the one Sigrid had fallen down. Crystal lamps lined the two walls running parallel to the bridge, the source of the orange light. On the far side, an archway led into darkness.

Eva raised the Wonder stone into the air, but its light revealed nothing other than bare rock. "At least there aren't any more runes," Tahl said. "We'd be doomed if we had to translate something."

He stretched his toe forward and tapped on the stone in the threshold of the entryway. When nothing happened, he pressed his foot down, applying some weight. Still nothing.

"Let me go first," Eva said.

Tahl grabbed her arm and pulled her back. Almost before Eva realized it, they were kissing. Her lips pressed against Tahl's just as she'd imagine it a thousand times. For a few brief moments, the gloom and dread all melted away. Her head spun, but not from the dizzying drop just feet away. And then it was over.

"Just in case one of us meets a sudden and gruesome death," Tahl said as they pulled apart.

In spite of their dire situation, Eva laughed and pulled him back. The second kiss lasted longer, until Fury forced himself between them and they parted.

With one last look at Tahl, Eva took a deep breath and stepped onto the narrow bridge. She tried to focus on the stone path before her instead of the gaping blackness on either side. Just thinking about it made her head spin and her legs wobbly. She'd never felt so exposed, not even on the back of a gryphon hundreds of feet in the air. A thought crossed her mind that it was not knowing what was below that made it worse.

"Let me cross all the way before you follow," she yelled back at Tahl and Fury.

About four paces from the other end, a thunderous crack filled the chamber. Eva spun around and locked eyes with Tahl, frozen by fear. The bridge shifted beneath her feet, and the narrow length of stone started to sway.

Eva's end of the bridge dipped, and Tahl jumped onto the other end to balance it back out.

"Fury, no!" Eva screamed in panic as the gryphon tried to follow Tahl. She feared the gryphon's extra weight would topple them into the chasm.

Eva and Tahl crouched down to maintain their balance as the bridge started to spin and wobble.

"We're going to have to meet in the middle," Tahl said from across the bridge. As soon as they started inching toward the center, however, the rock shook, and they had to throw themselves down and wrap their arms around the edges to keep from being thrown off. On the far side of the cavern, Fury screeched, pacing back and forth along the ledge, desperate to reach Eva.

"It's not going to work!" Eva yelled over the rumble. "I can't come back across!"

"I'm not leaving you!" Tahl yelled back. He took a step forward, and Eva's stomach clenched as the entire bridge dropped and teetered even worse.

"Stop!" Eva's eyes met his eyes again, and she tried to recall the memory of them kissing to push away the terror building in her. "This is the only way. Take Fury, and go get help."

Against her every instinct, she inched backward. The bridge sank, and Tahl had no choice but to do the same or send her plummeting to her death.

"I'll come back for you, I promise!" he said.

They continued to scoot back, trying to match one another's pace. Eva started to think they might make it when a sound like cracking ice filled the cavern. She looked at the middle of the bridge and saw lines racing throughout the dark stone, chunks of rock breaking in their wake.

"Eva, jump!" Tahl shouted over the rising din. "NOW!"

Eva twisted around and leaped. The edge of the rock connected with the bottom of her ribs, driving out her breath. She started slipping into the chasm and scrambled for purchase.

"EVA!" Tahl screamed. His voice sounded miles away. Eva clawed and kicked like a wild thing, fighting for any ledge, any crack she could find.

But the rock was smooth as glass, and she slid down to her elbows. Were it not for the strength in her forearms from years of swinging a hammer, Eva knew she would have gone over already.

Eva felt her arms inching backward. Her whole body burned from exertion, but she was helpless to do anything.

She fell.

Chapter

28

Eva's screams echoed throughout the chamber as the darkness rushed up to grab her. The air whistled by her, and she flailed, kicking arms and legs into nothingness. Soon the air left her lungs as her heart and stomach rushed up into her throat.

A screech split the air above her, and Eva felt a rush of wind before striking something beneath her. She felt feathers and fur and realized Fury had leaped after her. Although he'd managed to catch her, they continued to fall.

The air rushing past seemed to slow a fraction, and Eva felt the whoosh of his wings on either side of her. The thought struck her mind that Fury couldn't fly and now they were both doomed. Even so, they seemed to be slowing. Eva tried to hold on and balance out her weight across his back — an almost impossible task given the gryphon wasn't any bigger than a colt. Yet somehow they stopped. Eva felt Fury's straining muscles beneath her and knew it took every bit of his strength to stay in the air. Afraid to move and upset her gryphon's balance, Eva shut her eyes as they began to rise.

"*Eva!*" After several long, excruciating moments she opened her eyes. With the last of his strength, Fury pulled up to the opposite side of the chasm as Tahl. As soon as he reached the stone shelf, he collapsed, and Eva rolled off the gryphon.

"You flew!" Eva shouted, lifting his feathered head into her lap. Fury gave a weak chirp in answer, beak hanging open as he panted for breath, completely exhausted.

"Good boy." Eva stroked the gryphon's copper-colored head for several moments until Fury shook himself then sat up.

"Are you okay?" Tahl yelled across to her. "Maybe Fury can —"

"You're too heavy," Eva said at once. "He barely carried me. Go help Sigrid, and bring help!"

Tahl hesitated. "Be careful!" he shouted.

Eva committed the picture of him standing there to memory in case she never saw him again. She opened her mouth, but the words wouldn't come out. Instead, she pulled out the Wonder stone, the pale pink, gold, and blue lights a small comfort in depths of the mountain. She held up the light, and it grew, filling the chamber. He raised his hand to her, smiling and then, was gone.

A quick check revealed Eva's sword and knife had somehow stayed on her. Fury stood and looked at her. The gryphon's presence gave Eva strength, and she took a deep breath. The tunnel yawned before them, black and empty as the chasm behind them. She stepped into the void, Fury at her side.

The click of Fury's front talons on the rock cut through the stillness. Although she hadn't noticed any real turns, when Eva looked back after a while there was no hint of orange light from the crystal lamps in the bridge room. Outside of the reach of her Wonder's light, the path ahead looked endless.

"I guess I owe you one," Eva said to Fury in an effort to break the maddening silence. The gryphon looked at her and dipped his head. Eva laughed. "No need to be modest about it."

They stared at each other, Eva's light blue eyes meeting Fury's deep yellow. It seemed like a lifetime ago since Fury had hatched, changing her life forever.

"No matter what's ahead, I won't let anything a happen to you," Eva said. "We're in this together."

Fury chirped and nudged Eva's hand with his head, filling her with courage. The Wonder stone grew brighter in her other hand, and they pressed on.

What seemed like hours later, Eva had no sense of time or how far they'd traveled since leaving Tahl. She felt light-headed and stumbled often. She had no clue how long they'd been down in the Catacombs and guessed it had to be at least morning outside. Realizing that, her stomach grumbled, and her throat burned with sudden thirst.

"Almost there," she said, over and over. "Almost there."

At long last, Eva spotted a light ahead, an orange flicker in the distance burning like a fire. Eva paused long enough to tuck her necklace back into her uniform. With a light ahead, she felt the need to remain hidden as much as possible. She couldn't say why, but it felt like the end lay ahead. Placing one hand on the wall to guide her in the faint glow and the other on the hilt of her sword, Eva started walking again.

The orange light grew, and Eva realized the entrance to the room ahead was gigantic, at least twice her height and wide enough for several people to pass through side by side. She continued forward at a steady pace, eager to reach the Heart of the Mountain but dreading what she might find.

A few dozen paces from the end of the passage, a silhouette appeared, outlined in the orange glow. Fury hissed and shrank back. Eva stopped and drew her sword, heart hammering in her chest.

"Who's there?" Eva said, trying to sound brave. When the figure didn't respond, she took a hesitant step forward. Light reflected off the person's bald head, and Eva felt like she'd been punched in the stomach. "Ivan?"

No response. Eva took a few more hesitant steps, and her worst fear came true. It was indeed the Scrawl boy.

If he recognized her, Ivan gave no sign. He stared straight past them, down the length of the tunnel like Eva wasn't there. His arms hung limp at his sides.

"Ivan, we've got to go," Eva said. "There's something down here…"

The Scrawl boy still didn't seem to hear, so Eva grabbed his wrist and tried to pull him down the tunnel. Ivan took two faltering steps and then yanked his arm out of Eva's grasp. Fury hissed and stepped backward, but Ivan just stood there again.

Ivan's head turned, and his eyes focused on Eva. Raising a hand, he beckoned to her. Without waiting, the boy turned and walked into the chamber, toward the orange light.

Still grasping her sword, Eva followed, Fury at her side. When they crossed into the chamber, Eva gasped. It was the largest room she'd seen in the Gyr, hundreds of feet high and wide. The circular cavern walls were carved with gigantic runes twice Eva's height. They pulsed and throbbed, bathing the chamber in a fiery glow, and Eva felt like she was inside a gigantic smelter.

Eva realized they stood on a large round platform of stone that dropped off before it met the cavern walls. A rectangular stone table stood in the center, about twice the length and width of a person. Across from them, Eva saw another entrance: a long stone ramp leading up to a pair of massive rune-carved doors. Ivan continued across the room to the table then stopped.

"Ivan, we've got to go," Eva repeated in a louder voice.

As she spoke, the stone doors across the chamber opened, and Celina stepped into the light.

Chapter

29

Eva's mind tried to make sense of what her eyes showed her. Celina descended the ramp and walked toward them. As she approached, Ivan's gaze followed her every move. Eva took a step back, mind reeling. At her side, Fury hissed.

"How good of you to join us, Eva dear," Celina said. In the light of the runes, her face looked even paler and more drawn than the last time Eva had seen her, weeks before.

"You." Eva said. "I don't —"

Celina raised her hand, the one with the Wonder gauntlet on it. "All will be explained, Eva. You've done well to make it this far, but then again you've had a good teacher these past months, haven't you?"

She smiled that sly fox smile, and the runes on her gauntlet pulsed with orange light of their own.

"What's going on?" Eva demanded.

"Something very special," Celina said. "An event over a thousand years in the making, and you've got the unique opportunity to witness it."

The woman lifted a dark stone knife from the table and held her gauntlet over the table. As she did so, Ivan began to chant. Eva recognized it as the same deep, dirge-like voice he'd taken up in his chambers. His voice grew louder and faster, and Celina ran the knife through her palm. Blood flowing from the cut, she pressed her hand over a rune in the center of the stone table and held it in place until blood ran into the grooves. Ivan fell silent.

Eva took another step back. "This...this isn't right," she said. She reached for Ivan's arm and pulled, but the boy shrugged her off again, eyes transfixed on the blood-filled rune.

"He can't hear you," Celina said. "He's completely under my control now." She flicked her wrist, and the runes on her iron band pulsed. Ivan took a step back from the table. Somehow the blood from Celina's cut multiplied on the table and ran through hundreds of little grooves.

"You?" Eva said. She struggled to comprehend. Celina, who had stuck up for her in front the Council, had believed in her when no one else did and picked her up at her lowest. It made no sense.

Celina nodded. "Yes. "

Stunned, Eva took a faltering step back as Fury crouched down beside her, prepared to attack.

"Clever as you are, Eva you've only been shown a small piece of a much larger picture," Celina said, ignoring their movements. "Your gryphon isn't just a rare specimen, Eva. He's a powerful omen. I knew when Devana first laid the red egg that it would be the key to my work."

"Your...work?" Eva said, voice hoarse. Blood continued to run down the solid sides of the table, catching in a groove running around the base.

Celina nodded. "I told you before, my entire life was changed on that expedition to the east. There, among the ruins, I discovered a power far greater than my own." She raised her left hand and turned her arm to show the glowing bracer. "This ancient relic opened my eyes and taught me secrets none have known for centuries. And ever so slowly, a grand future revealed itself to me, if only I had the strength to make it so."

Eva struggled to sort through the hundreds of questions bombarding her. She halfway wondered if this was all some insane trial set forth by the Windsworn, but when she looked at Celina she saw nothing but madness in the woman's dark eyes.

"But Uthred," Eva said.

"Uthred? Ha!" Celina laughed, a cold heartless sound. "That loyal fool doesn't have the strength or the vision to do what I will do. He began to suspect me, of course, but he had no proof, even after he started following me into the Catacombs. The Scrawl boy here proved a lovely diversion, though — his unique power made him especially vulnerable to the power of my Wonder. Poor Uthred couldn't unravel what was happening before his very eyes, but he was persistent, I'll give him that."

"So, it was you," Eva said. "You killed Devana and forced Ivan to steal the egg. You attacked Sigrid and Cassandra, and you killed Danny."

Eva felt a chill run down her back. "Why would you do that? What did they ever do?"

"They got in the way!" Celina hissed, clenching her hands into fists. The runes on the wall flared like fires fed by a gust of wind. She stepped around the dais, toward Eva, closing the gap between them. "I used the powers of the gauntlet to place Devana in a trance for the Scrawl boy to steal the egg, but her motherly instincts proved too strong. I had no other choice. While I fought the gryphon, my hold on the boy weakened, and he used my secret knowledge of the Catacombs to escape. I feared then he would recall me when captured, but the Wonder's rune magic overpowered his memory."

"But why steal the egg at all? Why involve Ivan?" Eva asked.

Celina smiled her cold, hungry smile. "The theft of the egg and its subsequent discovery in the hands of the Scrawls would have made Rhylance go to war with those tattooed idiots. Unfortunately, Ivan brought the egg to *you* for whatever reason, and it hatched."

"Why would you want to destroy the riders?" Eva asked. She continued to take small steps backward every time Celina spoke, doing her best to get as far away from the woman and the table as she could. Just being in its presence filled her with foreboding. Yet she couldn't leave Ivan. "You're the right wing of the Windsworn, second

201

only to the lord commander!"

"Oh, I don't want to destroy them," Celina said. "I intend for them to serve me, when I rise to power. A great storm is coming, Eva, the like of which hasn't been seen in a thousand years. With the Windsworn and Rhylance weakened by war with the Scrawls it will come to pass that much easier."

Eva glanced at Ivan. She'd hoped distracting Celina would weaken the woman's hold on Ivan, but the Scrawl boy continued to stare at the table. Its channels all filled with blood, and Eva wasn't sure if it was a reflection from the walls or not, but it seemed to give off a faint glow of its own.

"And the others?" Eva asked. "What did Cassandra, Sigrid, or Danny ever do to you?"

"After that debacle at the court, I needed it to look like Ivan had made another attempt at the red gryphon's life," Celina said. "The Scrawl and your gryphon share a unique magical connection that allowed me to lead Fury from your room toward the Roost. Unfortunately, Uthred was snooping around and muddled things up. I used Ivan as a diversion, but by the time I got back to the Roost I'd lost control of your gryphon and was almost spotted by Cassandra and Sigrid.

"Danny was another unfortunate victim," Celina said, shrugging like she was talking about a flower killed by an early frost and not the murder of a young, innocent boy. "The king and the Windsworn Council weren't acting fast enough. And for the ritual to work the best I need both Ivan and the red gryphon, but your bond had grown too strong to overpower him — I had to lure you both here. Once again, Uthred would have ruined that if I hadn't sent Tahl to free you and sworn him not to tell. And now, here you are."

"I trusted you," Eva said. Behind Celina, the trails of blood were definitely glowing now, the same fiery orange color as the giant runes. Ivan started chanting — harsh, angry words that froze Eva's heart and filled her with dread — and the light grew brighter and brighter.

"Ivan, stop!" she shouted.

The boy ignored her.

"He can't hear you, Eva," Celina said. "My control over him is complete." The chanting grew louder, and to Eva's horror, Fury turned away from Celina and stared at the stone altar as well.

"Fury!" Eva tugged at him, but the gryphon ignored her, focused on the table. He started walking toward the Scrawl.

"*Fury!*" Eva screamed again with no effect. "IVAN, STOP!"

Celina blocked Eva's path, arms folded across her chest, eyes burning with a feverish light. "You have two choices, Eva," she said. "I spoke the truth when I said you had the potential for greatness. Join me, and no one will ever laugh at you again. You will be feared and respected and will answer only to me."

"I don't want that," Eva said. She looked at Ivan and Fury, tears running down her face. "I don't want people to fear me."

Celina sighed. "Such a waste of potential. Just like your father."

Seeing the look on Eva' face, Celina let out a cold, harsh laugh. "Andor never told you, did he? That cocky, loud *idiot* was part of our expedition to the east. You don't know how bad I wanted to shove a sword through him before we got back. And then, if that weren't enough, he had an affair, and *you* came along. It almost tore the kingdom apart."

Celina spat out the words like poison. Eva's head spun. Her heart hammered in her chest, and her mouth went as dry as the stone beneath her feet.

"Who?" Eva managed to ask in a cracked voice.

"If you can't see reason, then I guess you'll die never knowing," Celina said.

The block of stone glowed like an ingot of steel heated in the forge fire. Ivan's voice rose, and he started shouting now, his voice ragged and hoarse from chanting. Fury sat down beside him, captivated by the glowing altar.

Eva rushed between them, shouting and shaking each in turn, but neither the boy nor the gryphon felt her presence. Anger rising, she turned to Celina, sword clenched tight in her hand.

The altar exploded without warning. Eva flew backward, shards of rock slicing her body and the air around her. She landed in a heap on the ground, several paces away. In place of the altar, a giant, midnight-colored golem shook the rock free and struggled to its feet.

Eva could only stare as it took one faltering step and then another. Clear of the debris, it stopped in front of Celina. The woman raised her glowing gauntlet and pointed at Eva.

"I'm sorry, my dear," Celina said, sounding genuinely disheartened. "This is where your story ends."

The golem turned toward Eva, and her ragged breath caught in her chest. Built wider and taller than Seppo, the golem's eyes burned like hot coals in the fire instead of Seppo's deep, gentle blue. Its armor was built for war — thick-ridged plates designed to turn or catch a blade, inscribed with ancient, forgotten runes.

Eva looked at Fury and Ivan, who stared at her with blank expressions. The golem flexed its hands and curled them into fists in anticipation. Each finger was thicker than Eva's arm.

"This will be quick," Celina said from behind the golem. "I owe you that much, Eva." The woman waved a careless hand toward her, the automaton watching her every move. "Kill her."

The golem bounded forward, covering the dozen paces to Eva in less than four steps. Eva barely had time to grab her sword before it attacked. She threw herself to the side just in time, rolling up into crouch, weapon at the ready. Undeterred, the golem covered the space between them in a single step. It swooped down for her, but Eva was too quick. She dove between its leg and hacked at the small of its back with all her might. Her blade struck the iron armor with a clang, reverberating so hard in her hands that she almost dropped it.

"The Smelterborn is indestructible," Celina said from across the chamber. "There is no escape. Soon, I will raise an army of them, and all of Altaris will bow before me!"

Eva backed away as the armored golem lumbered toward her. She managed a glance at Ivan and Fury, desperate for any help she could get. "Hey!" she shouted. "Snap out of it!"

Before she could see if the words registered, the golem lunged at her, forcing Eva to dive out of the way just in the nick of time again. When she recovered, she saw Ivan had the same blank look, but Fury had his head cocked to the side, studying her with some intent.

"Enough!" Celina shouted. Her impatience seemed to channel into the golem. It came at Eva with more intensity now, seeking to grab, stomp, or crush her any way possible. Each time, Eva stayed a half a step ahead of her opponent, sweat running down her face and soaking her uniform. Each time, the Smelterborn came at her just as fast and hard, showing no signs of tiring.

"Fury, help me!" she screamed, rolling to the side as a huge iron fist smashed into the rock, causing the ground to shake.

The gryphon took a hesitant step forward. "No!" Celina shouted, looking away from the golem to Fury. The fledgling paused, but so did the golem with Celina's concentration split between them.

That gave Eva an idea. She retreated from the Smelterborn, all the while shouting at Fury. The golem followed her every move. She managed to maneuver it between her and Celina while keeping a direct line of sight to Fury. Each time he heard her voice, the gryphon shook his head, tail twitching and wings flailing, but Celina's control held firm.

"Fury, please!" Eva shouted. She tore her eyes away from the golem to focus on the gryphon. "Help me!"

"Kill her now!" Celina shrieked.

Eva's eyes met Fury's, and she stared at him, seeing recognition dawn on his face. Too late.

In her moment of hesitation, the Smelterborn's fist came out of nowhere. It struck Eva, and she flew across the chamber, hitting the stone floor hard and rolling.

Vision swimming and body aching, Eva tried to move as the golem strode toward her and picked her up by the waist in its iron hand. Weaponless, Eva pounded its cold, lifeless hand with her fists, knowing it was useless. The Smelterborn turned and walked toward Celina, holding Eva out in front of it like child showing its parent a toy. Through a dizzy, pain-wracked mind, Eva felt her breast bone burning and wondered if her chest had been crushed.

"I taught you well," Celina said, shaking her head as the golem neared. "A pity you won't listen to reason."

The burning grew sharper, and Eva gritted her teeth and arched her back in the Smelterborn's grip until she realized it wasn't her body at all. *The necklace.* She tore at the collar of her uniform, scraped and bleedings fingers clawing to pull the Wonder free.

"Have you gone mad?" Celina asked as Eva tore at her clothing.

In one last desperate rip, Eva latched on to the chain and yanked the necklace free. The rose-colored light burned bright as the sun, and she twisted away, burying her face in her elbow.

Celina's shrieks filled the chamber. "What is that? Get it! Get rid of it!"

The Smelterborn's grip slackened, however, and Eva fell to the ground. Scrambling, she scampered out of the way as the golem floundered around. Free of being trampled, Eva grabbed the stone's chain and thrust it up into the thing's face. Celina screamed again, and the suit of armor threw its hand over its face, stumbling backward from the light.

A familiar scream cut through the din, and Eva saw a flash of copper as Fury leaped and struck the Smelterborn's helm, almost knocking it off its feet.

"Get it, boy!" Eva yelled. Holding the Wonder aloft in front of her, other hand covering her eyes, Eva advanced on the Smelterborn and Celina, who hid herself behind the suit of armor, still shouting for it to attack.

Fury wheeled away and struck again, causing the Smelterborn to pull its hands from its face in an attempt to fend off the gryphon. The chain grew hot in Eva's hand, and the light flared brighter. Celina's screams of pain stabbed at Eva's ears, her world consisting of nothing but light, deafening shrieks, and heat.

"Please!" Celina begged. In the shade of her hand, Eva saw the woman fall to her knees behind the Smelterborn. "Make it stop. I'll do anything you want, just make it stop burning!"

Eva paused and lowered the Wonder, shielding the light with her other hand. Almost at once, Celina's screams ended, and the golem paused. From behind the golem's legs, Eva saw Celina's face curl into a snarl.

"CRUSH HER!"

Arms wide, the Smelterborn leaped forward. Eva dropped to one knee and buried her face in her free arm, thrusting the Wonder above her like a shield. A bone-shaking roar spit the cavern. Celina screamed so loud Eva's ears rang. The sound of thunder filled the air, and the ground shook.

Silence filled the chamber.

Eva dropped the burning necklace as the light from the stone faded. Head spinning, she sat the Wonder on the ground beside her, using both hands to keep herself from tipping over. As her eyes adjusted to the dying orange light, she saw the Smelterborn lying on the ground. Before her eyes, its armor began to rust and corrode away. A pale, twisted hand stuck out from beneath it.

The sound of feathers signaled Fury landing beside Eva. Seeing Celina's body trapped beneath the golem, she leaned over and retched.

"Eva!" Ivan's confused voice cut through the silence, sounding almost as dazed as she was. "Where are we? What's happening?"

"Celina..." Eva muttered, her voice distant in her ears. "Smelter... thing." Eva's vision jilted and swam even more, white stars popping up everywhere she looked. She shivered, drenched in a cold sweat. A part of her worried she might lose consciousness and tried to lean away from her pool of sick.

"Good...boy," Eva said. Her hand slipped from Fury's head, and oblivion embraced her.

Chapter
30

When Eva awoke, the first thing she recognized was light. Not the rose-colored light of her Wonder, but warm, soft sunshine, which didn't make any sense given that she was in a cavern. Where was the Smelterborn?

Gasping, Eva shot up. Her head pounded in protest, and the entire left side of her body throbbed. The pain snatched away her breath. Wide eyed, Eva looked around and found herself lying in a bed, her dirty, blood-stained tunic replaced by a large white shirt.

"Good timing."

Twisting her head around, Eva saw Andor enter the room. He studied her for a moment before taking a couple of timid steps to a chair by Eva's bedside.

"How do you feel?" he asked, sitting down.

"My head hurts," Eva said, squinting. "Everything hurts."

Realization struck her like a lightning bolt. "Sigrid! Tahl! Fury!"

Hearing his name, the gryphon's head appeared at the foot of Eva's bed, and he leaped on top of it, chirping and flapping his wings in joy.

Eva smiled and ran her fingers through his soft, dark fur until another thought crossed her.

"Ivan! Lord Commander, Ivan was innocent; he didn't do anything!

Please, you can't execute him, he —"

The lord commander held up a hand. "Everyone is fine. Ivan suffered no lasting harm and has been sent back to his own people, to cure any lingering ailments in his mind. He has been fully pardoned by the king."

Eva took a couple of shallow breaths and realized she felt almost as bad as she had after Sigrid's beating. She blinked hard, trying to focus on Andor's face.

"Tahl made it out to get help," he said. "When Uthred and Lord Vyr found you, they thought you were dead."

"Lord Vyr?" Eva said, confused. "What was he..."

"You should have learned already that he's more than meets the eye," Andor said. "He was helping Uthred search the Catacombs when Tahl ran into them — it's fortunate because I'm told Tahl seemed to be under the impressions that Uthred was the one who was responsible for the attacks. He almost drew steel against the commander until Lord Vyr intervened."

Eva blushed. "It's not Tahl's fault," she said. "I told him and Sigrid and Wynn that it was Uthred who'd been behind the attacks."

"No harm came from your mistake," the lord commander said. "And honestly, I can't say I blame you given Uthred's attitude toward you. He's extreme at times, but his loyalty is as unwavering as this mountain."

Eva couldn't help herself. "Yes, but so was Celina's, at least I thought."

Andor's face darkened. "True. She betrayed everything she stood for."

Not knowing what to say, Eva bunched her sheets in her hands and nodded.

"I've heard Tahl and Sigrid's account, as well as Ivan's," the lord commander continued. "But you're the only one who can finish the story."

Eva swallowed hard and recounted the dark moments in the chamber as best she could. When she got to the part about her father, she faltered. Tears splashed down her face, and her voice caught in her throat.

"Is it…is it true?" she asked Andor. "Am I a…a bastard?"

The lord commander's jaw grew tight, and he stared at Eva, saying nothing.

"Answer me!" Eva screamed, punching the bed. Her head reeled, and she almost collapsed backward onto her pillow.

"Yes, Eva," Andor said. "Your father was a man named Aleron, my youngest brother."

"How could you not tell me?" Eva asked, voice broken. "How could Soot not tell me? You storming liars! I hate you!"

Caught in a burning rage, Eva struck the lord commander across the face with the palm of her hand hard enough she thought she'd might have broken her wrist. Andor just stared back at her, face as stoic and impassive as the mountain he commanded. The rage died as quickly as it came, leaving Eva with a dull emptiness in her chest and a realization for what she'd just done.

"I deserved that," Andor said in a thick voice. "What we did was wrong, Eva. It was wrong to deceive you. But we did it —"

"They did it because they were loyal friends who obeyed the orders of a selfish, proud fool."

King Adelar stood in the doorway. Before Eva could even begin to think of what to say, he crossed the room and knelt by her bedside. "Please, Evelyn," he said, taking her clenched fist between his hands and bowing his head. "If you have to blame someone, have to hate someone, let it be me."

A sob tore itself from her chest, and tears poured down Eva's face. "Why?" she managed to ask. "Why did you do this to me?"

Adelar looked up, and Eva saw tears glistening in his cold, blue eyes. "I cannot be sorry enough," he said. "I've been…trying to tell you, and when I heard what happened in the Catacombs, that it might be too late —"

A terrible thought crossed Eva's mind. "Who was my mother?" she asked, voice catching in her throat. "What did you do to her?"

"She was my wife, the queen," Adelar said. "She died giving birth to you. Blinded by the pain of her loss and anger at my brother's betrayal, I sent you away. Marien's death almost destroyed me. I — I couldn't bear to have a reminder of her around, a reminder of what Aleron had done. I banished him from Rhylance and ordered you taken from the palace."

"You made me an orphan," Eva said through her tears.

"Soot is a close friend of our family," Andor said. "He agreed to take you in and raise you. Eva — he hated me for lying to you; he wanted to tell you so many times. He wrote me almost every year around your birthday, but I wouldn't let him. Don't blame him for this; he loves you like his own."

"I still don't understand," Eva said. "Why did all this happen? Why would my father betray his family and his king?"

"Love is a powerful thing," Adelar said. "Before the Great Eastern Expedition left, Aleron and Marien were betrothed. While they were gone — Aleron, Andor, Soot, Celina, and the rest — your grandfather, my father, the king grew sick and died. Over two years passed, and we didn't hear a word from the company. I waited and waited, thinking they'd all been killed. I'd lost my father and thought I'd lost both my brothers as well. Marien…Marien was a comfort in those dark days. We fell in love, and she became my queen."

"When we returned from the east and Aleron found out what happened, he wanted to kill Adelar," Andor said. "I love your father more than anything, but he was…headstrong, rash. He was the best of us, the best of the Windsworn, and he knew it. His pride made him…difficult at times. Over the following weeks, Aleron withdrew from all of us, but somewhere along the line he and Marien began writing each other in secret and then meeting. You were the result."

"You can understand my anger when Marien and Aleron came to me and confessed what they'd done," the king said. "By rights, I could have had them both executed, but something stayed my hand… Looking at you now, I know why."

Eva snorted and wiped the snot from her face. "Huh. How benevolent."

Adelar shot her a pained look. "And so, I exiled Aleron. Marien and I tried to put it behind us, but weeks later she realized she was pregnant. You know the rest."

"So, my father never even knew I existed?" Eva asked. For some reason, that hurt worse than anything else.

"Aleron left before, and no one has heard from him since," Andor said. "Trust me when I say if your father had known about you, an army couldn't have kept him out of Rhylance."

"Lord Vyr!" Eva said, recalling her conversation. "He told me…he said my father was alive!"

"He very well could be," Andor said. "If nothing else, Aleron was a fighter. I don't believe the Windsworn or anyone from Rhylance have seen him since, however."

Eva stared out the window, lost in an endless sky of hurt and confusion. Everything made so much sense, and yet nothing made sense. Everything she'd thought she was, everything she'd been, was all a lie. She unclenched her hand and pulled it away from the king and into her lap.

"I know your forgiveness is something neither of us, but especially not I, ever deserve," the king said. "But I will do whatever I can to make this right between us, Niece."

Eva jerked at being called niece, like she'd been stabbed. "I…I'd like to be alone now."

The king rose to his feet and nodded. Andor stood as well. "Soot should be here soon and will want to see you if you are able."

"I'd like that," Eva said in a small voice, not looking at either of the men.

She suddenly felt exhausted and wanted nothing more than to fall asleep and wake up to find the last two days had been a bad dream — or, better yet, to wake up in Soot's cottage like none of it had ever happened. But then she thought of all she'd learned and accomplished, of the friendships she'd made, and especially of Fury. He nudged her hand with his break from the other side of the bed, and Eva knew at once that she wouldn't trade her bond with the gryphon for anything.

Eva heard one set of footsteps leave the room, while the other paused.

"Eva," Andor said. She didn't turn around. "I'm proud of you. Your father would have been proud of you as well."

The praise struck her bittersweet, and as the door closed and she and Fury were alone, Eva curled into a ball. Tears of equal parts relief, pride, and pain ran down her face, and Eva cried until sleep overtook her.

The next morning, Tahl, Sigrid, and Wynn came to visit. They filed in the room, shy at first until Eva beckoned for them to come over. "It's not my funeral; stop acting like I've died."

Needing no encouragement, they joined her bedside, Wynn rushing forward to get there first, followed by Sigrid, hobbling along on crutches, her leg bound in straps and wooden shafts to keep it still. Tahl brought up the rear, unusually quiet and unsure. Eva caught his eye, and they quickly looked away from one another.

"You're the talk of the Gyr!" Wynn said. She reached out to pet Fury, who was lying at the foot of the bed, dozing. The gryphon raised his head enough to make a lazy snap at Wynn's hand, and she pulled it back, frowning.

"Oh no," Eva said. "What are they saying now?"

"They're saying we're storming heroes, and you're the biggest hero of the bunch!" Sigrid said. Her face split in a rare grin, and she leaned forward over the straightened leg and gave Eva a slap on the back. "That must've been some fight — the lord commander told us about the golem. I'm jealous I missed out on taking a crack at it."

"We're fine, I promise," Eva said, then added with a wink, "that golem was nothing compared to you."

"Eva, look!" Wynn said. She lifted up the corner of her cloak to show off the winged badge pinned to her uniform. "I passed the fledgling trials!"

"I knew you could do it," Eva said, smiling at the girl. She started to say something else, and then a sickening thought struck her. "Oh no...I missed the trials!"

Sigrid threw her head back and laughed, and Eva shot her a quizzical look. "Why is that funny?"

"Eva, do you think the lord commander was going to kick you out of the Gyr after what you went through?" Tahl said, the ghost of a smile on his lips. "You made it through far worse than anything the other first recruits had to pass."

Embarrassed, Eva mumbled something, face heating up. Truth be told, the last thing she'd thought of was the trails, until Wynn brought it up. The previous night had passed mostly sleepless as she tossed and turned, body aching, mind still reeling by the bitter truths she'd learned from Andor and the king. She'd made up her mind that when her friends came to visit she'd tell them about it. No matter how much she wanted it to, she knew the word would get out and her parentage wouldn't be a secret for long. Yet now that they were here before her, Eva hesitated.

"Eva, is it true?" Wynn said in a hushed voice, eyes wide. Sigrid and Tahl both shot her a stern look, but the younger girl ignored them. Eva knew then it was already too late. Like it or not, she'd have to face this issue in the light rather than burying it away like her impulse suggested. Either way, she'd come to realize in the early hours of the morning that this wasn't something she could untangle in a night, nor anytime soon.

"Shut up, Wynn," Sigrid said.

"There's a rumor going around that Lord Commander Andor is your uncle," Wynn continued, ignoring the other two. "That you're the king's *niece*."

Eva forced a dry laugh. "Well, if the lord commander is my uncle, the king would have to be, too, wouldn't he?"

Wynn's eyes grew even wider, and for once she seemed at a loss for words. "Holy sky! It's true!"

Sigrid gave a low whistle. Tahl, for the first time Eva had ever seen him, didn't seem to know what to say or do, his usually easy confidence gone.

"It is," Eva said, the words sounding strange coming out of her. "But I'm still me," she added, not sure if she was trying to convince herself or them. No matter who her parents were and what tragedy her family held, she was still Eva, the blacksmith's assistant and

214

Windsworn-in-training.

Unbidden, she began retelling the conversation between the lord commander and the king to her friends. The raw emotion of it all flared up, and she laid herself bare in between tears and encouragement from the others. It still hurt, but it didn't cut her as deep as it had the day before, learning it all for the first time.

"And that's it," Eva said at the end. "Now you know the whole story." She looked from face to face. Wynn still stared in amazement, and Sigrid's brow furrowed as she tried to make sense of it all.

Eva felt drained, watching them, waiting for their reaction. Nobody knew quite what to say, and when she looked to Tahl for some kind of response, his eyes darted away.

"This doesn't change anything between us," Eva said.

Wynn, surprisingly, still seemed at a loss for words, but Sigrid broke into a grin. "I'll still go the rounds with you in the circle whenever you want, your Highness."

"That's not funny," Eva said, lips twitching in a smile. "I'm just Eva, and don't you forget it." She looked at Tahl again, and he cleared his throat. Sigrid caught the glance between them and pulled herself up on her feet, fixing her crutches underneath her.

"C'mon, Wynn," she said. "Let's let Eva get some rest."

Wynn started following the older girl out then paused when she saw Tahl wasn't coming. "Hey!" she said, motioning to him. "Let's — ow!"

The younger girl hopped on one foot and glared at Sigrid. "Sorry, still getting used to using these crutches," Sigrid said, waving one in the air. "Tahl will catch up with us."

Eva felt a flash of excitement, then trepidation and nervousness as the door closed behind the two girls, leaving her alone in the room with Tahl. She cleared her throat and focused on Fury lying at the end of the bed, not sure what to say. Back in the dark of the Catacombs, it'd seemed so easy and simple. Now, here in the light, that kiss seemed a thousand years away, a fairytale story about two people in another life.

Tahl sat down and leaned over to brush a strand of Eva's golden hair out of her face. "I'm…glad you're okay," he said. "They wouldn't let me go back down into the caves to look for you, and when they brought you out I thought…"

He trailed off, and Eva saw him swallow hard out of the corner of her eye. *Say something, you fool,* she thought to herself. But the harder she tried to come up with something, the more her mind went blank. A few moments of uncomfortable silence stretched between them. Tahl's hand rested on the edge of the bed. Knowing she had to do something, Eva reached over and rested hers on top of it.

"Eva," he began, "That…moment, down there in the Catacombs. I —"

Eva prepared herself for him to say it'd all been a big mistake then decided she didn't want to hear it out loud, even if it was probably true.

"You don't have to say anything, Tahl," Eva cut in. "I understand."

Although it was the last thing she wanted to do, she turned and looked at him. Relief flooded the sharp lines of his face, like a knife tearing right through Eva's chest.

"We can act like it never happened," she said, trying to get the words out as fast as she could, to get them over with. She pulled her hand back and felt tears welling in her eyes. "I'm not going to hold it over you. Let's just —"

Tahl's fingertips lifted her chin to meet his eyes. He looked at her for a second and brushed a tear away with his thumb. "I was going to say I never want to feel like I've lost you again. I… I care about you. A lot. But now that you're — I mean, now that you know…"

Eva laughed in surprise and clamped a hand to her mouth when it came out as an unbelieving snort. Feeling the heat pulse from her face, she glanced down. "I'm just Eva," she said. "I already told you: none of that changes who I am."

He pulled her face up again and leaned over. She felt her breath quicken as they drew close.

"I wouldn't have it any other way," Tahl said in a low voice.

Eva didn't think any kiss could have been better than their first. She was wrong.

Chapter
🦅 31 🦅

Eva examined herself in the mirror of her quarters. She reached behind her back to secure the chain of her mother's Wonder. The stone twinkled, giving of a reassuring light that filled Eva with a comforting warmth. Why it had destroyed Celina's golem was anyone's guess. Eva tried to leave the explaining and deciphering of that dark night to higher minds than herself, determined to regain some semblance of a normal life in the aftermath.

"How do I look?" she asked Fury, who was sitting on her bed. The gryphon dipped his copper head in approval.

With a long sigh, she buckled on her sword belt, adjusting it over her uniform just so. Another deep breath and exhale calmed her fluttering nerves.

"I don't know what you're all worked up about," Sigrid said. "You're a storming hero! Now hurry up; we're going to be late for the ceremony!"

Sigrid wore her fine silver chain mail and the other armor of the Windsworn. Her hair was done up in an elaborate set of braids, a couple of feathers thrown in for good measure so that Sigrid looked like a fierce bird of prey herself. Eva doubted she would ever look so at ease in the trappings of war and shifted to redistribute the unusual weight of her own attire.

"That's what I'm afraid of," Eva said. "People don't expect a hero to trip on their own scabbard or forget the words or —"

"Eva," Sigrid said, placing a hand on her shoulder. "You're going to be fine. This is a lot easier than fighting a golem!"

At the moment, Eva thought she'd take her chances with the golem, but she put on a brave face anyway. Together, she and Fury followed Sigrid out of the barracks, toward the upper levels. Halfway there, Tahl waited for them at a junction in the hallway. He looked like he'd stepped right out of a Windsworn tapestry in his polished silver breastplate and royal-blue cape.

"You look…" His eyes were glued on Eva, but Sigrid gave a sharp cough and Wynn folded her arms, frowning. "You all look stunning," Tahl finished.

"Right, right," Sigrid said, jostling between Tahl and Eva with Wynn close behind. "Let's just get this over with."

Together, the four of them climbed the stairs past the Roost, to Eleanor's Landing, the open peak of the mountain. Outside, the sun shone down on a clear, crisp day. Eva swallowed at the rows of Windsworn standing at attention. A long row of guards in polished silver armor and wing helmets formed a tunnel all the way to the lord commander and the rest of the Council. When they saw Fury and the four people step into the sunlight, a rousing cheer when up.

Wynn looked at Eva, a big grin splitting her face. "Told you it wouldn't be bad."

Eva allowed herself a small smile, and they passed between the lines of armored Windsworn, who pulled back their spears as she went by. Looking every bit royalty in their gold and silver armor, Adelar and Andor watched them approach. To their left, Soot stuck out like a sore thumb in his plain clothes, sun shining off his bald pate. Even so, his presence reassured Eva, and she felt a small smile tugging on her face.

A strange feeling crossed her as she realized her entire family, both old and new, were gathered here. Although she'd promised herself to learn to forgive, Eva wasn't sure what to think of her two uncles, or how to act around them. At least now, in an official capacity, it was easy just to be a recruit to the lord commander and a subject to the king.

The four of them approached the raised stone area where the lord commander, Soot, the king, and the Council stood and stopped, bringing their fists to their chests in salute. Both Andor and Adelar returned the gesture, and then the king held up a hand to silence the cheering.

"Throughout our history, the Windsworn have been our mightiest champions — the brave defenders of Rhylance. Men, women, and gryphons whose courage and skill at arms keep our people safe," the king began. "The four before you today exemplify these qualities, and we honor them for their courage in facing our enemies and safeguarding peace. Step forward."

Eva felt her mouth go dry and her knees weaken as she stepped onto the raised stone area and sank to one knee, head bowed. A moment later, she felt Andor slip a medal around her neck, and her heart leaped. Glancing sideways, she saw him kneel down and place one around Fury's neck as well, the gryphon's head held high and proud.

"Arise," the king said. The four of them stood, and everyone but Eva and Fury took a step back. "Rhylance owes you a great debt for your service. As long as our people walk the earth and our gryphons soar in the skies, your deeds will not be forgotten."

The crowd burst out in a roaring cheer for several moments until the king and the lord commander raised their hands again.

"But we have one more order of business this day," Andor said, his voice carrying across the open rock. "One among these four has proved herself worthy to be called Windsworn."

Eva swallowed and felt her chest tighten. She glanced to the Council and saw them, the same men and women who had voted against her, nodding in approval. Even Uthred, catching her in his stony gaze, gave Eva a curt nod of approval. On the other side of the king and lord commander, even old Lord Vyr had joined the congregation, cackling and clapping, his remaining strands of white hair blowing wild in the breeze.

Eva looked between Andor and Adelar. The king smiled, an expression that looked unfamiliar and forced, but warm nonetheless. Even if she couldn't completely forgive them, she knew she couldn't hate these men.

The lord commander drew his sword and touched it to Eva's shoulder, then Fury's. "I am the sword in the sky," he said.

"I am the shield in the storm," Eva replied.

"On the wings of gryphons I fly."

Eva took a deep breath.

"And to the wind I am sworn."

Want to know what happened before Windsworn?

Thanks so much for reading Windsworn. The journey has just begun and I can't wait for you to read the next two books in the trilogy: **Windswept** and **Windbreak**! Before you get started on them, however, don't you want an exclusive short story about Eva's father? You can ONLY get this through joining my mailing list. I never send more than two emails per month, and they're always filled with other reading recommendations, special deals, sneak peeks and more!

Go to **http://derekalansiddoway.com/newsletter** to start reading this exclusive Gryphon Riders short story right now!

When you sign up for my mailing list, you'll also receive Out of Exile, the first book in the Teutevar Saga series and two exclusive Teutevar Saga origin stories.

Also by the author

Gryphon Riders Trilogy

Windsworn (Gryphon Riders Book 1)

Windswept (Gryphon Riders Book 2)

Windbreak (Gryphon Riders Book 3)

Teutevar Saga

Into Exile (Teutevar Saga Book 0)

Out of Exile (Teutevar Saga Book 1)

Return to Shadow (Teutevar Saga Book 2)

Other Works

Lone Wolf Anthology: A dark and heroic fantasy collection

Swords for Hire: A Frontier Fantasy and
Medieval Western Story Anthology

Valiant (short story)

Derek Alan Siddoway

Derek Alan Siddoway is the author of Teutevar Saga, a medieval western/frontier fantasy series, and Gryphon Riders, a young adult fantasy trilogy. He was born and raised in the American West at the foot of the Uinta Mountains. An Undaunted and Everyday Author, Derek spends his free time reading, obsessively filling notebooks, adventuring outdoors and celebrating small victories. He's also a sucker for Star Wars and football, namely the University of Utah and Minnesota Vikings.

For more shenanigans, find Derek online in the following places:

@D_Sidd (Twitter)
Teutevar Saga (Facebook)
derekalansiddoway.com

Made in the USA
San Bernardino, CA
29 December 2019